W9-BHL-192

MISTER
WHITE EYES

MISTER WHITE EYES

A NOVEL

by *HERBERT GOLD*

ARBOR HOUSE
New York

Copyright © 1984 by Herbert Gold

All rights reserved, including the right of reproduction in whole
or in part in any form.

Published in the United States of America by Arbor House Publishing
Company and in Canada by Fitzhenry & Whiteside, Inc.

Library of Congress Cataloging in Publication Data

Gold, Herbert, 1924–
Mister White Eyes.

I. Title.
PS3557.034M5   1984   813'.54   84-9376
ISBN 0-87795-636-7

Manufactured in the United States of America

10   9   8   7   6   5   4   3   2   1

This book is printed on acid-free paper. The paper in this book meets the
guidelines for permanence and durability of the Committee on Production
Guidelines for Book Longevity of the Council on Library Resources.

This work is a novel. Any similarities to actual persons are purely
coincidental, and all of the names and characteristics of all of the characters
in this book are wholly fictitious.

For Ann, Judy, Nina, Ari, and Ethan
and the lessons of history

*"In the fight between you and the world,
take the world's side."*

1

THE VETERAN JOURNALIST had covered sixteen wars or revolutions, he sometimes admitted. But then he looked embarrassed and changed the subject, which for him, but not necessarily for others, was: Well, how the devil else can a man spend his life?

He had to be trapped to speak of the wars and revolutions. His face turned ruddy under the gray and black stubble, and he deeply regretted the corner he was in. "I've written it," he said. "I talk better when I'm asking questions. I'm like a stammerer who can only sing. If I could do anything different, I'd do it. I've tried. From experience I've learned I can't."

By this time the listener, a young woman at the bar of the Grand Hotel Oloffson in Port-au-Prince, was smiling at such a long speech from a man who said he couldn't talk. Ralph Merian couldn't help it. He drank little, but sometimes a glass or two helped him to explain himself—a kind of cease-fire declaration from his internal peacekeeping force. He did his business, sent back his words by telex or by shout over awful ITT phones, used far less Scotch and grass than most, and had never fallen in love at a single war or revolution. Sometimes he thought his full name was Ralph Merian, Our Eyewitness on the Scene.

The current war or revolution was different. In the first place, it was strictly a maybe. Some Haitian exiles promised, as they had been promising for years, to land on the St.-Marc road down the coast from Port-au-Prince and dump "the perpetrators" of the Duvalier regime. This time it was the Haitian Peoples Liberation Front issuing battle orders from the back room of a furniture store in Queens. The Veteran Journalist's editor, Arnie Schultz, had sighed and said, "You need a vacation, anyway."

"I do not," said Merian.

"Go hang out at the Oloffson and tell us how Baby Doc takes it," said his editor.

"You really think it'll blow this time?" said the V.J. "What makes this time different from all the other times? And who cares?"

"Do the Boat People from a coastal village if there's no landing. Or a fighting exposé of the worms in the mahogany salad bowls—do whatever. And Ralph—don't start asking who cares."

"You're tired of me, darling?" the journalist asked his old friend.

Arnie had shrugged and turned away. They were fond of each other. Sometimes they spent an evening at Harvey's Chelsea Restaurant, not drinking too much, just talking about why such bright old dogs as they were only barked a lot and barked alone, both of them, and managed wars and revolutions and even publishers okay, both of them, and were just wiped out in closer encounters, that's all. Love shorted them out faster than eleven Chilean generals in full uniform passing through a metal detector. Marriage might be a feast for some, but for Arnie Schultz and Ralph Merian, the Sahara was safer, richer, and more consoling. They each had had two wives: one bad, who had given little but grief; the other mostly good, who had given them much more grief by giving up on them. Their second wives had made an intelligent judgment. Arnie and Ralph had learned to use the new word processors and video screens on rewrite—why couldn't they catch on to life with a modern woman?

The bugs lay deep in the equipment. What they needed was something in the software to improve operations—replace whole paragraphs, correct spelling, regulate alignment. And surely something more. Arnie said that too much geography may have smudged Merian's brain with excess deserts and mountains, too many piercing-eyed leaders and dull-eyed followers, too many of the ungainly dead in the streets and improvised morgues. Once, when he had dragged Merian along to dinner with the publisher, he accused him of being a spoilsport—"spoilsportism" he called it—because Merian had refused to tell the story about the English journalist he saw in the Congo, strolling through a hospital with hands cupped to mouth, calling out, "Anybody here been raped and speaks English? Anybody here been raped and speaks English?"

"Don't want to," Merian had mumbled, and Arnie had to apologize for his best reporter's rudeness.

Later, at Harvey's Chelsea, Arnie had explained his theory of the social utility of newspapers, how they make marriages work by stalling arguments over breakfast, sheltering the folks in their armchairs at night, giving them something to share. "A newspaper isn't something you read," Arnie said, "it's a warm bath you get into."

"Marshall McLuhan," Merian said.

"You're in the business of putting cold water in the warm bath," Arnie said. "Need that spigot, too. It's the tingly part of the warm bath."

"Thank you for that tribute," Merian said. "I'm not sure how this applies to you and me."

Arnie looked at him over his beer. Both of them were sweating with beer, with fatigue, with ungainly comradeship. "We need work. We don't have women. I guess I'm speaking for both of us just now. Don't you know we've both got to do something?"

The editor and the journalist had served hard time discovering that a bad wife is bad, but a good one is worse. If she chooses to dump a fellow, there's grief and longing and regret and a sudden leap of aging as the teeth grind in sleep and the guts burn and the arms are empty.

A good woman won't stay there quietly just because an old dog needs her there.

So the veteran journalist checked for visas and went where his friend and editor sent him.

Merian wrote his lead: *A little band of desperate men, firing Soviet-made AK–17 assault rifles and screaming "Death to Tyranny!" this morning failed to storm the National Palace in Port-au-Prince....*

This is not a story about another war or revolution. The invasion of Haiti, as usual, did not take place.

The V.J. hung about the bar of the Grand Hotel Oloffson, under the creaking tropical ceiling fans, studying the paintings and carvings and the smoky Caribbean light outside and his single rum-soda inside—followed, with the exceptional discipline for which he was justly famous and mistrusted, by iced tea. He had a brother, Charles, in San Francisco, who, last he heard, drank too much. He always thought of Chaz when he ordered his second drink and made it coffee or tea or high-fashion bottled water.

He listened to the chickens and the tourists.

He waited a few days to see if the little band of desperate men would come to help him do his job.

The signal from New York was that the lads in the furniture store in Queens had postponed the game on account of contract dispute, but that he could file a Situation Normal All Far-fallen piece when he got back. In the meantime, take seven. The Government-in-Exile had adjourned to a soccer match. "Jet lag hurts at our age," his friend and editor added. "And I just heard there's such a thing as male menopause. Do you feel any hot flashes?

Are your breasts getting flabby? Chased any *National Geographic* models up a coconut tree lately?"

So he bought a couple of paperbacks at La Librairie Caravelle—too hot in downtown Port-au-Prince unless there was some nice cool shooting to distract a person—and sat on the terrace of the Oloffson, reading and deciding he would not take up smoking again and sipping iced tea with lime and reading some more. He didn't mind. He kind of liked how novel writers tell lies and wished he knew some to tell.

There on the terrace at late breakfast, early lunch, he met the young woman again. Perhaps he had been looking for her. She was formally but tenderly offering lemonades of good-bye to her fourteen-year-old daughter, a thin plain gawky child, an English stem rather than a flower. She was delivering the child for the year to her father, the British consul, the lady's former husband. Her face was pale and stricken. Some war or revolution!

The consul drove up in a freshly washed Rover with droplets of water in the corners of the windshield. Impeccable whites. Impeccable kiss on the cheeks. The consul drove off with his kiddy in the freshly washed Rover, the impeccable whites, a few gatherings of muck where the water had been. Ta-ta, Mummy.

Now the lady was a little shaky and came to the bar to say to anyone who might listen, or perhaps to no one, that people might think it odd of her to fly from London with a fourteen-year-old, just to deliver her, but she felt jittery and worried and wanted to make sure everything went okay. Joint Custody was something new in England. Maybe learning French and experiencing the Third World would be good for her—don't you think?

The journalist listened. He didn't think it odd at all, he said. And experiencing the Third World was always good for a person, or so he had always assumed.

When he bought her a rum-soda for her nerves, he ordered one for himself, for his own nerves—now that was odd. That was odd because why did he have any nerves?

Ralph Merian Susan Pollet. Susan Pollet Ralph Merian.

13

Howjado. Quiet weather lovely spot fascinating history. We met the other evening. You were saying, Mr. Merian?

"Perhaps you wanted to take one more sighting on the British consul, too," he suggested. "Maybe that was a little bit of it."

She studied him over her glass, under her helmet of white-blond hair, with her large, long-lipped smile turned down at the corners.

"Not that I'm an expert mumble mumble mumble domestic relations," he added. "But I find I accept opportunities to see the former wife I always liked, on the principle that a scratched wound heals faster."

"But it doesn't, Mr. Merian!"

"What does that have to do with it?"

She met his eyes very shyly, first with fierce English reserve and then with fierce English *Oh, the hell with it,* and said, "Of course. You caught me. But I had this look at him, your *sighting* as you put it, and nothing. Dead. All dried up and blown away, so I could hardly believe he ever did his snoring alongside me."

Lady, that fierce English reserve! When it breaks down!

"I don't know if I should congratulate you," said the journalist, thinking of his own last wife, the one he had liked so much, and what she didn't remember about him.

"Anyway, he has another woman now. American, as a matter of fact."

"I congratulate you both," said the veteran journalist. He ordered a second rum-soda for himself (was that three?), a second for her, so they could drink to new love—her former husband the impeccable consul's new love.

But of course a procedure was beginning in the case of the sweet, sad, not so shy, pretty English mother of one and the veteran journalist. It could have been the normal procedure of lonelies finding someone for the old stories in the public rooms of the Grand Hotel Oloffson, and if the truth is told, they both assumed that such was the case.

No war or revolution—an emptiness.

No daughter for the year and no spark at all, either, when the

14

nice British consul stood by while she kissed her—an emptiness. When in all his strict linen he gave Susan those kisses on each cheek, an emptiness.

"Excuse me," Mrs. Pollet was saying. "After a person has been traveling with a child, a person might well seem to take advantage of adult company—"

But it was not quite the normal procedure between the lady from the United Kingdom, mother of one, and the man from the war or revolution, divorced twice, badly.

After five days, the veteran journalist asked the lady to come back to New York with him awhile. Her return ticket to London could easily be rearranged, with a small surcharge that was hardly discussable. Independent souls like them were not bound hand and foot to their travel agents.

Rhum Barbancourt played no essential part in this plan, although they both needed all the help it gave them. It turned out that Susan Pollet's professional work was on the similar Creole languages of Haiti, Guadaloupe, Martinique, and the Seychelle Islands, and one could also find traces of it in the swamp parishes near New Orleans, and now it was even turning up in Brooklyn, Queens, and the Upper West Side of Manhattan. Her research grant made it not a totally silly suggestion to spend some time in New York, although, of course, had she known, there was a friend who could have used her flat in Knightsbridge.... Ah, well. Not everything in this life is predictable. When her husband had been posted to Nigeria, and she was still with him, she had found an echo of the word for hunger, *agu,* in the Creole *grand gout,* which probably meant there was verbal reinforcement in the Ibo language for the French borrowings....

"Very touching," said Ralph Merian. "I could use a person like you, linguistically."

"Has anyone ever pointed out, mister, you're a nasty brute?"

"It's been implied. I've grown to take it for granted."

"Arrogant fellow, aren't you? But you won't find me one of

your typical cheerful American girls. Now just do that again."

He did; they did. She seemed like such a cheerful English lady. Perhaps only recovering from delivering her daughter, she was really a solemn scholar with not a frivolous nerve in her head, that shining northern helmet, and she was merely escaping the sun by moving his body over hers.

Sprawled on the bed together, Susan and Merian began to come back to life like a successful attempt to fly that had ended in a successful crash in the mountains and mesas of pillows, sheets, quilt, crumpled mattress cover. That night they crawled to safety in sleep, whispering into each other's ears. In the morning the rescue party found them awake and hungry for orange juice, papaya, crackly toast, jams and honeys, coffee. They were their own rescue party.

Lovemaking, Merian thought, can be as good as work. He wasn't so sure of love itself.

Mrs. Pollet noticed his embarrassment in talking about himself. He hoped it would not occur to her that his past was a merely flickering reality, like yesterday's newspaper, with the inconvenient difference that it occasionally bothered his sleep. He supposed dreams and avowals to Arnie Schultz over dinner at Harvey's Chelsea were a small price to pay for having a history. There was, however, a more pressing reality—today and today's newspaper. Sometimes a person could temporarily omit the paper.

She asked nothing about his wives, his brother, his work, himself; he asked very little about her former husband, her daughter, her work, herself; getting to know each other was not their business, not yet, anyway. They were just living from breath to breath, from fruit to coffee, from morning cockcrow to evening throb of drums. The most amazing thing, to Ralph Merian at least, was the calm touch and cooling of bodies into sleep of these two who had met only a few days ago. Susan did not mention what was the most amazing thing to her; perhaps nothing, perhaps everything.

He did not try to imagine, in this heat, what "perhaps every-

16

thing" might mean, although he understood clearly from experience what "nothing" was.

Exotic tropical efflorescence was not the basic business between them; neither was fanatic lovemaking. Yet they feared they were infected with bougainvillea, loneliness, the wiggles, lazy inventiveness; and in timid, regretful, disabused fashion, they were behaving like kids while the fan turned overhead and they awakened to a tray of mangoes and papayas, french toast, sliced melons, and dark Haitian roasted coffee with a steaming pot of milk. When they went out, she did happen to look lovely, delicate and English, pink from the sun, under the wide straw hat. And that shy smile with no curiosity in it. The pale blue eyes peered into his, letting him see the lines of sun and fret that she, girlishly, neglected to cream. Was she looking at anything or was she just resting? Was he just an occasion or was she, by some chance, looking at Ralph Merian, American grouch? So to leave the site of excess romance was important.

On the flight to New York, the lady said she had read someplace, in the work of a German social psychologist, she thought, that the first sexual excitement lasts only six months or maybe it was two years. At the time, she was only browsing and it didn't seem important.

"Does it seem important now?"

"Essential, absolutely, of the utmost," she said. She held his hand tightly. "I'm doing this because you might be fearful of great heights."

"What about the *second* sexual excitement?" asked the V.J.

The lady laughed. "As I said, I was only leafing through. It's not my field."

"So we might have six months minus one week, or two years minus seven days—"

"And then we'll see," said the lady.

But neither of them felt it would come to that. They were busy people who treasured their plans and habits. At a certain time in life, a person has ways and tracks to follow. Eventually her

17

daughter would be back in school in London, and she would be back at her job at the School of Economics. And although his wars and revolutions weren't exactly scheduled, a person could count on them. (A doctor told him most people get sick on Monday. Countries, the journalist answered, tend to blow up on Friday afternoon, and bus service tends to go first of all, sometimes even ahead of the radio station; a little-known fact.)

He enjoyed his wars and revolutions, the lady noted. But his own history of failure and loss he did not enjoy.

They felt they understood each other as much as people could on such short notice and with the full intention not to try too hard. "There is a rumor abroad," she said, "that life is not the Club Med."

"Or the reverse," he said. "I think that's what you meant."

"We're both interested in grammar," she said. "We can help each other. If we stick with the structure of language, I'm sure we'll go far."

He laughed. He liked intelligence and humor in a woman, and hoped to encourage some in himself before it was too late.

It seemed a short flight. They chattered; there was nervousness about what awaited them in the real, nontropical world. She held his hand more than he normally liked, but he liked it. The journey from Illustrious Savior of His People Dr. François Duvalier Airport to John F. Kennedy International should have been more of a jolt, but wasn't. "It's mostly longitudinal," said the V.J. "The latitudes are what kill you."

"What a storehouse you are," she said.

"On time changes and jet lag, yes," he said. "Are we going to cool out now, just because we're in New York?"

"No," she said. "But maybe we'll change. I suppose that's necessary—a pity, isn't it?"

Manhattan with its grime, noise, and boiling streets, without slow fans turning overhead, did not wear out their friendship. One of the first changes Susan made was to get rid of the rotting flowers his cleaning lady brought him. It was one of her quirks to pick up what she called secondhand flowers from the florist

18

near the IRT subway stop and leave them for him in a pitcher or a coffee mug near where he left her money. It was nice. Susan agreed it was a lovely gesture, another side to life in New York; but since Merian often went away and returned weeks later, there the flowers were, no longer as good as secondhand, stinking with no mercy, and he had the job of carrying the pitcher to the incinerator and putting detergent in it and hoping the smell would go away. "You could tell her when you're leaving town," Susan suggested.

"Sometimes I don't know. And I don't want to hurt her feelings."

"That's what I treasure about you—you almost make sense."

"With an Olivetti portable under my fists, I'm a terrific sensemaker, dear. It's just organizing my life that gives me trouble."

It was as hot as Haiti that summer. The old folks were wilting on Riverside Drive, while the vacationing youth of America returned to the state of nature, expressing their talents in the fields of sex, drugs, rock and roll. A multi-ethnic staff of adolescents broadcast a survey of current music from the green bench across the way. Susan and Ralph felt like college kids released into the first joy of living together, that innocent rage of total approval of another. They had grown older and ironic, and tolerant of their condition, and they understood it to be a form of acceptable self-love. Street fairs and cab drivers and breakfast with the Sunday *New York Times* for company, and watching the Hudson River oil by beneath Merian's high-ceilinged studio on Riverside Drive, and cool, cool, summertime movies and restaurants that pumped air conditioning like the arctic over them in throbbing waves. This was better stuff than organizing a life; it organized itself. "I'm noticing something," he said.

"Yes?"

"Do men get hot flashes?"

"I'm sure they do. It's only right."

"Arnie says to watch out—here, feel my breasts. Are they getting flabby?"

"Um." Unsmiling, she lay a hand on him. "I think not. Of

19

course, I'm not a geriatric doctor, but I think your editor must be a scared fellow."

"Arnie's my colleague and friend in all matters."

"I think he's jealous," she said. "That's only an opinion. It's rather warm in here, don't you find?"

"Aren't the English supposed to hate air conditioning and cold beer? Gives strep infections?"

"Not necessarily," she said. "We more youthful persons can adapt nicely to the energy-wasting Yankee way. Personally, I find it's better to adapt—"

"That's a hard fact, isn't it, ma'am?"

She smiled. They were at the place where no facts seemed hard. They were too happy. They were silly. They didn't know how to measure and apply to real life the several months that passed. They could do without both theories and facts about it, without history and even future, at least for a while; they just let what was happening ride over them like the blast of summer. Susan sometimes read her linguistics journals with the head of a pen tickling her lips, and then they went out or stayed in. Merian organized his files, thought about a collection of his reports, wrote a couple of op-ed pieces. And then they had a meal with Arnie or they went to the Village or they did nothing and Merian told her she had ink on her mouth.

Arnie didn't seem to be jealous—just suspicious was all— and obligingly kept Merian in New York, doing Special Reports and Backgrounders (outlook bleak on Tuesday, guarded optimism on Sunday), the sort of thing that didn't interfere with what was happening between Ralph Merian and Susan Pollet. *Haiti: The Land of Unlimited Impossibility.* The V.J. could view with careless sobriety for a few hours at his typewriter, and then view with earnest frivolity. Arnie judged Ralph and Susan with the forlorn amazement of a true pal. He recommended books about love, Stendhal, Denis de Rougement, Freud, which wouldn't cure the disease but could inform them about their companions in folly and the usual course of this plague that caused flushed cheeks, firmed thighs and arms, and unaccountable laughter, ignoring the conditions of history.

Did this mean they had four months yet to run in the typical infection—according to a German social psychologist—of a love affair, which brings silent midnight clinging and talkative dawns?

Did asking the question, which suggested normal limits, mean they were claustrophobic already? Getting there? Or were they simply taking on a new ballast of suspicion along with their training in doubt and disbelief?

They preferred to run with the silliness. "Let's," she said, and he felt himself shaking until he just put it out of his mind—a good solution in such cases.

Sometimes it was the dawn that was silent and the midnight which was filled with talk. Susan had a sudden, elbow-propped fit of information gathering. "What made you choose this line of work?" she asked.

"Arnie says a newspaper is a warm bath. He stole that from McLuhan and says it as often as he can."

"How about you?"

"I think it came from hearing the war on the radio. Do you know about the liberation of Paris?"

"In England we study history," she said reproachfully. "Besides, Daddy told me. I can almost remember."

Ralph Merian remembered his brother, Chaz, at every moment of their childhood; his mother and father mostly in their dying days. Some memories were like jealousy and did no good work. It was 1945, summer, and he was weeping convulsively at the liberation of Paris as he listened to the radio and Chaz played with an erector set and his father bent forward, cupping his bad ear. His father knew why Ralph was crying and smiled at him. And he was thinking that's what life should be about—somehow being present with General Leclerc and the gaunt, blackened faces of the freed French when such things happen. Somehow managing to be in the city when the enemy is driven out. But such things don't happen very often, not like the liberation of Paris, so he

21

was merely present during other killings and didn't weep. If a woman made the tears start, or Chaz, or a dream of his father or mother, he did not treasure that experience of ache behind the eyes as he treasured the arrival of De Gaulle at the Cathedral of Notre Dame. At thirteen, it didn't really hurt; those were tears of joy.

Now he liked to be in Chad or Beirut or Chile, and to be a professional about it, telling the truth, the piece of it defined by the conventions of newspapers, cool-eyed, unmucked by sentimentality, maybe even calculating, pushing the sweat away from his eyes and scribbling, getting the details ripe and right. If a person does that, it's enough; he doesn't need the truth about himself. Merian suspected there might be pain and longing within, beneath his normal teasing hard-working good humor—his character that dealt so well with Arnie Schultz, so adequately even with the wife he had liked. Better than he could deal with Susan or Chaz, who didn't want a styled arrangement of the truth as defined by words everyone could agree on.

With Susan, when she slept, he could look upon something without translating it into something else. He bent his head to her sleeping one, that shining helmet of hair spread on the crumpled pillow, that dear light turmoil of a dream making her eyelids quiver; he quieted her by bending his head to her sleeping one and touching the warm brow with his mouth. That ache behind the eyes. Thank God she didn't awaken. Let her sleep, let her go on sleeping. If she caught this gesture, his tenderness, it would be a knowledge of him and an incorrect knowledge. It was something he dared to give her in her sleep.

Outside, it was still and hot all night. There was barely a ripple on the black river beyond the park. It could stay hot until Halloween, but Merian lay there looking at her, not waking her, knowing the summer was nearly over; and despite his joys, the shock of unexpected joys, he did not dread the next season.

Some men needed women to tell them who they were. Merian needed his peculiar work. It might be preferable to find the answer to the question elsewhere, just because life was sweet.... "In

22

the next island along, in Jamaica, they have a song—'Oh, Sweet Life,'" Merian had said, and Susan answered, "They *would* put an 'Oh' in it. They're right to do that. It's a prayer, isn't it?"

Maybe he should have had a child to tell him, maybe he should have listened to his mother and father until they told him, maybe even Chaz knew something about him, maybe he should just continue on his way and not assume the truth about himself was somewhere to be found. Finding it in a woman's arms had not been a correct procedure in the past.

"That would be nice," Susan was saying a few weeks later.

"Pardon?"

"You should listen, dear. If life were only sweet and that was all. We're not ready for that, are we? Could you sit on this suitcase until it shuts, your big burly weight, please, and then not break the zipper when you zip it up?"

When it came time to say good-bye, although the taste of fall was not yet in the air, he described the leafy scent and she said it sounded like England. He said Indian summer was different, a totally different smell. They were stuck. And then after a pause, looking at her neatly packed bags, she said, "Well, well, it's been nice, and now you've got your wars and revolutions."

"And you've got your kiddie squared away and your job in the ethnological linguistics department. Isn't it wonderful how failing England can still afford you."

"Yes," she said. Her face went cool, smooth—her superior English face, he called it. What does *she* want? Would Ralph please consider Susan?

That English way under stress works well in wartime, he thought.

He heard himself explaining gently and pompously, "We begin selfish; then when youth has finally begun to work for us, we have enough energy for others—then like babies we think of ourselves again. I'm afraid I've reached that stage. But at least, my dear one, I'm trying to warn you."

She kissed him. The superior face was gone. Her smile became more and more tender and desiring—loving, why not use the word?—as he confessed his weakness to her. Had she turned stupid? Was she a nurse? What cause for smiling was this?

"Warning! Warning! Warning! Warning!" he said. It was the wrong time for that loving face; he didn't want it.

And then she laughed. Perhaps he was the stupid one. "Don't worry," she said. "I know they miss you in Beirut."

In this rapid, distracted conversation among her packed things, with her ticket flapping near the telephone in the direct line of the air vent—ticket not to be forgotten on the way to the airport—he felt certain they had come to no clear understanding at all. She needed and he needed and he said and she listened and he gave her a dire warning and she only blushed gorgeously and smiled, and then rapidly punctured the heaviness with her sly offhand dismissal, so that he couldn't tell whether or not she even took him seriously, or herself, or them.

This way lies trouble, he thought.

At John F. Kennedy Airport he said, "Used to be Idlewild—that's how I still think of it. I'll be in London in a few weeks." She looked astonished. Her eyes hadn't filled with tears yet and he said that. "I'll arrange something, you'll see, maybe a plot to overthrow the Queen."

In less than a month he turned up, as predicted, with ample warning, of course, so that she could make her arrangements in case she had taken up again with her former lover, a prof at the London School of Economics. She hadn't. However, there was a complication anyway. It seemed her life had not just been invented for his convenience.

Hearing about her American—that heavy greedy gloomy fellow—had caused some turmoil in her former lover. He had suddenly taken to promising (a) to cut down his drinking and (b) to marry her. Surprised by so much interest, she had considered giving Paul perhaps, oh, a week or two of reprise in order to test it out, just to see what it felt like. It seemed logical. It wouldn't hurt. Any sensible young woman adrift in the nonswinging London of the 1980s, where only the Arabs and the Iranians were secure, would have to consider following through what had been, only a few months ago, her most tidy plan.

Just thinking about it was enough. The prospect of the prof, even nondrinking and an eventual homebody for her daughter, chilled her. In fact, she told him to go away, please, and when he bothered her at strange hours, to bugger off, mister. At two in the morning, when the need grows extreme in a man who had just preferred to take what was available, give what was convenient, because the American had not yet come into existence—and *now* thinking that his lost homeless jealous thoughts should be of interest to the lady—well, rudeness was in order. She knew he was alight with jealousy, of course—especially of a bleeding American *journalist,* for Christ's sake—but even if he promised to do everything right, she didn't want him. Even if (miracle) he *did* everything right, which of course never happens. Even to try, for fairness and old time's sake, even to give it one more shot—which did make a kind of sense, she reasoned—would only confuse her daughter, herself, everything.

Because she hoped Ralph Merian would come visit her in her semidetached in London.

Which he did.

She had hoped not to tell him about her problems with the prof because she feared it might put some sort of burden of gratitude or responsibility or pressure on him. After all, maybe the prof *would* give up his overabundant eye-openers and his reckless sundowners, and he *did* have an office conveniently down the hall from hers, and someone like that *could* provide a more normal nest for her and Cynthia than someone who was constantly whoring off after the slightest little pretty coup d'état—an American, besides, with grown former wives in Miami and Michigan, America, plus a brother in California who managed to keep in trouble. . . .

Well, it did lay a trip on the V.J.

How ladylike of her to hope she could resist telling him, and then to take all the credit for not telling him, and then to tell him. It could almost make a fellow nostalgic for the old days, growing up in the games of romance at Cornell football weekends.

He had a familiar impulse to head out for Ouagadougou, Upper Volta, because someone needed to inform the world what the goddamn Libyans were up to next.

But on the other hand, he didn't need to.

Screw Qaddafi (Khadafy, Gadhafi); even the stylebooks couldn't settle on a spelling for the name of that sand-scoured maniac.

He was staying in London instead and anyway.

It wasn't a war or revolution that provided his excuse for this visit, but a droning meeting of first-world monetary fundholders. His friend the editor was cooperative, although Arnie had it firmly in his mind who needed to write about OPEC and the World Bank and who (the V.J.) about boundary feuds and dust in the equipment and sand fleas and ravines full of bodies and palace murders that decided almost nothing. Monetary fund meetings didn't change too much either, and the gore was less picturesque. Ralph Merian had a nice controlled touch with gore. But since they were such old pals, growing old ungracefully together, the friend and editor obliged Merian by sending him up again into ozone layers that lay strips of cholesterol like *crème brulée* along the arteries. No fool like this fool.

More and more forlorn, Arnie was still a pal.

The assignment would be an exercise in on-the-spot back-grounding, the usual bleak outlook, guarded optimism, Tuesday and Sunday combined, plus a description of fawn-gray bankers' camouflage suits and emissions of soothing baritone prevarication. In the end, it would cost the USA a few billion and rescue a couple of consortiums. So no one could claim it was entirely without result.

The V.J. liked Susan's daughter. The kid turned up for a flying visit during a school holiday. She was a well-mannered English kid, no doubt like both her parents, with nice skin and shrewd looks, like Susan's. She missed her father and seemed to like the

American. Shyly she admitted she liked him better than the prof with the ginny breath no matter how many mints he sucked.

One night, middle of the night this time, the lady and the V.J. were awakened by a telephone call from the prof at the London School of Economics. Gin or Scotch speaking, of course, uttering pleadings and awful prayers to remember, remember—

She slammed down the phone. But it kept coming back, what she had done, closing that door while she waited for the American who might not even have turned up.

"Perhaps you shouldn't have done it," he said. "I'm not sure I would have."

"I lost interest," she said.

"But you must have had interest. You liked him. Just to give him another chance. I can see you were tempted. And I . . ." His voice trailed off, growling or muttering, as if he were sleepy, which he was not.

"I like you," she said. "Aside from how much I don't believe him, I like you."

"I'm not reliable, either." He sat up suddenly, although at his age a person needed to get a decent night's sleep, and said in a shockingly loud middle-of-the-night lover's quarrel voice, "Your kid! Your job! Where the hell am I? Who the hell am I for you?"

She was a lady in London town, S.W. 5, semidetached, and he was a person with a large one-room rent-controlled studio on Riverside Drive, in the middle of what was now a cocaine distribution free port for Bolivian diplomats, because one large room was all he needed during the few weeks a year when he went home.

"Home," he said. "As the song says, there's no place like home, and that's why I prefer to be elsewhere. So why didn't you at least give the poor lush a chance, since you must have approved of him in some ways and you surely read about the case where a lush gave it all up for the love of a grand, grand, wonderful woman—by the way, do you like losers, is that the deal?"

There was a moment of anger. She sat up, too. At this moment

27

she could have socked him, and he could feel the twitch in her arm, the rage, the willingness to take a swing. He was ready for it. He had asked for it.

She soothed him by kissing his chest, by licking his chest, by moving all along his body, as if somehow *he* was an aggrieved party and *she* had to make amends. In fact, of course, it was he who had declared he was about to give up, it was impractical, out of the question for people at their time of life, especially for him, of course—it was obvious what was on his mind—

"We can talk about this another time," she said.

And a long while later: "Or not, as you wish."

And again: "You're not a loser."

At last, near dawn, with the phone off the hook against eyeopeners, they slept. But first he remembered a Jaguar 3.8 he once owned, ran smooth, smelled warmly of leather, purred and sped. But oh, when it broke down, transmission, drive shaft, *clunk!* Impossible to fix. Never ran properly again.

First he remembered this—it had happened in Buenos Aires or Beirut—and then he slept.

In due course, the Petro-International Council of Aftershave Skinflints and Cutpurses finished its deliberations, folded its umbrellas, crawled into its Mercedes 280–SLs flying the national colors from the aerials, and dispersed to a little recreation in the gaming clubs of Knightsbridge. Conciliation of the have-not nations, upholding the world's economy in a period of turmoil, providing for spot recyling of oil, gold, and such less desirable commodities as the dollar, plus sitting there with simultaneous translation crackling into the ear, a shitload of boredom and babble, demanded one hell of a lot of nonrenewable energy. Some of the delegates took their new English girl friends to Monaco on strict doctor's orders. These girls really like the Mediterranean sun, and the distinguished delegates really wanted to be nice. Recycling of hard currencies begins at home—preferably at Prince Rainier's home.

The V.J. thought it might be time to return to New York. He didn't want to, and so he wanted to. "I wonder if nonswinging London is an aphrodisiac," he said.

"Our six months will soon be up."

"Don't count as a run if it's not consecutive, as any good Kraut social psychologist can tell you."

They clung to each other.

This thing between us, he thought, is a distress signal. It should bring us together. But I'm sinking and she is bouncing off the runway, trying to take off.

"We like each other. That's something we have in common," she said, "which the Kraut doesn't know about."

He wished to consider liking each other enough. But also he didn't want it to be enough, not again. He had loved another woman, a wife, and she him, it seemed, and now she could barely recall him, although he was no lush or spick-and-span diplomat or other disregardable person. He believed he should do his best to learn from history—also had no choice.

"What's this about distress signals?" she asked. "Don't you have fun with me?"

"Yes, that's true," he said. "Goddammit, you're right! I should make allowances. Want to just sit home and read by the fire tonight?"

"Yes," she said, smiling, "that's true. It's what I really want."

She knew how to construct an English coal fire in the grate. He knew (American know-how) ways of adding wood. They locked eyes for a moment, friendly readers about to read, and then opened their books. After a while, he said he was hungry and she said they should have tea, as if it were the afternoon, because in London they didn't usually just sit at home reading like this in the evening. They could get used to it gradually. She cut thick slices of bread for the tea; it seemed unlike her and it was nice—thick rough bread from a neighbor, honey from France, marmalade from Scotland, heat from the fire, heat from the teapot nearby. They were lazy together and had sticky fingers. This should be happiness, he thought—why isn't it?

Scared. In this good comfort with a lady who smelled sweet, who kept strict limits on pains, who arranged for good bread and marmalade, who let go in the dark with him and screamed, screamed so nicely, he felt his legs twitching with the desire to run. He thought with longing of Beirut, of Chad, of Angola, even of the junkies screaming so non-nicely outside his window on Riverside Drive. He wondered how this, which he had sworn to his friend and editor, and even more stubbornly, calmly, contentedly, to himself, would never happen again, had now happened again. He looked at her with her book in her lap, pouring the tea, slicing the thick rough pieces of dark bread from the neighbor, and tried to remember. Tried not to remember. Retraced his steps as a warning to himself.

A hotel bar. Port-au-Prince. Heavy heat and a civil war that didn't happen. What's so complicated about that? Him almost a nondrinker and her just handing over the kiddie to an elegant, too-elegant diplomat in too-clean whites. So there was this accident of running into a woman when he had happily given up all such accidents, either bar friendships or dwelling upon the him and her of it, the hairy him and the sweet-smelling, fair-foreheaded, long-smiling-up-from-the-pillow her. Old fools, he decided, are the best fools.

With her sweet fair lonely kid that he liked.

With her sweet fair gregarious body that he so much enjoyed liking.

Why not be willing to love and turn tender, taking chances, like a young man again? Why blame it on the landing at the St.-Marc road that didn't happen, leaving him with nothing to do at the Oloffson bar? Why keep on remembering other women who made him unhappy? Why not just remember this aforesaid present one, her sliding walk, her clever cautious shy attentive jokes, her helmet of hair, her kindness?

A veteran old fool didn't have to be totally terrorized, did he? Especially one who could crouch calmly under fire, spitting in the dust and scribbling with a pencil: *Half grenades unexplode...Russian and WW2 Italian rifles...17-year-old scream-*

ing for his mama.... If Merian could do that, he should be able to sit near a coal fire in an English grate and drink tea and eat thick good bread and sometimes smile at the other person.

The conference over, it seemed that a tide was pushing him back across the Atlantic Ocean. He needed to sit and discuss with Arnie Schultz. He was a professional. Something stubborn said this was plainly what he had to do.

She put her book on the floor. "I see," she said. "Because the conference is adjourned, you want to go to New York."

"What other excuse do I have?"

"I'll look it up in my German social psychologist."

He didn't enjoy disapproval. He didn't enjoy displeasing her. He didn't appreciate her chilled turning away. He had learned love was like this, and he didn't like it.

"Do you want to go out for some wine? Let me take you someplace funny—that tavern, the Hungry Horse—"

"No thanks," she said. "Oh, never mind. Sure. Do you want to go out?"

It seemed a marriage all at once. The straining to please and the hopelessness, that doggy following after the lady to please her and knowing he was doing it wrong. Bad doggy. Her not meeting his eyes. The evening was backing up through the windows of her narrow house with a heavy wash of old-time London bad air, the night backing up on his chest and belly. He was a dirty mutt. She didn't like him at all.

It passed. In fact, they really weren't married, and sulking could serve no purpose. She looked at him and shrugged and smiled. What can a person do? What can a person do with a dirty old dog? Well, what can she do?

He remembered, in that row house in London S.W. 5, a house of bricks painted white and Brancusi posters, the different house, one with a screened porch and sprinklers squishing on the lawn, where he had lived with his last wife, the one he liked, who said to him one summer night: *I don't know why I married you anymore. I'm sorry, dear.*

He remembered a priest who used to drive by in a convertible

Mustang, radio playing blue-eyed rock music, on his way to softball practice.

He remembered her sons who used to come to visit their mother and her husband on their vacations from school, and fondly called him "the wicked stepfather." *I can't remember why, dear.* Just like his brother, Chaz, those boys were now invisible. He never saw them anymore. They might have troubles, like Chaz, but he was busy elsewhere.

Merian had excess recall. It was useful for interviews with sergeants who had just declared themselves heads of state. It was more than he needed now. He didn't want new warnings. But the sprinklers squishing, the happy priest, the vision of his wife's sons so pleased about him, were warnings to make no future, not again, to keep close to the present, to abstain from plans, projects, hopes, and inevitable grief; especially that, since he still stubbornly wanted to go on, to keep his arms from the emptiness of holding an angry woman.

"You're staring into space, my dear," she said. "Do you want to go to the Hungry Horse?"

"It's the fire. That blue and green from the coal. It's a different color from American fire."

They wouldn't even have had to ask the neighbor who made the bread to come sit with the sleeping daughter. Cynthia was old enough to stay alone. But they didn't really need the Hungry Horse. After a while, without discussing it further, they went to bed.

The daughter flew back to her father, and Susan cried a little at Heathrow Airport, but only after the child had gone through the gates. She waved a handkerchief—another departure—as if it were a shipside farewell. A kid can't stand at the railing of a 747 and wave back.

And then Ralph Merian made his own reservation. And then his flight was in three days. He gave Susan two days' notice, but of course it wasn't a surprise; it just hadn't been mentioned a lot.

Even her daughter had been sad to leave him. He was a case just like her real father—presents, funny T-shirts, jokes, departures. He recognized, not praising himself, that it was partly the consul she missed, avoiding his eyes at the moment of goodbye, despite how polite she had been raised to be.

To the lady Susan Pollet he said, "Well, I'll be back, or you'll somehow—"

She shook her head. She indicated it was not worthy of him to throw these courteous promises into the vacancy. She drove him to Heathrow, parked, and it turned out his flight would be an hour late. So she phoned in to cancel her appointments at the university and he found a quiet place for them to sit in a room reserved for the press. Surrounded by tables with identical beat-up Hermes typewriters, dirty ashtrays, an urn with cold coffee, a pile of Styrofoam cups, he felt quite at home. But where was UPI, Reuters, Agence France-Presse, the *New York Times?* Where were Novosti, Ed Behr from *Newsweek,* the *Time* guys with their Smithsonian Abercrombie suits and the pockets filled with electronic equipment? Where was the old *Life* with its angelic expense accounts?

He thought about her sliding way of walking, like a girl, just gracefully sliding by—he thought about her for a moment as if she weren't there with him in a room that was more like home than any place he knew. But she was there.

He planned to write to her what he now had to say, filling the hour until flight time. He had warned her about him, but she didn't—that cool light pink fair intelligent English head of hers—she didn't want to pay attention to warnings. So now he had to spell it out.

"Go ahead," she said. She folded her hands primly on the tartan skirt, in the tartan lap, and requested of him that he proceed.

WARNING! WARNING! WARNING! THIS IS A LAST WARNING! he wanted to shout at her, *not* holding her hand, as he had shouted with fear and exasperation in the middle of the S.W. 5 night, after a drunken telephone call from the lover she had, in his considered, careful, warning view, unnecessarily given up. From a lover she might give up if she liked, but not necessarily for the V.J. "I like it sparse," he said, "without too much going on in my private life besides war and revolution, avoiding any more trouble. You know? My brother, Chaz, has a lot going on inside. It's very busy for him, and what good does it do? I prefer to spend my time when I'm not at work looking out the window, watching the old world grow older, like me. I like to work, too, but that's easy. One disaster at a time. I've given up complication."

Why that lovely smile? Why these inappropriate signals? Was it some kind of transatlantic communication he didn't understand? Was this any way to take a serious conversation seriously? He soldiered forward.

"So for me to try complication again, I want a guarantee—no grief. And no such guarantees are available."

"No," she said. She did understand after all, without his pedantic fight-picking.

"I can do war and revolution, plenty of energy left for that. Or I can just stare out the window—patience for that. Or I can whine and joke with my dear editor. The one thing I can't do is get myself in the way of being cared for and then lose it. Cherished—and then she decides no. I had that a few years ago. It would finish me for it to happen again."

Long wait. She was feeding it into her system. He could almost hear the intelligent computer checking all the discs.

"You make hard conditions," she said. "Are you asking me to predict the future? Promise for sure?"

He shrugged.

"I would try."

Let her retrieval find its own way.

"I feel," she said, "I feel, but I can't promise forever what I don't know forever, dear."

That was wise of her. It was his turn to contribute some silence to the discussion. There had been so much talk. A little down-turning smile played at the corners of her wide shy mouth; it flickered and went. There was something further on her mind. "That habit of yours," she said, "that really irritating habit, now I know what it seems to mean."

"Which one?"

"That little joke. That little pretentious joke, dear."

"Yes?"

"You don't say 'I' or 'me.' You say the Veteran Journalist. If you're in a hurry you say the V.J. 'The V.J. is happy today.' 'The V.J. would like some dinner.' I think you really really *really*, as you announced in your editorial opinion recently broadcast from Heathrow Airport—how did he put it?—you want it sparse and not too much going on because you're afraid of complication, dear, and yet you know you can't claim absolute treaty guarantees."

She was breathing fast because she normally didn't make speeches, didn't make breathless parody speeches, an Attack Speech like this one.

"The Veteran Journalist is sad today," he said. "The V.J. has been hit by an accurate volley."

She glanced up with a friendly social smile as the Heathrow press hostess stood by them, saying, "Your flight has been announced, Mr. Merian. I'm sorry about the room. You know there's a slowdown of the Pakistani cleaning personnel. They call it a slowdown, I call it a strike. Gate Eleven, sir."

He hoisted his Lettera 32 with the clever shoulder strap improvised by a local helper in Uganda. He waited till the hostess took the hint and clacked away. Then he said, "He'll miss you." Susan refused to meet his eyes. With an effort, he added, "I'll miss you."

"Old man," she said.

"Can't I just be a veteran? Do I have to be old?"

The stream leading to Gate Eleven was a straggle by this time. A man in a striped worsted suit was running, and it seemed like the first time he had ever seen a striped suit running like that.

Usually it was the seersuckers that ran. He would have to hurry, too, or miss his plane.

"No," she said. Was this an answer to the question, *Can't I just be a veteran?* Her eyes were wet. The smile was long, shy, and unforgiving.

"I'm not too old to fall in love," he said. "For me it's more dangerous than that. I'm too old to fall *out* of love."

He ran, the lightest practical typewriter in the world banging at his flanks.

2

ARNIE SCHULTZ, WHO knew Ralph Merian better than Merian knew himself—this was only fair and symmetrical, since the Veteran Journalist knew Arnie better than Arnie knew himself, also—understood when the V.J. needed a serious change of scene, a fresh war or revolution, a greening riot in the capital streets, a U.S. Marine or CIA incursion preparing to happen. "I'm looking at you," he said to Merian, baring his teeth.

"I notice this," Merian assured him, "and why? You're usually nervous about such things—eye contact isn't your strong suit, Arnie."

"Your sticky little toes are caught on flypaper."

"Okay."

"It's not the pest strip is sticky, it's your feet. That's my opinion. But you're stuck there."

"Okay, you don't win the insight prize this time, pal, but okay."

Arnie rolled back onto his chair, arms behind head, stockinged feet on desk, nudging coffee cup, feeling insulted. He did a silent paragraph jump and then stated, "Do you have any allergies to Native American messing around? That fine brave mistreated people that perhaps crossed the Bering Strait, trickling down through Alaska, growing Eskimo puffiness and generosity with wives up north, feathers on the Great Plains, picking up horses, a brilliant civilization rivaling the Egyptian in Mexico—Aztecs, gold *chashkas*, magic mushrooms—exploited and murdered and alcoholized but never once crunching a twig in the forest?"

Merian stared at him. "That's an ongoing story. Another backgrounder for the high-income zip-code insert? Jesus, Arnie. Fishing rights, minerals, water, Russell Banks—it's local bureau stuff, isn't it? What are you telling me? I'm demoted to how the original inhabitants of this fair land finally want to get a fair shake?"

"Have I got a story for you," Arnie said. "This is *entertainment*. For you, have I got an assignment!"

Merian wrinkled his nose at the stockinged feet playing with the scummy coffee cup. Just because Arnie had an office with partitions and a door that closed he didn't have to take on airs. "Has this been kept from me previously?" Merian asked.

"Not like we got it now you didn't see it, my boy. I promise you racial prejudice, injustice, pathos—what we call Major Tragedy on the editorial page—filmland scandal, hucksterism, and possible syphilis and embezzlement in high places."

The V.J. was growing interested. How could his own life compete against such a list of blessings? "Injustice," he murmured. "That's always a thrill."

"Injustice and rampant abuse, my lad, among the former brave hunters."

Ralph Merian was slouched in a chair opposite his buddy Arnie Schultz; he too had a scummy coffee cup on Arnie's desk, but he kept his shoes on, his feet on the floor—this was where Arnie lived. Surrounding them on five floors of the News-Press Building were the silent word processors and less silent electric typewriters and telex machines and the overpopulation of very whispery telephones. Blue screens were glowing like immense bland eyes, blocks of unnecessary intelligence were passing through equipment, lights on untended phones were flashing, waiting for secretaries, who sat elsewhere, to pick up. Merian was thinking that the solution to the problem of comfort, ease, delight, and pleasure with Susan, claustrophobia with Susan, agoraphobia with Susan, was to head into some nice international crisis again. A war would do, a civil war would do even better, being so much less organized, uncivil, in fact, although of course some of the Arab wars were almost as good as civil ones for their terrific virulence. Give him Iraq or Iran any day, and Syria doing a job on Lebanon, neat!

Formerly he didn't like such thoughts. To fly someplace where sallow foreigners in shiny white nylon shirts ran the shops, people different from the people who bought in the shops, who then came crashing through in various nights of long knives or mornings of bloody buckets or noontimes of dynamited mopeds—an efficient substitute for the thirty-day credit plan—he wasn't supposed to visit such scenes just to get away from a woman. That wasn't intrepid. That wasn't Columbia School of Journalism John Foster Dulles Spring Lecture. That wasn't very Nieman Fellow of him.

Ralph Merian was supposed to be a cunning wire contraption for getting into tight places and prying around and fishing out the good stuff. And then get out quickly. That was also a necessary part of the trade. The contraption worked because it didn't bother with the self out of which he could not get, did not wish to get, mucky as things were inside. He didn't enjoy dire predictions, News-Press Building backgrounders. He liked telling what he saw, what was unavoidable, with a little thrust at what was sly. But this made a problem with a Susan, didn't it? He was trained to do his work, leave at the appropriate time, no entanglements, on deadline, keep his personal muck within borders. But that's not how a person proceeds with a woman. Not with a woman who has her own decent line in life, her own responsibilities and steadiness to keep in order.

When a fellow has come to a truce with the world, why upset things and risk war? Merian didn't know if he was ready to cause so much trouble.

"I want to believe I can always count on you to carry the banner of the Fourth Estate," Arnie said, "a quill dipped into the skull of Richard Halliburton, inspired by a generally unquestioned expense account, and take arms against a sea of ennui, and—"

"Shut up, Arnie."

"Why should I? Were you even listening?"

"Just fill me in. Off the starring role in your motion picture, Arnie, okay?"

"Okay." Arnie leaned forward with his gap-toothed, yellow-toothed grin. Although he had recently launched his fifth or sixth lightning campaign to give up smoking, he hadn't yet given up yellow teeth. He said, "Omens, maledictions, incantations, and fried corn bread."

"Pardon?"

"You weren't listening, buddy, as I talk about this Stony Apache tribe, they call it a Nation, Capital 'N.' Would it help if I pushed your cuticles back or whatever special that nice lady does for you? Would you listen?"

"You may proceed."

"You know about Danny Grand?"

Merian dealt the name into the meat computer. He tried to keep up with American culture, priding himself on his memory for lint. "The most popular American in the Christian quarters of Beirut, that's a detail," he said. "Let us now join our guitars in a duet of..." And the two men sang:

> I went downstairs
> And I drank two six-packs
> And I ate some fried chicken
> 'Cause my baby don' love me no more

"You got it," said Arnie, "that's his platinum. Country-western rock, not quite so big as Willie Nelson but bigger'n Johnny Cash, or maybe it's the other way around, and doin' his own damn thang. A scam artist beyond anyone in your wildest dreams, Horatio. Now let me tell you the pot of luck our Danny fell into."

It seemed that Danny Grand filled an idle moment on the Johnny Carson Show by remembering that he was a son of the Apache people, although he had mentioned to *People* mag that he was a Cherokee with some Sioux in there someplace—that was a previous interview and a different record wanting to climb the charts. Danny's voice wavered when he sang, too; it was beer, loss, and a nose habit on top of all that takeout fried chicken that caused the mental variation.

"My brother, Chaz, used to say he was a crazy Indian, too. He was wild."

"I know about your brother, Chaz."

"He had border grievances, too. Even though he was my brother, I absolutely believed him. He was the Indian in the family."

"May I proceed?"

Merian nodded. The steady employment of news served partly to distract the people of America with a nice warm feeling of chaos in the world. Merian enjoyed exercising his skill at putting the chaos together. Effort irrigated the capillaries of the skull, which made the brain crop grow; this was what was meant by keeping the juices running. He felt the old thrill of work. Distraction from Susan or Chaz was not a worthy motive. "Please," he said to Arnie, "I'm listening."

Arnie looked at him with a lover's reproach for his wandering attention, waited a moment to indicate very slightly bruised feelings, scrubbed his knuckles across his front teeth in a nervous cleaning gesture, sighed, continued.

As it happened, with one of those delicious serendipities that come into the karma of every country-rock star worthy of the name, the Tribal Parliament (formerly Council, formerly Powwow) of the Stony Apache Nation in southern Arizona had been debating around the time of Danny Grand's confession on the Johnny

Carson Show—well, whether to spend the Nation's funds on a cattle fence, a water dig (lack of sweet water was poisoning both the cattle and the people), an electronics trade school, or just a passel of new Ford pickups. Many a cement-block, poured-concrete, corrugated zinc wigwam had to make do with brackish, clay-colored water and no Ford pickup out beyond. There had been earnest discussion of the matter and earnest fistfights on the subject and one earnest knife duel (carotid artery, careening life-saving rush to the clinic in Tempe). There was a problem of angst and loss of identity within the Nation.

But then, around the big Great Spirit Rec Hall Advent screen, a group of Stony Apache elders and parliamentarians happened to be watching Danny Grand tell how the Establishment allowed him to be a country-western star, go platinum, get a good rep for philosophy and truth-telling in the ballad form. Sure. Okay with those eastern money boys, but owing to prejudice against his Founding Braves blood, nobody would let him make the Indian and Cowboys movie that he had written or at least carefully outlined on the back of some old envelopes from his business manager. It lay down the funky stuff about Native American oppression and that was why. The big foreign-born bankers, Russian and Greek—Tel Aviv, some of them—who financed the movies out of New York and Century City didn't like hearing any down-home truth from a real part-Indian was why. All he needed was a million or two, plus he would invest his own time and effort and a share in the soundtrack record, and he'd be on his way. The first Americans to own this great land of ours, only they weren't called Americans in those days, wandered the Great Plains, killing the bison-buffaloes and their enemy peoples, but only enough to eat, never for sport, in keeping with the dictates of the Great Spirit—well, maybe a few ceremonies and sacrifices in case of drought—but no, the big boys in those high-rises in New York City, the Apple, didn't want the story about Danny's heritage on his mother's side. All they cared about was (rubbing his thumb and forefinger together).

"You heard about the Bottom Line?" Danny asked Johnny. "That's what it means" (thumb and forefinger).

Danny had the old envelopes in his pocket right here.

He held them up for everyone to see, all over this great land of ours; later, in syndication.

"It's a great filmic epic," said Danny Grand. "The Truth Shall Make Ye Like Free, only for modern times. But do you think I can tell it? Do you think they'll let me?"

The Elders of the National Parliament, foregathered in the Rec Hall for a few cold Buds, felt an Idea growing among them like the hump of fat on a buffalo's back. Danny Grand was one of them.

Serendipity zapped across the filthy East, over the flat and smug Midwest, around the poisonous industrial cities, past the slow Mississippi, over the green and Rocky Mountains, around the sparser but still cursed western towns, and then through the desert with the hot speed of a microwave oven into the outsize Advent screen that the Nation had bought itself for Christmas from a salesman in Tempe—no, this show originated in Hollywood. Well, same principle, slightly shorter distance, but still worlds apart. Nevertheless, the Stony Apache Leaders and Elders happened to be Johnnies on the spot. . . . Since Arnie didn't get to leave the News-Press Building and gather the story himself he liked to inspire his best reporter with a little imaginative projection; creative editors are like that. Arnie beamed, motioned Merian to relax and hear him out, and continued, ignoring the tattoo of buttons flashing on his telephone.

With the telepathy of their ancient ancestors on their side, plus help from an Advent, the dignitaries of the Stony Apache Nation tuned in on the spiritual connections between all of them and the totality of Danny Grand. Plus, linking up with Danny would settle the dispute about cattle fences, wells, schools, pickups, which could wait. You can always dig a well or teach a kid. The Bureau of Indian Affairs brings in the gamma globulin for the hepatitis, the special welfare programs for some boy who is cued in to the ancient traditions of his people even if he can't write too good or hold his whiskey. (What the white man calls "firewater" has all sides to it, including some derogatory ones.) But Danny Grand there, Danny Sings-in-the-AM-Radio-Night, one of their own, was getting damn impatient. The Native Americans in this slave country have been waiting too fucking long. Danny's sideburns already looked a little purple, due to the passing of time, just like the Rev. Jim Jones, who was also one of their own, partly, although of course he couldn't sing so terrifically plus write many of his own ballads. And, besides, Danny wasn't into mass Kool-Aid suicide.

The Elders gazed at one another with that special look of timeless, big-sky tribal serendipity. Not serendipity, that's not the word here; wisdom and laissez-faire of the race; no, there must be another term for it, Arnie thought, grasping: "Ralph, you give it to me."

"Fatality? Mythic communion?"

"Maybe."

"The word usually depends on what you're trying to say."

"Well, never mind, let's just call it . . . serendipity? and get on with it, okay?"

So the Elders closed down the screen after Johnny and Danny signed off with a little ripple from the band and they just looked at one another, the truth revealed, but not shaking their heads from side to side; that's a white-man gesture, a round-eyed form of hysteria. They sighed in great earthy rumbles, what vulgarians call saying "Uggh." The Decision came upon them like a spring breeze, a nightingale song at dawn, a clean start-up of a cold motor. The Great Spirit was bringing peace. The dispute over the treasury ended not in a vote but an acclamation. They—and with them, the Nation—would invest in Danny's Vision.

Naturally, the details took a few months. It's hard just to dump a couple of million from the treasury of an Apache nation, untried in film production, on an unsuspecting future movie star with high country-western standards. At first Danny Grand thought they were vulgar publicity seekers or groupies who wouldn't actually put out. They had to work on him, make a lot of long-distance calls, send Jarls Coyote, President of the Stony Apache Nation, as an emissary to Century City, wearing his itchy leathers and feathers—round-eyed people go for shtick. In the parlance of the space folks from Century City, they took a meet. Jarls gave him a ceremonial stone mug—"Drink deep, Danny"—and Danny offered Jarls a pinch of white snuff.

At last Danny guessed they were serious, first-class, honest braves like himself, not just bullshitters. The white snuff made President Coyote giggle, something he previously had not realized Native Americans could do. They can do anything round-eyes can do, if you give them a chance and a line or two.

Danny got the proof positive pronto in the form of a certified check from the Tempe National Bank in downtown Tempe, assigning the capital surplus of tribal funds to Danny Grand Offshore Productions, and asking only for his promise to bring the film to the Nation for its world premiere. "You got my handshake on it, boys. You *got* it." And he stuck out a finger and a knee at them in a sealing of the bonding gesture he had learned from his deep personal friend, Sammy Davis Junior.

The bankers and trustees also insisted on inserting clauses about repayment from first gross receipts (changed to "net"), shares of profits (changed to "after certain other shares"), stuff Danny and Jarls, being braves together, didn't like to quibble about. Danny realized these were not only serious folks but also friends of the ancient art of truth. He thanked them kindly, much obliged. He sent them a complete set of his video tapes, and promised a better machine to play them on as soon as he could get around to it. They already had a hi-fi for his mono records. The Nation was poor in goods, but rich in spirit. Only recently had it taken control of its traditional communal funds from the Anglo bankers in Tempe who had been sitting on them and extracting round-eyed percentages. The Advent screen in the Rec Hall had been their first investment in high technology and already it was paying off. Danny's word was his bond—a brother (on his mother's side, he said).

The drinking water, which had been trucked in for generations, could be trucked in awhile longer. People ought to learn not to drink from the goddamn old wells. Out of the profits from the film, they might dig some new ones where the BIA engineers told them. That was only their opinion, but what do geologists know? Liver disease was a kind of tradition on the Nation. So the water might get to be less polluted, and the weaker children, who tended to die from soft stomach, might live a little longer. If they reduced hepatitis, it might even turn out to be a good thing. But why tamper with a way of life that had endured for so many generations?

And as to the cattle, chased all over the range and sometimes stolen by rustlers, they were Native American cattle who don't like to be cooped up. Someday a federal agency might build a fence. Who had gone into the locoweed and talked to the bulls about it? Why should the Stony Apache Nation tie itself and its cattle down with barbed wire? That wasn't the Way of the Ancients.

The kids started fighting the battle of the bottle at age fourteen or so. So why give them schools and schoolyards to drink in? What was the point of teaching them to use tools they would stab themselves with? The goddamn Bureau of Indian Affairs meddled in everything, issuing opinions, sending advisers and inspectors, eating their fried bread and asking who has this or that funny disease, which tends to fade away in the fullness of desert time anyway, leaving only a little arthritis or paresis. The BIA had no sympathy for the Way—patience, acceptance, calm, plus revolution.

So the Great Advent Color Teevee Serendipity solved the problem of the money. Danny had already written the words to a little traditional rain-dance ditty, but he couldn't sing it to them right yet—not registered with ASCAP. "Y' unnerstan?" he asked, and the Elders nodded their heads with the proud, ancient, and traditional dignity of not knowing what the fuck ASCAP was.

Ralph Merian listened carefully. Arnie was in a frenzy of salesmanship; he had stood up and taken to walking around the

46

office, arms waving. On the Great Plains, he shouted, people didn't weave any barbed wire and they didn't read about any Little Jack Horner going to the well with Dick and Jane. For emphasis and punctuation, he didn't take a single call, despite the angry flashings from his telephone. He really wanted Merian to do this job.

"They have a weltanschauung," he said, calming himself a little, getting practical, "just like a regular philosophy of everything. You might want to get into that. Religion, culture, the economy on the mesa. The Carter Administration gave 'em a pilot electronics assembly project and an air force contract. Life expectancy lower than Upper Volta, but they have their pride. I see this for a series that could start on Sunday and continue maybe five days into the week—a veritable eternity of syndicated exposure."

"Weltanschauungism," said Merian. "You think I'm getting too old for details? I have to get into meaning because that's all I'm good for, just a ragtag of my former self?"

"No. I'm just not ready to send you back to the Middle East with a stopover in London. I don't need that pink lady on your expense account."

"Thank you very much."

"You can get thoughtful and all those good things," Arnie said. "America repays thought as much as Lebanon, sometimes more. Just make sure you step *gently* on Third-World toes and support every accurate observation with a touch of balanced hope. Don't leave out the alarm. I'm not saying you have to be as boring as James Reston, as doctrinaire as Alexander Cockburn, as jazzy as Hunter Thompson, as—but do I need to explain? I want a *major* Ralph Merian."

"Then I'm your man," said Merian, "the Miss Lonelyhearts of Investigative Reporting."

Arnie peeked at him sideways, wrinkling his nose in that flirtatious goading way he had. It wasn't a sexual taunting, but it said that Arnie had reservations about his old friend; the reservations were what made him so fond of the V.J. Besides, they were close in spirit. Arnie valued the inwardness and doubt that seemed to keep Merian's metabolism going. He actually liked to trundle off to places where he knew no one and to smile earnestly and listen to peoples' yadda-yadda. Merian's mistrust of himself led him to take other people seriously.

Arnie, on the other hand, lived by a kind of brooding outwardness. He had borrowed his style as a joke from the Legend of the Snotty Editor, green eyeshades and gartered sleeves, but it seemed to suit him as well as anything of his own. (He actually did own a fedora with a sweaty band.) Once he had thought to be not a journalist but a poet, stupid college shit that he was, and so he drifted into this merchandising of words—not his own, but others'—while he waited for *Ulysses* or at least *The Waste Land* to come to him. They didn't come. He had heard that Ezra Pound just yanked *The Waste Land* out of the hands of T. S. Eliot (spells "Toilets" sideways), and then cut and spliced a little, edited. But for many years now, since his first wife left him, there had been nothing to yank out of Arnie's hands, and so Arnie had entered the business of yanking pages out of other people's hands. But not poets' hands. Just wordsmith private eye investigative fast-pass hands. Arnie had become a *lovable* snotty editor, straining for the curmudgeon title.

The perfect journalist was ready to write two to eight thousand words about anything—the first two to eight thousand that came to him, depending on the amount of advertising, time of year, glossiness of the supplement. He could tailor to that. The V.J., Arnie's closest buddy, best reporter, finest writer, a veritable "correspondent," tended to go on thinking about his last war or revolution or even his recent love affair, and therefore he tended to contaminate the next project with shadows and theories, details and images, "some fuckin' gestalt that has disappeared from the scene already," as Arnie put it.

"You still teaching your night course at the New School for Social Research?" Merian inquired.

"Up yours," said Arnie.

Merian wrinkled his nose right back. Old pal, old pal.

If he was still teaching at the New School, he had a right. A fellow's lonely, the bed is empty at night, any remedy will do.

The Veteran Journalist would never have thought of the Stony Apache Nation on his own. His malicious editor, deskbound, squirming and possibly hemorrhoidal in his chair, liked bad jokes. His job was to think of such things and point out that *there*, in fact, in silence, exile, and cunning, lay the uncreated conscience of the race of newspaper readers. The rest was college-boy and coffeehouse stuff. Danny Grand, tapping into the Stony Apache Nation tribal funds, was a story that sharp-nosed editor Arnie Schultz considered a worthy challenge for the V.J. How to avoid intimations of racism while dealing with a Hollywood and Nashville shuck artist taking an isolated band of poor Indians for a ride in his Bentley with customized trailer? "Play it for pathos, longing, hope, yearning, living in the fantasy of media, software feedback on the reservation—those things you ought to be able to do in your sleep by now," he commanded.

"You know I do blood and terror better," said the V.J.

Arnie shrugged. "Well, maybe you'll get lucky. Where you go goes gore. I'll bet, you stay on the reservation a week, there'll be some force and violence turn up someplace. Dig, pal. Poke and prod. Those things you favor."

"I've got a visitor coming back to New York first. This thing'll keep a minute, won't it? I like the idea, I really do, but you've got to give me a little time."

Arnie stared. "Okay. How much?"

Old friend with the new doughnut-shaped foam pillow in your chair.

"But Ralph. You wouldn't think of taking the lady with you, would you? 'Cause don't."

3

SUSAN POLLET AND Ralph Merian had come to an agreement. They had been lovers and they would remain friends. There were shadows, but that happens. At Heathrow it seemed to both of them that he was running from her, but that happens, too. She could as easily have been running from him— her life settled into its own routines, that of a graceful young scholar with a bright helmet of hair bent over her journals or fiddling with her tapes, certainly not needing a clumsy and lumbering American to fix her Sony or take care of any other chores. She had a beat-up old TR-5 for running around London with the chores. When the top leaked, she just wore a raincoat. What she did in the smoky London evenings, after the bending at her desk and the meetings and the errands, was no longer his business. Neither was what she did, if anything, on the long weekends. (But why did she keep going to Great Wilts? The fact that it was near Wiltshire did not answer the question. What kind of friends or country relatives did she have in Great Wilts or Wiltshire?)

They wrote letters. The letters were friendly and communicated partial truths.

Merian did not repeat the error of the ginny prof from the London School of Economics. No midnight telephoning, just because it occurred to him to want her by his side, just because it was midnight in his time zone, Eastern U.S. and Canada all the way down to the Caribbean, and Lord knew what she might be doing at whatever hour it was for her. Surely not pining after a stupid journalist. Surely none of his business. In his distress at midnight, and in the mornings over the instant coffee and instant bachelor's milk and instant peeled banana, before he got down to generating the op-ed and feature eight- to twelve-hundred-word items with which he was holding Arnie at bay, he was smarter than at least one other man. He was smarter—more cautious, more coddling of his stupid self—than the ginny prof who just tossed out his self-respect like a chewed-up olive pit. He was smarter than that. He had trouble sleeping and he was smarter than that. He had trouble waking up, but he was smarter than that.

Although he wrote more letters than she did. But it was only because he grew a little garrulous when he longed for a person and it didn't help to talk to Arnie and his brother, Chaz, had been no help for many years now and he liked writing letters when he wasn't on a real story. Not this thinking and digesting old investigations and viewing with concern stuff. Since Arnie didn't want him to wear out in the service of war and revolution.

Writing two or maybe three letters to her did not necessarily indicate his lack of intelligence. It might have been a sign or signal, though. Writing hugely unspecific letters about the changes of New York and Riverside Drive and the condition of his high-ceilinged room (did she remember?) and the old couple fearfully tottering outside his window (could she grow sentimental about muggings?) and all that wary mood shape of the transatlantic letter did tend to indicate a sort of dumbness. Describing the tottering neighborhood couple as wrinkled and shrunken, like apples left on a radiator—surely she wouldn't read that as the poet in him, longing for a young woman with a helmet of hair like a lamp spilling light over itself, shaking free in sparks as she bent over phonetic lists comparing Ibo with Haitian Creole with South Carolina Gullah with Louisiana parish French. Oh, he was feeling lonely, although he was supposed to be beyond this disgrace, else why specialize in the mere trivial splendidness of hair? In the recollection of bright hair and nape of neck? Shampoo and longing and stupidness deserved the credit.

His letters bordered on public mopery. He hoped she didn't read them as such.

She might have.

So when it happened that she received her grant to study the Creole-speaking community of New York, Haitians mainly, but also a scattering of Martiniquais and Guadaloupeans, whose language was almost the same despite the lack of contact, she explained that this was one of those things that sometimes comes to pass in research. She hadn't really expected the grant. It should not terrify either of them. (But didn't she apply for it? Well, not to mention details.) In New York there were some interesting developments in "the demotic culture and script," whatever that might be (Susan was better educated than Merian). She would be very busy, trying to accomplish a lot in a limited time with the Empire's paltry resources for essential sociolinguistic reconnoitering; poor Albion, no longer possessing the strength of perfidy.

Both the lady linguistic scholar and the gentleman journalist agreed that living in the same city would neither end their friendship nor force it onto any other downward path. The weeks in the same narrow row house in London S.W. 5 had probably been a mistake; too good for such as them—mature, grown-up, experienced, well-bruised citizen and subject. They would proceed from a more sensible level, just gathering data and passing the time. They were friends. They were friends who happened upon a fluttering of the heart when they touched. This was probably a matter of sociobiology; nothing to worry about; just what occurs when certain exogamous types meet under circumstances similar to spring. Odd how curious climates and weathers can come to resemble the springs of extreme youth and ignorance and foolishness and hope. How a song on a portable radio from a fire escape across the way can drain all the caution from a person. "You took my arm as if you loved me." How happening to hear the song again tells children that they own a shared history.

The town of Manhattan was large enough for them to keep their distance. They were intelligent. Songs are mere ballads and end; spring passes, even the spring of extreme youth—a disease that time cures. Could he, she inquired, live with that? Could she?

They certainly could.

Excellent. It would be nice to see each other now and then.

Her own self, by mail, in a trade with a resident English alien, even found a place to live crosstown, with no help from him, with Central Park as a buffer zone between them.

What discretion. Such an intelligent person.

And he would frequently be away on assignment, as usual; she would be busy with her work, might even travel to South Carolina to listen to some Gullah speakers, plus a few informants in Charleston, to try to chart more of the lines between Creole as a French and African language and Gullah as a similarly developed English and African verbal code. Very interesting, very curious how little basic work had been done on the obvious parallels. It occurred to her that cognate vocabularies might exist, and possibly one might even find an individual who had learned both Creole and Gullah. . . . No wonder the British Council grant committee just pushed her proposal right through. How lucky they just happened to have matching funds from Laurance Rockefeller to foster international communication.

With Merian and Pollet both so busy with their separate occupations, they might even during some conjunction or other

54

enjoy a love affair with each other. Why foreclose this option? Why indeed?

So it could work out nicely.

In this world, nothing remains the same and everything moves along. For example, Susan's daughter turned fifteen. During the time between Merian's leaving London and Susan's arrival in New York, he had had a birthday, too. Nobody knew it except his brother, Chaz, who sent him a postcard from San Francisco of The Crookedest Street in the World. ("To the Crookedest Brother in the World—hi! and many others like them!") Merian's last wife, the one he still liked, also had a birthday, and out of kindness to himself he neglected to call her. Why was this a kindness to himself? Because she would have said, Oh, dear, I forgot yours again, didn't I?

Susan was still aged thirty-five: "*Nel mezzo del camina di nostra vita* or something like that," as she said, "it's not one of my dialects." One of these days she too would have a birthday and he asked her the date. He wrote it on a matchbook and later transferred it to his calendar so that he could remember to do something about it.

So he hadn't asked her to move to New York and it just happened. They made no promises to each other. She was an independent soul. He just wanted her.

Her grant would enable her to complete a stage of her work, although of course the work is never done. If you added the ethnology collections at NYU to the Columbia library, and didn't mind the subway too much, they had excellent facilities in New York. There was also that large Haitian émigré colony in the West Nineties, her major resource. And the ones in Brooklyn. And the older group in Queens. Merian could count on her not staying, of course. Cynthia would be coming to live with her again. This was a kind of sabbatical for study. One should not fret on that score—that she might be deposited in Manhattan forever, a stone weight on Arnie Schultz's best friend's freedom of motion.

Anyway, she knew the town from the three years when her husband was in the consulate. She had a few friends, including an RAF hero who was now the darts champion at the Rose & Thistle on East Sixty-sixth. She even had favorite restaurants of her own and remembered the name of a grocer in the East Eighties. It wasn't as if she needed any attention.

Of course, Susan Pollet and Ralph Merian might see each other if they so chose and decided. Though they had not been acquainted very long, their friendship felt like an old friendship. At his age, even at her age, one doesn't make good friends easily.

The news felt like a wounding. His chest pounded with hasty desire as if it were an illness. Love did not seem agreeable to him. But he could think of nothing else during the weeks before she arrived.

He was only resident in Manhattan when he was not elsewhere. There was no need to take care of her; she was a grown woman and researcher. The grocer was named Sanchez, Isador Sanchez. He was Dominican, but he had a Haitian wife.

Of course, New York was an excellent center for her field. She would be very busy with her studies of written and spoken Creole—in the 1950s, UNESCO had done some reasonable work systematizing the spelling of written Creole, before it got distracted by politics—and in no way was Merian obliged to entertain her, just because they were in love with each other and neither one believed he or she understood the meaning of the word. When they were younger, they had understood. And it had led to many misunderstandings, several marriages.

So now they would just proceed with the more reliable business of life.

She refused to let him meet her at JFK. She knew her way around airports as well as he did. Anyway, this sort of thing, long trip out, flowers or whatever, long weary road in, was the sort of thing that implied engagement or commitment or...

Whatever, he had work to do. She could take care of herself.

He told her, when he showed up anyway, that he had hired

an ambulance to carry them into town, siren screaming, so they could make love on the expressway through Queens. She laughed. It wasn't true.

"But it was something I thought of," he said.

"You would," she said.

And they both fell silent over the next little idea: He thought of it, but he didn't. The prudent man that he had become enjoyed a good idea but chose not to carry it out. She should go directly to her new digs.

On the East Side, near where she used to live with her husband—only now it was different; under the recent city administration there was less dogshit on the streets—she had found an apartment to exchange with a returning Britisher. She had left her place in London for him and he had left his place on East Seventy-second. In response to Ralph Merian's question, no, they didn't know each other but had mutual friends and perhaps had met once or twice but weren't sure. "Over warm drinks," said Ralph Merian.

"Tu comprends," said Susan Pollet. "So much world traveling experience."

"But now, even in England, they have discovered the ice cube."

"Got it. Despite economic ruin."

"Due to oil," said Merian, "despite the North Sea discovery. It's the higher science of economics."

"Not our field," said the lady.

"May I propose to you," he said, proposing, "an evening of C, C, and F."

"See See and Eff?" she asked. She wasn't sure of this supercilious grizzled person.

"Culture, Charm, and Food," he said. "Dinner."

His bad jokes worked as an Intimacy Retardant. Sort of like mosquito lotion. Antifeeling Oil.

"Just the thing for serious jet lag," she remarked.

"You tell me what you want," he said.

She wouldn't tell him. He would need to discover for himself.

English reticence, English pink flush on the cheeks, English good cheer, English gloom held in check. Susan let him help her unpack, anyway, and explore the overdecorated little apartment where a man she didn't know had pushed his own things into corners of the closets, not leaving much room for her. "He's an old bachelor," she said, "probably poofy, very nice, and couldn't find where to put his things and figured I wasn't staying for more than six months anyway...."

Ralph Merian noted this. She was scheduled to return to London in six months. He need fear nothing, although he was not a poof, but he too was an old bachelor with everything in its ordained place and not wanting to be crowded.

In fact, they didn't go out to dinner for a while.

Afterward she sat on the edge of her English sabbatical landlord's bed, wearing a Chinese robe that belonged to him because she hadn't finished unpacking, with the sleeves turned up over her wrists, gazing down upon dozing Ralph Merian with eyes of no particular expression when he awakened. He blinked at her and remarked that he had fallen asleep, it seemed.

Some kind of expression came back into her eyes as he looked at her and reached for her. They were both cautious. He offered to help her unpack before the wrinkles got etched into her English clothes. "Good English wool," she said, "shakes out. Good English lady doesn't fret too much."

He understood that this was the case. Yet they were speaking this peculiar pidgin.

Were they developing a joking relationship, as primitive peoples sometimes do? Haitians joke a lot; maybe their chance meeting in Haiti had infected them, as with some kind of encephalitis. She was claiming to be a neat portable foldable English convenient town-and-country lady, when actually she was not; that is, she was something besides the sort of young woman about whom, among wealthy New Yorkers (Southampton people, for example, and Connecticut people), it was said: *She couldn't be nicer.* Susan kept secrets and had secrets to keep. That was not part of the character of the sweet girls who couldn't be nicer.

"This is upsetting," she observed at the signs of contentment and settling into Manhattan. She remarked about how upset she was, not equipped for the habits of ease. Pollet and Merian didn't really have the same or a similar heritage—his clumsiness, for example, her grace; his thickened skin and persistent mucking in the past, her fresh pink untouched coolness despite all the obvious troubles of marriage and child and trying to make her curious career in dialects, jargons, and creoles, which she insisted should be called languages. He was American and didn't know what that was. She was English and it never occurred to her to ask the question. She seemed to know who and what and where she was. He felt he belonged in a communications satellite, spinning over the nearest war or revolution. When he was there, he knew who he was: reasonably clever eye, reasonably clever meat computer.

Before getting acquainted, Susan and Ralph had shared personal alternations of turmoil and boredom. It was something they had in common. This bad habit was not enough for a long-term meeting of the minds.

At the moment Susan was content to think neither of the past nor of the future.

He, of course, had long ago turned away from belief in this good luck he was having. If she loved him now for no reason, she might with just as good reason stop loving him. In the mists of antiquity—his childhood—he had learned that people took to him and then went about their business, which might mean taking to someone else. (He was the first child of his parents. There was another. He was the first husband of his first wife. There was another, and then a third.) He had learned that his health was excellent, his skull competent, and he could do his work reliably. There were ample wars, revolutions, and brutal national leaders to keep him occupied.

People, when he was a child, didn't stop caring for him. It only seemed that way to a selfish elder son. They went to work, they had Chaz, they needed to exercise their talents in a pharmacy, for example, as his father did, writing prescriptions. Personally, Ralph Merian avoided prescriptions; he wrote descriptions. He guessed that his father must have had time to love his mother, and even to love him. It just seemed he wanted more when he stood reading the magazines in the drugstore, careful not to muss them, while his father took care of the customers and his mother, at home, took care of the difficult littler one, who screamed, held his breath, and turned red for attention.

Merian suggested to Susan that they go out for dinner to a little neighborhood place; surely there was one, Italian or Hungarian, in these blocks. Or a tavern that served acceptable steaks. "Such as you Americans still like," Susan said. "Yes, let's. Anything to stop your thinking and looking so worried."

"That's how thinking goes," he said, and pulled her to him for a quick cuddle that stops the thinking.

How his heart stopped when he looked at her was not a sign of impatient desire for her body (he had known that with other women), or love (perhaps he had known something like that, too). It was regret because he felt certain he would lose her. How odd, when she loved him, and waited for him, and came to him, and he shook loose of her, that he should suffer this secret twinge of loss and regret already, when he had lost nothing. It must have been that his heart suspected something about himself.

There was a dark grave between her breasts, surprisingly soft mounds, a woman's not a girl's, where he needed to die for a while. He thought he only liked it. He needed it.

"This is also what I need," he said. She didn't interrupt his mumbling at her in the dark booth at Angelo's, as they cut into steaks—his rare and American, hers well done and English; his with thick grimy steak sauce, hers without. There were large graffitilike signatures on the walls, the names of East Side celebrities who had previously taken steaks in the place.

"Where's yours?" Susan asked. She meant *need*.

"Right here," he said, and pointed first to his head and then to hers. "I wish."

"I'd like to know," she said, "what's in your head."

"I'd like to tell you," he said, and didn't. They sipped their espresso and she remarked that even the taverns in New York now serve espresso. She chattered because he didn't want to talk. She knew he was trying to get used to her being here now that the convulsion of the first days of greeting her was over.

The little red lamp affixed to the wall in their booth glowed, and so did the little red lamps in the row of booths. It felt cozy to be out among others, where scenes were not appropriate, at least not too many tears or too much lovemaking; a little laughter wouldn't hurt, and occasionally he stroked her hand, she touched his, they laughed at the pleasure of each other.

He was thinking that love is a way to say farewell to death, and also to the past.

That's for romantics. For sensible people, love passes the time until dying; it means living till I die.

Some people who didn't love their partners loved their children. Since it seemed he loved mainly his words, his reports addressed to strangers, a timeless abstraction, the news of the world—this became very crisp and too clean! Perhaps he should have tried what poets and novelists try in their needy boyish state: to appeal to women, charm them, make them laugh and cry and love.

His contrary choice may have been (this remained to be seen) a loss. (He saw it. A loss. It was seen.)

When he watched a child's winsome sadness, a child playing alone in wreckage someplace, in Beirut or Harlem, he knew certain sadnesses were not available to words. Dire grief, mute it was, very accepting, and the sweet smile of play, which was why amid so much grief he sometimes wanted a child like that. But then he gave it words again, telexed ones. He wanted his young marriage again, his brother again, even with the dire griefs Chaz harbored against him. That late-afternoon feeling of death in the heart, the rhythm of loss that afflicted him often in Manhattan and afflicted him when he was a yearning boy, disappeared when he was at work in some climate of irrelevant disaster. At the martini hour in New York, the hour of calisthenics and flirtation, of too much smoking in people's faces, everybody needed escape when the day was done and the night not yet begun. Merian had made a profession of his escape.

Could he still have a child, and was loneliness a good reason to bring more dire griefs into the world? He looked into Susan's pale, fatigued face, with its premonitions of sag, a fine-looking woman's face like that of other fine-looking women, only with hair more naturally light.

He still hadn't answered her question about what was in his head—probably nothing.

"Let's go home. You're tired," he said. "First three to five days in a new time zone, mustn't make fine-tuning distinctions. Of course, I always do."

She laughed, took his arm, and said, "You are one of the great fine-tuners of our time."

"Come to my place," he said. "Get your work started tomorrow. Let me take care of you, think of yourself as a jet-lag invalid, because maybe you are, although, me personally, I'm older and it gets worse, but let me bathe you and massage you—"

"Tricks you learned in the popular democracies of the Third World," she said, "or maybe the kingdom of California."

"There's an alternative for you. Taxi! taxi!"

The cab slid toward the curb, the door fell open, and the driver listened to Merian's address over the reggae beat from his cassette player. His car was hung with signs saying YOU MAY SMOKE IF YOU WANT TO GET THROWN OUT and CAUTION! SMOKE MAKES DRIVER EXPLODE.

Susan curled up in the shelter of Merian's shoulder in the approved taxi posture of contented lovers. They entered the park at Eighty-sixth Street. He marveled at his bringing her across town, which now committed him not only to a night but also a slow morning, long breakfast, dawdling, not hurrying her home or hurrying himself out. She knew what he had done and she was smiling into his shoulder. While they drove in silence, except for the anticancer reggae tunes, fragments of a visiting journalist's weather passed through Merian's head—the leaf-heavy acrid

62

burning of Riverside Drive in early autumn, the wet and blowing rains that drove him to bars and coffee shops when he wanted to walk off the mania of long hours at his desk, those magical white snowfalls when even the buses stopped and he wrote someone's name in the frost on the window as the someone stood behind him (was it Christmas eve? he remembered carol sounds outside), the flowering flagrant dogshit smells of spring—ah, ruin his romance, would he? For Merian, passport in his jacket pocket at all times, air tickets handy, credit cards at the ready, Manhattan was a city of longing and waiting, not of gain; yearning, not love—sailing high on nerve and isolation and one word leading to another. Summers, when the air conditioner hummed, the streets howled, Ralph Merian sat snug away from the howling in his high-ceilinged lair, behind the labor of the old Fedders that shook the window, and tried to make sense of things by expanding notes he had brought back from some even less protected, even more worried place.

He lived on his notes like a West End widow on her capital.

Merian wasn't sure a man could do this much longer.

The cabbie didn't believe in taking tips without giving something in return. He handed Merian a sticker, suitable for office or dashboard use. CANCER BUT NOT FOR ME.

They were home, they were in his high-ceilinged large room, which was more of a hall for the meeting of one person together with himself than a dwelling. When the building was a luxury house, this must have been an important center for the family. The Spry sign on the Palisades, which Merian used to consider both a verb and a command, had disappeared. As he looked that way now, housing projects were clinging to the soft cliffs and slopes, and his eyes found the city and beyond unfamiliar. There is something there that loves a lack of neatness, he thought. And a man learns to accept that or he settles into comfort and a guaranteed old age.

Well, am I ready to take a chance again? Just when everything was so depressed and nice? Do I still feel spry?

Normally he left this troubled city in quest of the troubles that nourished him, but Susan was right; they were the troubles of others and he battened on them, he lived off them, just as Yasir Arafat battened and lived off the fears of kings, sheiks, and displaced persons. The Veteran Journalist did without the fleets of Mercedes, however, and without any personal bodyguards.

Now came another chance, maybe his last, to see what benefit his own troubles might bring him.

Susan had fallen asleep. Her head lay sweetly on his shoulder. The sound from her mouth was that of a child's light snoring. He was sure his own snores were heavy, grumbling, and annoying, or so the wife he had liked informed him, with great concern to tell him exactly how she felt about him.

"One flesh." Isn't that what people imagined love to be? And what they remembered? Yet it wasn't usually what they found. And yet it was true about love. The bodies really did contain each other, soaked into each other, became one. He wondered if the biologists have studied this. How about old people who have loved each other a long time? Do they become so much alike just because they've been watching and listening? Or is it some physical exchange between them?

Of course, the bodies really don't become one. The V.J. knew both that they did and they did not. Ralph Merian believed that they did.

Since he still felt young when he made love to her—then he forgot his eyes and teeth, and how they were not so young—he could still imagine becoming one flesh with someone. Perhaps he didn't want this. He was impatient on a long Sunday afternoon with her. And yet, Monday morning, when they clutched and squeezed and sweated together, he wanted to cry that he loved her, he was one with her, he wanted to cry out something that would last longer than his wail of pleasure.

So people die for love, which meant that they love what they are not but hope to be, they are transformed, they die. Their ideas passed into animal noises and were no longer theirs but everyone's.

Ralph Merian's father's last breath, when he decided life had gone long enough and it was time to die, sounded like this. Having heard this breath, Merian never made love in the old way except when he was travelling, wandering, out of touch, doing his focused job. Then he was the V.J. and had no father or mother or wives or brother, and he made love in mainly tropical places without a loved one.

Not only Susan was asleep. Merian had been sleeping, too, for he had just waked himself. He heard himself suddenly crying out in the dark, as if talking to himself and alone, It's so beautiful! It's so beautiful! As if it were a sunset, a summer rain with dustlets settled and cleansed, or a snowfall at midnight in the city and the moon swollen over white towers and turrets—yet all he had done was hold a woman in his arms.

It's so beautiful!

It's so beautiful!

A familiar woman, with smells and liquefactions and the points of teeth that were not a surprise to him—much of her mysterious to him, as Ralph Merian was to the V.J.

She said nothing but watched with those teeth glinting at him. She was silent. She understood the risks. She was sad, too, because she wasn't sure how much he liked surprises from her. It was unlike his first day in a strange place, although also filled with surprises. A hotel in a war or revolution, or returning tired and half-deafened to his dusty flat in Manhattan—they were all strange places the first days. Before he could sink deeply into sleep, he woke suddenly, legs jumping, with the sensation of a woman's arms around him, his around her, a sweet holding of each other. Light was leaking through the shades. He woke, got up, dressed, made coffee, did nothing.

Why did he dream last night of finding a newspaper on the beach, dry, October 1954?

His friends from that year were dead or living in the Sun Belt or disappeared. The wife he met that year was fat and still angry with him, robust with rage. Why did he believe that? He never saw her anymore. He assumed. He assumed she should be.

His friend Theo, who used to tuck a flower behind his ear and dance sweatily, crazily, like a dervish, and was married more often than anybody, now was quiveringly small and old and dying, with his congested heart and his thinned blood and his leg removed from the gangrene, diabetes: "The quality of life is shit," he said. "No, I don't like it. This quality of life is shit, but thanks for making me laugh, pal. You don't have to visit anymore. I'm out of it half the time anyway. Pretty soon I'll be out of it full time."

Susan came up sleepily behind him, tiny in his robe with the cord knotted tightly. She took the cup from his hands so she too would have coffee breath. She sipped from it and asked him, "Why do you fret so much?"

"I never worry when I'm working."

"When you're in the way of armies you never worry at night?"

"Even less when I'm in the way of guerrillas and terrorists."

"Isn't that strange?"

He touched her mouth to shush her, saying, "Not when you think about it. Not when you're me."

The look in her eyes, the anger she did not mention, said that killing and anarchy were expensive distractions. And what luck for him that he was exempt from blame, since it wasn't his killing he used as distraction. He only profited from it.

Her stare was not news to him. He knew that he traded in people's thick lives, smelly, soaked in semen and blood, bricks and plaster falling, straw in flames, booby traps everywhere, parents desperate for their children's present, never mind the future; he plucked sentences out of fire and blood. He played a trick with death, like an adolescent hanging grenades from his belt. He pulled a feature out of bombing, and the dust of the city settled into death helped his words grow quick and lively. Kids on Vespas, flourishing steel, made him feel at home, at ease.

Those nice clean words that went into a computer far away earned him these lonely nights. There was a price for ease. So far he still thought his words were as real as the booby-trapped

Vespas. So far Susan was merely hurt because he could not always sleep when he was tired, even in her arms.

There were those who thought Merian firm and reliant because he had lived so long without a woman. Merian was not one of those who thought this. He had learned to live in this way because, for him, the alternatives were more troubling than war or revolution. Of the women he had known, he had found takers, who simply drained him, and givers, who gave so fully, as Susan did, that their loss terrified him. He knew what happened with the takers; his early wife was one—a rattler of kitchenware, a demander, complainer, off-balancer. And the giver made him happy, she taught him to live with her, she taught him to depend on her. And then she removed herself and left him bereft. She wanted someone who gave as richly as she did, and he believed he was not one of those. She wanted someone to be a father to children, to care, to stay by the fire, and he was someone who wanted to be a father, to care, to stay by the fire—but didn't want it enough. It was only a good idea. So the bad one tormented him and the good one also tormented him.

Better to depend on the V.J., who was always present and usually loyal. And his judgment of himself might be unrelenting, but he would not give up. Merian would not abandon Merian. When he started to go—illness, say, or, say, old age—it would be time to resign from the earth. Fair enough. He had learned. He would not buy again the rotten chance almost all men bought, which was not much of a chance, since almost all men lost at marriage.

So it seemed to Ralph Merian, veteran journalist, observer of sixteen wars and revolutions. When he thought of what lives fast, loves hard, and dies young, he thought of guerrillas and mice. When he thought of what lives and loves very cautiously, growing old and still persisting, he thought of himself.

So it seemed to him.

Wars don't usually end in clean decisions. There are victories, reversals of advances, stagnations, truces, treaties, and peace conferences. And then violations of the solemn promises. And other factors come into play. On different sides of the border triumph and sacrifice are defined in opposing ways. Love was not war, but it was just as confusing. Merian never lost a woman only once. Sometimes he left her, and then to his surprise she also left him—didn't care! Once, with his second wife, he must have treasured the pain of her leaving, because when the pain disappeared, he missed it. It turned out that a person doesn't necessarily love forever.

He discovered this on the way to interview Solzhenitsyn when he was first shipped out of Moscow to Germany (another peculiar idea from Arnie Schultz). Jet lag, plus trying to discuss things with the Messiah and Savior of All Civilization, was so uncomfortable that it made being lovelorn easy. He concentrated on his headache and coffee tremor, his stomach and his itching eyes, and on the ranting hero, who gave him lessons in Truth with flecks of saliva at the corners of his mouth. He wrote that Solzhenitsyn expected someday to be shipped back in a closed railway car to Leningrad, hatch himself out to the chanting of a mob (chanting in Old Slavonic), rename the city St. Petersburg, and declare himself Czar of All the Russias, King of the Universe. And then, of course, it was necessary to be responsible: But nevertheless Mr. S. has suffered, borne witness, and the world should be grateful.

Firefights in blacked-out cities were easier to handle than lost love and Alexander Solzhenitsyn. To Arnie he said, Give me desert gnats and a coup by corporals next time, please, dear friend, not that I fail in gratitude for a chance to do Deep Political and Cultural Significance.

He arranged a little dinner at the Ginger Man for Susan and some friends. He wanted the approval, not wanting to confirm anything, of Arnie, who shrugged and said, "I told you she's nice. She still is. Nice. I like an intelligent woman." He met a few English couples. Once they watched the dart throwers at the Rose & Thistle, including the former RAF hero, now a darts champion. She got her library privileges organized. She started to cultivate her network of Haitians, Martiniquais, Guadaloupeans, and even a Marxist half–Sri Lankan Creole speaker from the Seychelles, who worked for his country's economic mission, trying to sell the Isles of Love as a location for soft-core porn movies. Susan was ready to enjoy her research; when she talked about it, she actually rubbed her hands and giggled.

When he looked silently at her across a table, eyes meeting and turning away, hands fluttering and reaching, it was as if he remembered things to come—not just lovemaking, though these gazes were brimming with that, but also the blessed dailiness of staying with someone in boredom and routine, distraction and the wish to be elsewhere. She smiled. They told their stories. When the evening ended, sometimes they ended doubt in gasps and embraces, kisses, mouth to mouth, deep sleep. "Was I snoring?" "Maybe." "Was I?" "I was asleep."

And they both sank again, content with good luck.

Yet as he looked at her tonight, his hand touched hers, he felt trembles in the chest, doubt, dismay, a wish to be elsewhere, his V.J. solution. She smiled; her mouth welcomed him. She was mysterious to him. There was no good reason for a grown woman who had already suffered a few bad deals to care about him. Yet she seemed to. She didn't know him yet; that must be the reason. Their eyes hunted each other like lazy mistrustful children; their eyes raked the fields of face. In risk and turmoil he asked, "I love you! I love you! Answer!"

"That's no question, sir."

"That's no answer," he said.

When he was younger, he thought he would conquer the world, be certified marvelous by himself, find a girl who said, Hey! You're right!

Arnie and he agreed they don't really chirp like that anymore, now that all the girls are women. And since they couldn't really certify themselves marvelous without that *Hey, you're right!* they might have to reevaluate the whole concept.

Now Merian thought, I'm tiring, it's harder to suck in the gut when I'm walking naked across the room and she's watching, I haven't done what I wanted to do—no, worse, I did it and maybe I picked wrong—I'm worried, I'm in doubt...

Was that what Susan liked about him? Another reason to go cautious with her. Why should she settle for him as he was now, when there were so many like him as he was then? Full of hope and ambition, full of optimism, full of shit. To Ralph Merian, the last twenty years of serious endeavor had added shanks and frazzling. What was wrong with Susan Pollet that she didn't run from a man on this other slope of the metabolic inevitability? (Old man! Old man! he thought. Isn't that a cleaner way to say it?)

"In the eyes of God," Susan said slowly and deliberately, "we are all created with equal expense accounts. You've got a plot afoot. Are you—please tell me absolutely straight—are you going off to cover the riots in Polish Guyana or someplace?"

"I think you mean—I'll tell you absolutely straight—Gdańsk."

"I know what I mean. I mean Serbian West Africa or wherever else you make shooting and filing stories stand for real life, instead of—"

"Stand for?"

"Instead of just a part. Let's get organized, Mister V.J. It's an unfortunate part, all that killing. I don't mean words are bad, V.J.—"

"Let us stipulate the fact."

"I feel you are packing. I feel you are talking to travel agents. It might be Afghani freedom fighters this time, or anything else to get out of how distracting you find being with me."

He lowered his face, lowered his eyes, lowered his voice, and felt lowered. "I care for you. I care for you more than—" And no comparisons came to mind. No honest metaphors or rankings occurred to him. A joke he had heard in Lebanon came to mind:

70

Why is lovemaking better than masturbation? Because you meet people.... His face felt hot, as if the sun had been pounding it. He didn't like it when she used his secret name for himself. He should never have told her. The V.J. trusted her, and she was trustworthy, but did that mean he should trust her?

It made him sweat. It was like the time he hid with a bunch of kids in an Israeli air-raid shelter when the rockets came over from Fatahland. The kids were doing their homework and the one soldier in the shelter, a white-haired fifty-five-year-old infantryman, was saying, "If your neighbor shoots at your children, you have to tell him to stop. And if he doesn't stop, you have to go in and shoot the gun out of his hands." And Ralph Merian was sweating, not because a direct hit on the shelter would cause a serious concussion to the kids inside, and to him, too, but just because it was hot in there. The air pump was working, but it was a hot day on the Lebanese border and the old infantryman was saying, "We're going to go in there. I'm a grandfather and I hate sleeping underground with a bunch of kids who aren't even my own. We're going to go in there."

"You were saying you care for me, but your attention wandered," Susan said.

"I'm embarrassed."

"You're soaking wet."

It was an animal flight reaction, this change in time of fear or shame. An overage Israeli border guard or a young Englishwoman could bring on the flow. And he trusted her even as she dissolved his overattentive view of himself, like soaking the starch out of a new shirt, by saying he wasn't any special cut of meat for doing what he chose to do. He was merely fleeing what everyone else put up with—love. Or sought to put up with. He deserved no credit for his efforts at evasion.

He had nominated himself V.J., but Susan had elected him by acclamation Permanent Boy, O.F., which stood for Old Fart. He didn't see what she saw in him.

"You're as hard on yourself as anyone," she said.

He shook his head. He knew what was there, knew it better than she did.

"You're not objective. Neither am I," she said. "But I'm stupid enough to be disappointed because all you mostly care to do is pinch me now and then, not that I mind being pinched, not that I mind being stupid, but all you care to do, my dear..."

What about his clinging to her last night, saying nothing, his face hot with what he was unable to say?

"...is pinch me, lick me, stick me, make me happy, leave me. Like some old hero you read about. That's not enough."

"I never said I was a hero."

"And you're *not*," she said.

"I'm a coward?"

"Don't be an idiot, Ralph. You're a man like just under half the population of America. Of course it's your work and you have to do it. You're not even leaving the country this time. Arizona is where? Nevada? Why are you making so much of it?"

"I didn't think you'd want me to go."

"Who said I wanted you to go? But I don't want you to stop your life, either. Send me an Indian postcard."

"What will you do while I'm gone?"

"What I usually do, whatever I always do, maybe I'll miss you. That's normal. What's bothering you?"

"I'm not sure I want to go."

"Don't send me lies, Ralph. I don't want you ever to say that again unless you mean it."

"You think I don't mean it?"

"Oh, my. Oh, my, this is so much like a marriage. I think you really mean it, Ralph, but I think you don't mean it more. And thank you anyway for being so polite. What on earth makes you think I don't want you to do your work?"

"Maybe I'm trying to get away from you."

"So what? Doesn't everybody? Is that all?"

"Is that all for you?"

"Do you want me to hint I'll be at the Rose and Thistle looking around for some neighborhood linguist with a few hours to kill, because his wife is slaving away overtime as a computer programmer?"

He shrugged. "You do seem to have a specific picture of the subject. You have someone in mind?"

"Dear American friend."

"Okay, can we just live from day to day?" he asked.

"That's all I intend. That's all we have in mind, either one of us. That's all I even want in life, Ralph, is one victory per day."

"Can we make love now?"

She turned her back on him. "What are you waiting for?"

4

INSTANT MIGRATION BY telepathy would be a mistake for Ralph Merian; he was one of those creatures who felt at home on commercial aircraft. No phones, mail, or friends to distract him; the hum of other people making all the decisions to soothe him; a tray of microwave minicuisine to nourish him— why, a few hours, half a day, even more, in a Boeing or Lockheed floating spa left him feeling vigorous and happy. Something about the ozone worked on his hormones. The massaging of his soft cranial tissue, traveling a millisecond more slowly than the rest of his skull, bumping around at the back of his head, tickled his spirit.

Travel time was invented and kept cozy, he confided to Arnie Schultz, so that the Veteran Journalist could do his research. He confessed to Susan Pollet that he liked long flights—it was part of his craziness, she should be warned. And she replied that perhaps it was part of a genetic modification that would eventually produce a race of foreign correspondents with marsupial pockets for storing notes and halazone glands under the tongue for emitting water purification directly into the cheeks.

And then she said she would profit by his absence to spend more evenings in a computer search for various African vocabularies. There was late-night time open at NYU and they were glad to help a visiting scholar. Have a good trip to the West. Have a good computer search.

He had ordered a couple of books and also some Xeroxes from the *News-Press* librarian, and over this helpful background he dreamed away the idle hours on the flight to Phoenix. It turned out that the Stony Apache Nation of northern Arizona, unlike other fierce but proud small nations, enjoyed no fighting air force of its own but was the satisfied possessor of an airstrip for use in breech births, extreme Saturday-night knife damage, and other emergency medical need. Merian could charter a snubby little Cessna to carry him to the secluded high-desert ex-reservation, now (reminder, please remember) called a Nation since the angry independence movements of the late sixties. The Magic Mushroom folks from Harvard, Berkeley, and UCLA had wandered elsewhere, but left this mark of their passing.

Merian had gotten through most of the early Xeroxes, which were arranged in chronological order, by the time he boarded. An alert United Airlines ground-travel manager at JFK put him in first class, which wasn't strictly legal, because he had read *Coups and Countercoups,* Merian's book—collected dispatches was all it amounted to—about Chad, Benin, Zaire, and Gabon. The nice person with the name "Stan Ground Manager" pinned to his official blue blazer remembered the title as "African Cooze," and on the whole, Merian preferred that to "Cups." He was grateful for literacy beyond the call.

He stretched out with all the liquids, orange juice, beer, and coffee, plus unsalted nuts and cheese snacks, his habitual defense against hydration problems; no lemons to suck, but we've licked the scurvy plague; stretched out his legs, nice first-class leg room—it happened sometimes; buried his attention in the basic research material handsomely supplied by the *News-Press* librarian, whose name, Ann Rand, bemused him, as funny names did, even his own.

Almost all names seem funny to their proprietors. In the air Ralph Merian found any little detail of history entertaining. It must have been that bumping of the brain in its unyielding canister.

The Apaches were the last tribe, along with the Navajos, to emigrate from Asia. That's the best theory. They used to be warlike. They were bold fighters with bow and arrow, with spears, and then when the white man started to slaughter a little, thereby teaching the Apaches about guns, they killed for their first guns and bought others from enterprising traders who saw markets opening up. They were bold fighters on horseback with their new muskets, slipping out of their taciturn ways in favor of enraged shrilling and screaming. Guns just brought up the whole temperature. "Apache" is the Zuni word for "enemy." Proudly they still call themselves enemies.

But then they also have a real, a secret name. *"Dine,"* which means "The People." They don't speak it, but they use it. (Merian scribbled notes on this mystical stuff.) Their language, which many of them still spoke, was more subtle in its tonality than Mandarin. They taught it to the kids. They had three-day ceremonies sometimes. Yet the other nations among whom they lived didn't realize how complex their thought, consideration, and religion was. Many judged them dirty and irresponsible; such was the dominant opinion of the white people, who were the original dusty interlopers, bringing rats and cockroaches to the land in their covered wagons.

The Navajo nation had another name for Apaches: The Mountain People. Because they came late, they couldn't claim the good lands for farming. Out of hunger and living on irregular slopes, they became raiders and preyed on their cousins, the Navajos. The Navajos, who had settled the lower and flatter areas, went into the farming and craft lines and let the violent Apaches gnaw on them because they didn't know how to stop them.

The first great war with the white interlopers started near a copper mine. The whites trapped the Apaches by inviting them to a feast, then successfully butchered a large number. It might have been called genocide if people had thought in such terms. It was just clearing the land, plus a little bit personally satisfying to the white heroes of the Indian Wars, a name they gave it because they also wrote the histories. "Holocaust" was an idea yet to come. The white soldiers and settlers with their smoking breechloaders had simpler thoughts in their heads. Clear off the buffaloes and the Indians; don't even shoot them for meat. The Apaches got the white man's attention by being stately, proud, and silent, and how the white man responded to notice was by appreciating their death and encouraging it with the weaponry available in those times and at those latitudes.

Now and then Merian looked up from his reading and made notes in his spiral pad. Generally he didn't use much of the stuff he got from research, but sometimes it helped him to ask the questions, to feel secure in a strange place. Since he read about fried corn bread, and even Arnie had brought it up, he was ready to taste it. In Haiti he drank hot bull's blood at a voodoo ceremony, in Biafra he chipped off a bite from the ceremonial kola nut when they passed it around (and got one hell of a lip infection), in Algeria he watched an efficient young fellow stick, skin, and cook a little black goat that looked more like a skinny pig, and they ate it with roasted sand—that was the best gourmet delight, except for the sand.

Sometimes, as he read, a detail would sharpen something in his mind, would engender a thought: about fried corn bread after he read about it, above love as he woke from a sudden beer doze with a turbulent dream of being locked out in the dark in some viscous, paralyzing loneliness. Merian and Susan. Not yet home, were they?

Geronimo was an Apache. The great chief, the great tactician, the great hero, was finally hunted down by other Apaches, by Indian police. They trapped him and got ready to finish him off, like Che Guevara and the squat dark unsmiling Bolivian police who stood for their portraits around the body. Geronimo knew tactics, but he didn't find the right strategy, so finally even his tactics failed. Was he scalped? His tomahawk, headdress, and vest are in a museum in New Mexico. Maybe someone has a piece of shriveled skin with a few hairs clinging to it stored in a trunk in Albuquerque. There you go again, Merian thought, dreaming and lying like a New Journalist instead of a V.J.

Geronimo was put away to spend a long time dying in captivity.

After the Indian Wars, which the Apaches fought with energy and intelligence, and also some of the savagery people think they remember—Geronimo's warrior band only numbered about a hundred fighers—the Apaches sank into the lethargy and melancholy of a defeated people. Warriors became worriers, shamed before their women, their children, and their gods; shamed before the past, the present, and it seemed, the future; shamed before themselves. They were tuckered out. In the cities, when people saw them sprawled and drunk, they looked small. They didn't look so much depressed as broken: broken bottle glass sparkling at the curb, broken capillaries in the eyes, broken hearts. How odd that the war cry of paratroopers leaping from the sky in World War II should have been "Geronimo!"—a ritual shriek from melting-pot boys over Dieppe and at Anzio beach.

The Stony Apaches—an offshoot band—went from hunting, warfare, and predation to handouts from the government. They accepted the barren desert hills and accepted that it be called a reservation. The Bureau of Indian Affairs got away with that one, but in recent time they took to calling themselves a Nation again and insisted that the Chief was not a Chief but their President. While the Great Spirit ruled, a bank in Tempe ran the tribal (national) funds, which were held in common—a cooperative, a commonwealth, a complication. That stuff with the Anglo bankers was just detail. Actually, the Great Spirit was biding its time, waiting for a Danny Grand to come along and give them back their dignity.

For years the Indians hadn't understood how to get their money out of the bank, and so it didn't matter about the fees, the commissions, the management charges; the money accumulated anyway, despite the best efforts of the Anglo custodians in Tempe. Then what happened about Danny Grand: The Elders—the senators—discovered they had all this capital and they could get at it and achieve a great modern victory for one of their own. They could make a sound movie in living color! What a revenge! An Indian, backed by Indians, could do this!

Merian suddenly barked out his short doggish laugh, startling the first-class steward, who asked, "Sir? I'm amusing you?" He was carrying a bowl of fruit and a tangerine had rolled off.

"No, no, no, I was just reading," said Merian.

"A book?" the steward asked politely, peering down at this not entirely unfamiliar object. He was used to either better or more frankly drunken manners. "Sir? In your opinion?"

"It says here the Apache kids root for the soldiers when they watch movies about Indian wars on television."

"That's nice," said the steward. "Would you like some grapes? I have these new blue seedless miracles of modern grape science. I've not read that one yet, sir. Is it available in paperback?"

Beginning to doze again under the steady persuasive throb of the jet, which he always found peaceful and calming, reducing the entire world to a crisp clean isolation, plus simple nourishment and no place to go—why did flying make some people nervous?—Merian lay back to dream of the Great Spirit. It (He? She?) was still worshiped despite the defeat, disgrace, and murder of Geronimo, and the Nation now transformed into a lumpen corporate welfare enterprise with a bank in Phoenix, a branch in Tempe, which translated its former glory into great high-risk securities with special percentages to the custodians. ("In some cases we make a market in these issues.")

At last the tribal gathering of power and guilt money in the high mesas was determined to reenter as a conqueror over the hostile white world by backing the hard-riding country canary in a singing western. In fact, Geronimo hadn't been killed; he had only been exiled to Florida, or was it Oklahoma?—check this— where he instructed children in moral behavior.

Merian slept. Moral behavior'll bring this reaction every time. He woke and ate a blue seedless modern miracle. He copied into his spiral notebook the words of Captain John C. Bourke, the Indian fighter, who wrote postslaughter: "The Apache commanded in peace respect for his keen-sighted intelligence, good fellowship, warmth of feeling for his friends, and impatience of wrong."

The extermination hadn't really stopped itself, despite these kindly sentiments. The Apaches resisted, became skilled guerrillas, and it was expensive to try to kill them all. Reconciliation commended itself to Washington as superior policy. A few centuries after women, children, and perhaps American dogs were deemed to have souls, and at about the time when it came to be suspected that Negroes were also in possession of this commodity, the Indians began to be seen as Native Americans who had preimmigrated to the western United States of America. The crude beginnings of conscience were shipped to the frontier in the wake of hardtack and the firewater trade. . . .

The Boeing 747 landed in Phoenix, and Merian received a fond farewell from the steward. Merian congratulated him on his mile-high seedless grapes. He promised to fly the Friendly Skies on his next journey.

In another part of the airport, presenting his *News-Press* card and his magic sheaf of credit plastic, the Veteran Journalist found the charter, which had already received notice by telex. They knew the way to the Stony Apache airstrip—"A piece of cake," said the Owner–Operator–Ticket Clerk–Baggage Handler. To drive would take four hours, but from aloft he could comfortably survey the terrain for twenty minutes, arrive freshly rumpled, and save time, which is a diminishing resource. Susan would approve of this consideration, he hoped.

The pilot said they would leave in ten, make that twelve, "minuetoes"–Latin influence?—sharp. He waited a half hour, diddling valves and transistors, to see if anyone else wanted to fly to the Nation this afternoon. Nobody did, so Merian benefited from a personally escorted, private trip in a Beechcraft, not a

Cessna, with not a word spoken after they got off the ground. The pilot was wearing a tan bush-pilot safari suit with epaulets and short sleeves. Merian figured he was too chicken to be a dope smuggler, not attractive enough for corporate planes, and had fallen into the short-haul business. A teamster of the air, with a mesh cap that said "Xtian Broadcast Network" on a decal. Merian thought with his V.J. satisfaction: I'm in the Far West; this is another country.

The sky reverend's interest was in getting there and back. The small-craft rattle would have forced conversation into a shout, anyway, and the pilot didn't look as if anything further pressing to say would occur to him for about five to ten years, when he might gaze up beseechingly at the paramedic, uttering the brave words, "Level with me, Doc. Does it look real bad?" With his broken veins, hollow eyes, yellow fingers, the silhouette of a lean cowboy and the colors of a liver-haunted former abuser of substances, Merian figured he must have lost his smuggling license. Born Again was a fallback position. Today, legal bush planes, backcountry charters; tomorrow, crop-dusting.

They followed the ribbon of state road down below as if it had been painted on the desert to lead them to the Stony Apache Nation. The rocks were brown and a hard yellow in the sun, the shadows were purple. They couldn't move the road on this pilot, although life had played other tricks against him. He didn't trust maps—the Lord had done without them. He found the reservation. He pointed his thumb in a gesture that could mean either "Kill" or "Down there." Merian saw low flat brown buildings, blazing corrugated tin roofs, spurts and puffs of dust where pickups moved off the roads, serrated gullies and hillocks, and a few green strips where trees and grass followed a crooked, half-wet stream. No, not strips, irregular patches; probably a stream only when it rained, a watering hole the rest of the year. Gloomy, gloomy, gloomy, Merian thought happily, itching to begin.

The pilot banked the Beechcraft sharply—he was beyond elegance in the matter. The engine went into another pitch, a nasty whine; Merian deflected the slight panic that other people seemed to suffer during landings by watching a small green Fiat Spider with an open top—they were low enough to identify the vehicle—speeding toward the airstrip.

He thought—could such a thing be anything but the usual pig correspondent's fantasy?—he thought he saw two lovely nut-brown maidens in that open Spider, with long straight black hair streaming in the wind, hastening to bid white man welcome. Two Sacheem Littlefeathers in a moving holding pattern, preparing to accept Academy Awards in the name of their people, its water rights and film residuals.

The Beechcraft hit the ground, skidded, and turned, and the pilot bowed his head for a moment of silent prayer. He didn't even plan to descend for a cup of boiled Apache coffee before pointing back to civilization in Phoenix. He knew Merian could figure out how to unlock the hatch and climb out himself, and he happened to be fully on line about this. "Thanks," said Merian. No reply, not even a grunt or a Praise the Lord. Too busy reminding Jesus to protect against leaks in the oil line on the return leg, checking the altimeter. Eventually he would have to close things up again. Merian jumped out with no further sociabilities because the pilot was lighting his after-worship cigaret and somehow Merian didn't think this was a good idea with the engine still turning and smells of grease, gas, petroleum products, plus unidentified fluids, some of which smelled human, which are the worst fluid smells. Who were those girls out of the Fiat Spider?

This definitely commanded the V.J.'s attention. The welcoming committee was a group of the two young women in the Spider plus one young man who looked as if he belonged in juvie hall. A dancing clump of tumbleweed in lieu of red carpet. Searing wind. Chapped lips coming.

One nut-brown maiden said, "I'm Sandra," while the other rode in on her as if she belonged in the same sentence, "And I'm Claudia."

"Sandra," repeated a nut-brown maiden with whited mouth.

"Claudia. Sort that out," said Claudia. "These Native Americans around here have trouble telling us apart because we all look alike. We're taking you to the Guest Hogan."

"Thank you for meeting me," said Merian, who also thought they resembled each other.

"You could walk if you knew the way. But you have a typewriter, old Olivetti Lettera 32, isn't it? And a bag—what's in that little one, a camera? They don't like that around here."

"Not too much," Sandra said. "Steals their souls shadow image blah blah blah. Here, let me save you some pain and grief." She reached up with a Vaseline stick to paint his lips. This was new to the V.J. in the line of welcoming rituals.

"Forms of hospitality are a characteristic of human beings in groups," said Claudia. "You've experienced that before?"

He remembered the shared bites of kola nut from an Ibo chief in Biafra. "Yes," he said, "among the Eskimos. But you're not members of the tribe?"

"Shrewd," said Sandra. "No secrets from you, are there?"

"The Nation. Remember that. No, Sandra here and Claudia, me, we're social workers from Chicago, graduate project on family acculturation, female dominance, male blah blah blah," Claudia continued, rolling her eyes toward the boy or young man who was standing frankly too close, frankly listening, frankly uninvited nearby.

When they all stopped to look at him, and for a moment even Claudia and Sandra were at a loss for words, and it was one of those moments when everyone forgets his native language, and the young man surely was not going to help by speaking—prisonyard biceps like that don't go with amenity talk—Ralph Merian himself, despite his experience and maturity, his *savoir faire* and *savoir vivre,* that unflappability that comes as a bonus to old correspondents because nobody is really responsible for anything anymore, and it doesn't make any difference if this is true or false, a fellow can live by it, in fact *must....* Merian thought his boyish stammer would surely reappear after all these years if he tried to squeak out a hello. *Where'd you get those swell tattoos?* wouldn't be the right approach, either.

Grit blew in the air near the gently turning propellers. The

84

pilot had decided to descend after all and work out a kink in his crotch; maybe it was just in his Xtian Broadcasting undershorts. What was more itchy to Merian's eyes than the hard air and grit was the silent, cold, compressed stare of the young man.

"You're taking something in," Claudia remarked.

"Get used to it," Sandra said. "They like to know what's going on in their territory. Hi, Ward," she said. "You've seen this light plane before, haven't you?"

"I'm Hawkfeather," said the young man. "Don't like it when you call me by my BIA name."

He turned and strolled around the Beechcraft as if it were a Ford pickup he was thinking of taking for a test drive, or of hot-wiring it off the used-vehicle lot with pennants flapping from the wires as he lurched down the curbstone. He kicked the tires. What a Hawkfeather; not tall, but brown and knotted with muscle, with purplish tattooing on both shoulders. "Geronimo," it said, not "Mother." A bow and arrow. A fish. An arrow in the fish; probably meant to be a spear. His denim shirt had been cut down to display these delights. His eyes had fine lines from squinting into the sun. He was missing a front tooth and God knew what that came from squinting at.

Hawkfeather stepped too close to Merian. The two graduate students held their distance. He came close to Merian like a lad who knew a pair of pretty girls was watching his every move. He touched Merian's arm. It was not a friendly closeness or touching. "How much you pay for a plane like that?"

"I don't own it."

The kid smiled a little. He preferred opposition. This Anglo made the game better. When he smiled, the lips looked almost lavender, like the tattoos. "Didn't ask you that, own it," he said. "How much?"

"About a hundred dollars to fly here from Phoenix."

"A-*bout*," said the lad, and spat into the orange dust at Merian's feet. A fleck of mud leapt up. Hawkfeather grinned. "A-*bout* touched you, didn't I?" he asked. "How much them shoes? Not per each shoe—both shoes together. A-*bout*, mister."

Merian believed this was not the time to start a discussion of rich shoes and poor shoes and the needs of a man who enjoyed extensive use of his feet in middle age. He didn't remember what shoes should cost these days, in New York or on a Nation. He made up something. "Forty-nine ninety-five," he said, and stopped.

"Maybe 'bout fifty dollars?"

Merian said nothing.

The young man waited and got tired of waiting. He squinted across at the two women watching for the fight to begin. This wasn't the time.

"What's your full name? Mine's Ralph Merian."

"Hawkfeather Ward No Middle Initial Brown."

"You've been in the army already?"

"Few weeks. Veteran for a few weeks till they found out 'bout me."

"I see."

"And your name's Merian. Isn't that a cunt's name? I'd have given five dollars your name was more Schwartz or Kaplan, like the Anglos at the Trading Post."

And he turned and disappeared, kicking dust, not your typical light-treading redskin from *Hiawatha,* as sung by Henry Wadsworth Longfellow. The two young women realized this concluded the traditional airstrip greeting ceremony; there were also practical arrangements. "Now we take you to your room. Did you bring any papers from the outside world?" Sandra asked. "You didn't happen to pick up a *Tribune,* did you? Chicago?"

Claudia said, "Sorry about the welcoming committee." She shouted over the roar of the Beechcraft revving up for departure and held her hair back and down in the sudden gritty swirl. "They'll do that sometimes! Hawkfeather is Jarls's cousin!"

"No, nephew!" Sandra shouted. "Get your kinship straight, dollface."

With one further screech the Beechcraft started its short run; it lifted; they watched it a moment in case of disaster—shrugs—no disaster. Another victory for Jesus.

The young women were nut-brown University of Chicago maidens, due to sun and ceaseless wind over mesa and through pass, but they weren't Indians yet; Darwinian adaptation works more slowly, needing millenniums, at least; they giggled and jiggled in their wispy shirts and winked at each other when Merian admitted he hadn't realized from the sky they were Anglos. They said he would learn to recognize Anglos from Stony Apaches on the ground.

They had straight black hair, ironed straight, skin weathered by a long season of sun and wind, and wore Indian folk embroidery with beads and headbands in the hair and dust in the ears. Genuine Stony Apache maidens would be wearing cutoff jeans. Kaplan's Trading Post had plenty of dresses and decor, but couldn't keep soap and shampoo in stock. This crazy high blowing like a khamsin or mistral made a hiss in the ears besides the grit that settled everyplace. Sandra and Claudia looked like sisters, but they were only friends. They looked like Indians but were not. They shoved Merian into the little open Fiat Spider, where he sat hunched over a cramped shelf seat meant for no human long-legged reporter, and they were still laughing about things he couldn't be expected to understand; dumb-dumb one-shot reporter; they delivered him to the Guest Hogan, the tribal motel.

Cinder blocks and prefab it was, not teepee architecture, or hogan, or pueblo, though closer to the last. The cement was cracking enough to let in samples of the wind and dust and half a coyote snout in the space where building materials had shrunk away from the window frame. Before they left him in his comfy room with the rust-streaked sink basin and, behind a plastic shower curtain, a commode used by some previous visitor who believed in water conservation, the V.J. had a few questions for Sandra and Claudia. They didn't seem to be the questions Sandra and Claudia wanted him to ask. Why did this remote tribe—"Nation," said Claudia—want to get into the film financing business?

"A place in the sun," said Sandra.

"Why Danny Grand? He's never even done a movie."

"You know the answer to that one. He said on their TV he's one of them."

"Isn't there more? Didn't he say they won't finance an Indian in Hollywood? Didn't he say he wants to tell the truth about his people, plus sing a few country-western Zen Buddhist Indian rock songs?"

"Since you know all the answers, why are you asking?" Claudia sweetly inquired.

With the innate grace and hospitality of her nature, Sandra had ducked past the shower curtain while he was talking and, wrinkling her nose a little, flushed the toilet. She returned in time to contribute to Claudia's thought: "Because he's loosening us up for the questions he *really* wants to ask is why, is that right?"

"Caught me again," said Merian.

Claudia, giggling, said, "Really really *really.*"

"I've got an appointment with the President of the . . . *Nation,*" said Merian, "but I like to ask different people the same question. Sometimes a person gets different answers. It's all useful. What do you two do here?"

"You can believe it if we tell you," Sandra said.

"Goddamn but we're useful," said Claudia.

Embarrassed, they admitted they wanted to help the Stony Apaches. They came for their research project, but then they saw the children in the Head Start program, those big burnt-almond eyes. Silent depressed kids. "It's more like a Fall Behind Program," Sandra said. Usually the fathers were fighting the battle of the bottle and losing. If they were lucky, the mothers were not fighting the battle of the bottle. If they were really lucky, sometimes, but not too often, the father won the battle of the bottle. But usually by that time he was forty and the kids were started the way they were going to go, sort of like Hawkfeather there—he was enterprising for one of them. Tried some schooling. Enlisted in the army.

Claudia let drop some of her Chicago smartass. "They're cute before they get to Hawkfeather's stage. They're like dark grief dolls. We keep them clean and talk to them. The parents don't have much time for that. Wiping their noses is a big step up. We read to them. We try to get through them to the mother."

"The father," said Sandra, "is a lost cause. He's got better things. He's worse'n our kind of fathers. The ravine is filled with pickup truck wrecks. You know why they allow drinking on the Nation now? Because this is a democracy, all persons equal under the blah blah blah, plus it was too expensive in national funds. They were driving to town, they were crashing alongside the road in the gulleys, they were smashing each other going back, sometimes they were rear-ending and snapping their necks for fun. Which cut down both the men plus the family pickup. They buy patriotic American, not too many Toyotas."

"These kids," said Claudia. "You'll see their eyes. It's a hundred and fifty years of war and losing. We've been here for six months now; it's supposed to be only a project, not get involved. A little cabin fever in the desert around here. Are you going to have to work twenty-four hours a day?"

"That's not my usual schedule," said Merian.

"So we'll play," Sandra said. "You'll hear from us. We're the ones who look like Indians to you with our nice even tans all over."

"Don't need to plan," said Claudia. "This isn't a huge Nation. It'll happen."

They had a way of presenting the smartass pinched face and then the earnest do-good soft frown and then this intimate private giggling. It was intimate and private, just between them. Ralph Merian was not included. He wanted to share a laugh with these ladies who were not Susan and stipulate that he worked twenty-four hours a day, but not all in the same day.

Too bad. They were gone.

Before he unpacked and set out his few things, toothbrush, typewriter, and vitamin pills, turned around a few times in his lair to make it his, he peeked out the window, which was like a viewing strip in a blockhouse, and there was still an angry swirl of dust where the Fiat Spider had taken off. Laughing Lady and Mouth-of-Chicago were gone. In the road, instead, cans, bottles, a piece of pink plastic breathing in the wind, a paperback book whose cover looked familiar to him. A shopping bag whose bottom had fallen out, due to smashed tomatoes or broken eggs. A stocky kid with tattooed biceps just strolling and ignoring the grit blowing in his face—that stuff had points like flint, and yet the steady gusts kept it levitating. He'd bet the clinic was lined up with eye problems, conjunctival irritations, but maybe they just slop in lubrication.

And what was the kid from the airstrip wanting?

Merian put his back to the sights. He stacked a couple of yellow pads next to his Olivetti Lettera 32. Certain things he liked to get ready, in case inspiration struck, a fit of comprehension or industriousness.

The water in the shower ran brown. What does brown water matter, brown from muck, not rust; what does it matter when you're a nation of big-time film magnates with cigars that don't quit?

He blotted himself with the towel. It wasn't long enough for scrubbing and wiggling against his back. It was nearly transparent with laundering. Was the kid still outside?

No. Empty road; a worn dimming path enlarged by trucks that had taken liberties with the curb mounds; wind tumbling plastic and paper, budging soft-drink cans. Maybe it was feeding time on the Nation.

The V.J. figured he might perchance meet Mr. Hawkfeather, Ward NMI, in the course of their unfinished business. As far as Merian was concerned, he was perfectly ready to call it finished and leave it, but friend Hawkfeather may have had nothing better to do than getting to the bottom of things he started. There was so little going on in the world, and so much turmoil to be soothed, that the few distractions a brave turned up needed to do double and triple duty. The V.J., on the other hand, would have preferred to put their entire airport greeting behind him. It reminded him of the faces at Sheremetevo Airport outside Moscow, which kept reappearing as cab drivers, icon pimps, or cleaning men in the hotels—sometimes the same cleaning man at the Astoria in Leningrad as the one leaning on a broom outside his door at the Hotel Natsionalny in Moscow.

Well, Merian couldn't avoid himself in the mirror, could he? So why should he try to evade the one whose business and pleasure it was to be his double, keep good track of him, make him more nervous than his own face very gradually crumbling in the mirrors of hotel rooms?

Hawkfeather might have to keep on the move. So would Ralph Merian. So intended Sandra Laughing Lady and Claudia Mouth-of-Chicago, those nut-brown non-Indian maidens. Only Susan, having a clearer idea of what she was and wanted, could afford to stand still and patiently. Hawkfeather's impatience—what was he asking?—worried Merian. Stump-headed, stubborn, and road-worn, Merian didn't even mind being worried (what kind of a genetic error produces a Veteran Journalist?).

When Claudia said nobody needed to plan, good things would just happen, she must have meant on the Stony Apache Nation, because this world was an astral projection of desert and mesa, whereas elsewhere the world was enormous and daunting, and if a person drifted, letting things happen, there was a certain amount of peril. Peril doesn't just fade away with time like, say, the wounds of childhood (his poor brother, Chaz, in San Francisco) or an old marriage (what's-her-name in Coral Gables). Risk grows sharper. Witness Ralph Merian and Susan Pollet.

Before his appointment with President, formerly Chief, Jarls Coyote, the President had invited him to take a stroll down Lyndon B. Millhouse Street to the new Stony Apache Smokeless Industries shed, the light manufacturing and fabrication center. The President's voice was flat and toneless on the telephone. The President was very busy during these difficult times of national and international Third-World linkups, but he had already consented to see the reporter from the capitalist press. A traditional Stony Apache saying applied: My word is my bond. First, however, to make the most of his background information, the President advised the reporter to survey some of the other irons the Stony Apache Nation had in its fire, besides film financing. He sincerely suggested this.

There was an old Stony Apache saying that applied: Keep the bugger waiting.

Merian changed into dry socks, a fresh khaki shirt that used to be a Bolivian air force officer's shirt. South American sky aces were far ahead of the U.S., the Soviet Union, and even Italy in their shirt technology. Outsize epaulets, pleated pockets, fine long-grain cotton, adequate tails, first-strike macho power. Merian's socks were just regular North American, First-World socks.

The main street of Stony seemed to lack a credit jeweler, but otherwise it was a miniature main street from any backcountry western town, except that the paving only ran down the middle of the road, a kind of paving strip, symbolizing the possibility of actual street paving, dirt and gravel on either side. Something creative in the government bidding, Merian guessed, and a contractor who needed the paving materials for his Spanish mission ranch place in Phoenix. The buildings were prefab and cinder block. There was no Greek Revival or Student Unrest bank; it was an army surplus building with "Tempe National (Stony Apache Nation Branch)" stencilled on the rippling Quonset siding. There's a reason, Merian thought, banks try to act like temples or forts and this one doesn't. This one was more of an afterthought than the Purefit Union Auto-Truck Tire & Parts next door.

Merian stretched his legs and hoped he looked like anybody else. He did not look like anybody else. While he was above medium height in most places except northern Europe and California, here he was tall. The Apaches may have been mighty once, but now they were less mighty, with gnarled and bumpy faces, too much flesh on the women or, sometimes, on both women and men, the skinnied, cooked-down diminishment of liver trouble. Blue jeans, surplus shirts with chopped off tails and sleeves, straw hats, boots or running shoes, and pretty much the same fashions for men and women. It could almost have been a Tex-Mex border village. Average number of beads. Those cute button-eyed kids of Claudia and Sandra must have been in school or day care. Here, the infants strapped to the backs looked like bundles of laundry, but of course Merian was not a close admirer of newborns. Once he reacted sharply, recoiling at the sudden wail from a nearby swaddling, although fly-covered starvelings in Africa, leech-infested rain-forest safari visitors, even the fisherman he saw at the shore of Petit-Goâve in Haiti, with a gaping hole in the middle of his face where his nose used to be—yaws, an unfriendly form of leprosy—could fit into the Veteran Journalist's system. In general, information soothed him. Classification, organization, and words served to civilize suffering. Therefore no reason to jump like a convent girl at this peep by his elbow; it wasn't a mouse.

Merian did not appreciate his new jumpiness. Probably, with Sandra and Claudia to protect him, he could handle a cute button-eyed brown child, play a little trick with a coin or a card, make the creature laugh. Merian, as usual, was busy accumulating for his story; and as usual, he was wasting energy accumulating what he didn't need; and finally, as usual, he agreed with himself that this so-named waste was actually a part of the resonance and depth that some people, including the Nieman people and some of the Pulitzer jury, had claimed he managed to bring to his subjects. They called it resonance, depth, complexity, feeling; he called it feature material. The condition is not always treatable and a player has to run riffs on it.

The Tomahawk Shopping Center looked like an army rec hall. Inside, a beauty parlor ("Unisex Hair Cutting"); the Stony Post Office, advertising money orders and a career in the U.S. Army; the Stony Branch of the Bank of Phoenix (two banks, that's progress); and a marine recruiting desk with a Chicano sergeant testing his hand strength on a cylinder filled with navy-issue ballpoint pens. He was wearing a bright dress uniform that would glow in the dark. The poster above his desk depicted a white college boy with hair brushed forward on his forehead and a V-neck sweater and his black buddy in a cardigan, both of them about to sign up for the bright Marines future.

Next door there was the CLINIC'N DISPENSARY. Merian hoped it dispensed better'n it spelled. Probably a psychedelic nurse had passed through: the Clinic'n was pasted over with decals; rainbow colors shaded the BIA stencilling. Entire families were lined up, looking dazed at the rainbows. Merian figured the event—a cold, a running eye, a baby hangover—was a time for relatives to hang together in mom 'n' pop solidarity. Pickup trucks were spinning in and out of the cusp of dust that served as a parking lot. One truck had a Confederate flag and "Go Navy" stickers on the bumpers, and a "Peace No Nukes" insignia on the front windshield, where the driver would have to peer over it and through the grime. More prefabs, air coolers pumping, desert water bags hanging from Ford or Dodge pickups and a splattered GTO Pontiac.

Merian sniffed hot Bakelite decomposing, shedding blackness under the sun from the heaped junk in a ditch. It was the smell of the kazoos Chaz and Merian used to play as children. There were also tires, a thickness of oil and rubber beneath the flat sun-scoured plastic. It might take a hundred years for Bakelite to disappear; yet enough of it was dissolved into the air for his nose to find it.

The open range had gone automotive. Especially at the cross-roads of Sitting Bull Boulevard and Warren G. Harding Alley, oil and tire and transmission smells came up strong. Old cars (flivvers, jalopies, in the days when Chaz and Merian shared one) ran on oil drained from other cars and gave off this perfume. The one Chaz and he had bought together was a Chevy. They used the mottled oil from giant cans at the Texaco station at the corner where they used to get gas, because when everything is worn so nicely already, a car doesn't need unused oil. It was the smell of no more damage to be done.

People moved, stood, opened and closed doors, pushing against the wind, ran machinery, carried shopping bags, just as in so many elsewheres, but it wasn't because they were American Indians, different from him, that Merian felt strangely dimmed and isolated. Not drowsy, but a kind of deafness, although the trucks revved, the wind blew, the cash registers beeped, there were thin desert sounds. The gravelly whine from somebody's tape deck was the voice of Danny Grand. Merian walked back past Nation Elementary, where children were standing in line for the midmorning school event, citrus-aid and graham crackers, and now he knew why he felt this selective deafness. Even the children were silent. A dense herd of kids and almost no voices, no chatter, no shouting or whistling. There were too many souls here for so little use of voice. Merian believed it was not just a case of strong silent Indian braves living up to their billing. It was melancholy. Despite the surrounding mountains, mesas, distant forests, skies, and the daily traffic of the sun through heaven— all that splendid artistry of nature—Merian had contracted a virulent case of sadness. He believed these people were sunk. They wanted excitement, they wanted to take arms against grief, and here was Danny Grand, one of their own, reaching through the TV with his complaint about the big boys in Hollywood who ran everything—they knew about big boys from elsewhere— and he promised to bring them some thrills in living color and on the big screen. These would be personal thrills, owned by them, paid for by them, the best American kind.

In the meantime, they shopped on this strip and waited in line for their diseases to be treated in the Clinic'n. At the intersection of Territory Road, people had made camp in tar-paper shacks and beached trucks. You take off the wheels and you have real estate. A man who seemed to be called Wildcat, taller than most, with streaked blondined long hair under a straw hat, was weighing himself on the nickel scale in front of the Great Spirit Notionette and shouting, "Wildcat! Wildcat!" He was only getting the first few pounds that you get for free.

An Anglo in an apron ducked out of the Notionette and answered, "Wildcat!" and Merian hurried over to introduce himself and explain his mission. Man to man, a fellow Anglo, Fred Kramer showed him the fun to be had shopping—the Character Reading Your Future machine, the Indian dolls from Taiwan, the Ouija-board and tarot-card counters, the motorized display of watches, ever in motion ("good as Timex but more for economy purposes"), the nonstick cookware sets, the Daisy BB guns. "These are starter guns for kids," said Mr. Kramer. "These are entry-level guns."

"Not for doing any harm," said Merian.

"Not yet," said Mr. Kramer, showing teeth like yellow late-winter icicles.

He walked Merian back outside, remarking that this was about it, just about the whole shmear, except for a few other items, like the frozen pizza back there in the case, a kind of ritual Eye-talian fried cornbread, as he understood it. Wildcat was still weighing the first few pounds of himself. Mr. Kramer hooked his thumbs into his apron and said, "He's a clam. Hey, Wildcat, what do you know?"

"Wildcat! Not smoking! Need a smoke!"

Mr. Kramer shook his head, reached into a pack, extracted one item, and held it toward Wildcat. "Means no harm," he said while Wildcat waited for a light. "They tell me he used to be intelligent. That was before I come onto the reservation."

"Nation," said Wildcat.

The President received him at the end of the afternoon. The temporary National Red Hogan was in a prefab World War II infantry company headquarters. No GI cans at the door, but half a Quonset in lieu of portico and vestibule. Strolling toward the door, Merian felt a nervous dizziness in his stomach over meeting a Leader of His Ancient People with a spiral loaded with questions. He had similar premonitions when he met Muammar al-Qaddafi, too, and when he woke up on a Sunday morning with Susan and the whole empty day stretching ahead, despite the

Times and the promise on Station WQXR of a glass of Dubonnet Blanc whenever he so desired.

Here, as he stopped a moment before stepping through the Quonset gap, he could see the land stretching in all directions, coppery and blue tints of mountains, and green slopes far away. Above, firm dark chameleon clouds absorbed the late sunlight like sponges. They might predict rain, but it didn't rain this season. It was a land to dream in, expect rain in. A pickup hurtled by with a "Red Power" insignia, five men on the flat, and a banner that read "Stony Apache A-Go-Go." Merian did not understand the dreams of these lovers of Danny Grand.

He is not Qaddafi, Merian commanded himself. Down, stomach.

Jarls Coyote, President, heard the reporter coming and shut the door to his office so that he would have to knock. Presently, using a device in his desk drawer, the President opened and beckoned him in. "Sit," he commanded. He was a short man in his late thirties with a shock of lank black hair falling flat across the forehead. He had a pair of telephones on his desk, one yellow—for emergency powwows with the Colonel of the Third World?—and a coffee-can ashtray filled with butts. There was a thick folder, edges of papers sticking out. He shut the office door by pressing the device in his desk drawer. Merian had seen the thing advertised in the back pages of magazines.

He had never before noticed drifts of sand inside a building. In the Sahara, they tended either to sweep the sand out or move the tent. This building was more like a *structure*. Quonset siding reinforced the prefab Stony Apache Red Hogan. It shouldn't have admitted grit, but the wind blew unceasingly on this mesa, poured ceaselessly through gaps in the mountain ranges, and there were doors and windows. The President was aware of the problem. He had an answer for that, too. A broom stood in a heap of sand in the corner. The broom had been used in history; it was irregularly worn and eroded, like the mouth of an old man. All but the most recent sand was swept up in the corner, and with the room so bare, only surplus metal furniture and wastebaskets, a smell that wasn't beer and yet wasn't not beer, Merian thought of an army dayroom, of something temporary and blank, through which many men passed on their way.

The other phone on the desk was an executive model—a panel of buttons. There's a touch of permanence for you.

The President leaned back and waited for Merian to approach his desk. "Howdy, Mr. Merd."

"Merian," said Merian.

"Howdy and shake, Ralph." But he didn't extend his hand.

Okay, one of those, Merian thought; I've dealt with some experts in this line. He said, "We want to deal fairly with the question, Mr. President. Why, given the needs of your people for certain basic amenities and necessities, you are committing yourself to a potentially, uh, speculative investment such as film production."

If it's a matter of knocking a person off balance, well, two can play at that game, the V.J. decided. Normally, of course, he would do at least ten minutes of politesse. But with different folks, like this here President slouching in front of him, Merian had different strokes.

"You okay in the Hogan?" the President asked. "Not too anything for you?"

"Fine. I'm used to living away from home. It's not too anything."

"Good, very good. Hospitality is a must for The Enemy. That's my people, you understand. So what you want to ask me? Then I ask you a couple."

"Okay, about Danny Grand, what I just said. I'd just like to chat—"

"Danny," stated the President. "You come look in on us if it wasn't for him? No, you wouldn't. See what I mean? Danny Grand, that's our ticket to national attention. You want to arm wrestle, Mr. Merd?"

The President sipped from his cold coffee in an oversized mug with a piece of lettered adhesive tape stuck to it: JARLS COYOTE, PRES. As yet there was no offer to share. The boiler-sized coffee maker in the corner was making exhausted gurgles. The President propped his feet in their boots in an open drawer of his desk, papers heel-crumpled there, and said slowly, "We need just about everything you can name. This is the Third World in the U.S. of A. So what we need first most of all—like the black people are only starting to find out, they are so far behind us, not that we have any feelings against them pro or con—is honor. Honor, Mr. Merd. That BIA shit, vocational training, what does it get us? They put up an electronics assembly out here—I hope you saw it already but you didn't—and we get laid off soon as the contractor be paid. Honor they can't give. Honor they can't take away. That answer your question now, Mr. Merd, so you can charter your airplane take you back to New York City?"

Merian was grateful for the speech. It had unwound slowly, in a compressed monotone, as if thought through and then read off a prompter hidden in the cold coffee; in a low slow rumble with ignored red signals for emphasis. But there it was. "Honor through this means, sir?" Merian asked. When he didn't reply, Merian repeated the question. "Through this means, Mr. President?"

Still reading off the prompter, the President said, "Through any available means. Stealing. Dynamiting. But drinking don't do it. I switched over from drinking." Finally he raised his eyes from the oversized mug. "A big success sure would. Fame and dollars is the American way, isn't it? And if we combine it with the Way, our Way... He paused. "I don't take so much to how you just look at me and don't write down what I say. Aren't you suppose to be one of those reporters from New York City, Mr. Merd?"

"Merd" rhymes with "Turd," Merian thought. He could at least rhyme it with "Merde." But he doesn't care, doesn't talk too much.

Jarls Coyote explained that the Stony Apaches were not sophisticated revolutionaries, like the Iranians, who paid for weapons in the holy struggle against the Zionist Imperialist Great Satan with opium deals. "You can cook opium into heroin with garage technology," he said. "We looked into it but we're more organic. Our ancient name doesn't mean exploit the People."

"You're more into entertainment?"

"This could be a revolution in the entertainment field. Where else does a Third-World nation called The Enemy get to make a big Hollywood hit? You don't have to answer that question." Merian accepted the invitation with gratitude.

The President extended his arms. They reminded Merian of the Popeye forearms of the kid at the airstrip, Hawkfeather—at the airstrip and outside the Guest Hogan. Did all these Apaches eat their spinach? "Hey, come on, mister—a little arm wrestle just for fun, no money, okay?" The challenge seemed to be a gloomy form of greeting. Hawkfeather and President Jarls Coyote couldn't be expected to understand he was here partly to throw the gloom off his own trail.

Men with their own glooms don't have the repose for such considerations. Claudia and Sandra might—those chipper young persons.

Merian ignored the challenge. He didn't want to say no; he also didn't want to arm wrestle. There was a knife at the wide leather belt of the President. It was not in a folk-art scabbard; it was a business knife, and as if in touch with the spirits of clairvoyance and Indian inseeing, President Coyote extracted the knife—a snakelike sliding noise—and began to tend to immediate business, which in this case was the dual purpose of cleaning his fingernails with the point and avoiding Merian's eyes.

"That's a nice piece of steel," Merian said politely.

"Switzerland. It's not a nice knife. It's a weapon."

Merian was beginning to understand. The man's approach to politics was not friendliness, affability, and charm, like so many of the Presidents of the country that surrounds the Stony Apache Nation. The V.J. had a way with informants and interviews when his own affability broke down. It was to use no charm at all, a bit of *60 Minutes* hammering instead. "Mr. President," he said, "let me ask you one more time. This is poor terrain. You have considerable tribal funds, and now you have access to the trust accounts, but you need fences, wells, better roads, equipment for your schools. You need an employment program. With a cooperative system of investment, and a treasury augmented by grants from Washington over the years, why choose so risky an investment?"

"You don't understand that, you don't."

"No. I appreciate many things about it. I remember about honor, sir—not that what I like or don't like is important, I'm just a working journalist—but you don't even have a movie theater on the reservation. I mean, how people on the outside see it—you'll have to throw it on the wall of a rec hall when they bring it to you for the world premiere, is that true?"

"Danny's gonna construct a computerized minitheater. We're gonna have Danny bring us a premeer right here on the Nation. He's gonna shoot on our lands and we're gonna get extra jobs, acting jobs, commissary jobs, and all the other stars'll live right there in our Guest Hogan you're living in, you know that? Danny might not just set up a prefab, he might just build us a movie minitheater so we don't have to spend all our time on that rotten Anglo television. I talked to Danny's business manager personally last night at his personal home. He's a Hollywood mongol." The President paused. "And it's not *reservation,* Mr. Merd, get that through your head."

Merian stared. Did the President of the Nation mean they would show American Indian movies instead of Anglo TV? Did President Jarls Coyote see himself as a movie mongol? Was the gloom that bad around here?

He asked the President if he thought the movie would be a success and serve his Nation's other purposes, moral and psychological, spiritual if you prefer, and if it would return the investment, and if it was, all things considered, prudent. And if the promise to build a minitheater was in legal form. He meant to ask again—a certain hammering was in order—if the drilling of wells, the educating of children, the improving of public facilities, might in some people's view (oh, pompous reporter) take precedence over the financing of a motion picture for a country-rock singer who happened to remark on television that he was part Indian and proud of it. "Creative as this might be, of course."

"Tomorrow I will see," the President said. "When the sun rises and the vultures circle in the sky. If I want to see tomorrow."

"Uh-huh," Merian said. Redskin shuck and jive was new to him, but shucking and jiving in general was not. He wondered if a straight adversary reporter might do better than a pompous one. "Have you heard of the hippies, President? If it's righteous, it'll happen, Mr. President?"

"They come to eat our cactus. They have big freakout here. We know them well, we push them away, male and female."

"But tomorrow you won't worry—like those folks, sir?"

"That was the hippie way. This is the Way of the Indian. Do I look like one of your white-eyed mushroom and cactus eaters?"

Along with the boyish lank flat lock falling across his forehead, Jarls Coyote had a tuft of long hair tied behind in a ponytail, a liverish face, the skin tight and matted, large widespread teeth. His arms were ropy and strong and the shoulders twitched when he spoke. He looked like a man who worked out in a prison yard; the sobriety around here was solitary confinement followed by weight-lifting-in-the-yard sobriety. It was a style, like Hawk-feather's, Merian decided; he didn't think the elected President could be an ex-con unless they followed different customs from their brother nation (perhaps they did).

Jarls Coyote may have wanted to quarrel with the white man and finally win the Indian Wars. He watched the winds under the door, through the cracks in the building, scattering the grit— the broom stood like an explorer's marker.

"Am I a hippie to you?" he repeated.

"Of course not, President." Later, when he was far away, Merian could write anything he liked. Neither adversary nor pompous seemed to be the preferable tactic just now. And besides, agreeable was the courteous way to save getting slugged or thrown out on his behind.

The Veteran Journalist believed violence against his body should be avoided whenever convenient. He didn't enjoy violence against his mind, either, but modern life had not been entrusted to his keeping. And as to his spirit, battering came with the course he had chosen, which was to continue. Merian wished he were smarter, had learned a few things despite his stupidity. This was one of those occasions and places—an Indian nation in the scrub desert of Elsewhere County, Arizona—where it would serve no good purpose for his remains to be found battered and bruised and drying in the sand. Although the idea of the sun rising and the vultures circling appealed to his sense of the picturesque. *An Indian native male is the alleged perpetrator.* The county sheriff's report would strive for objectivity, just like the journalist. *The alleged perpetrator is the culprit.*

"Mr. President," Merian said, "may I ask you a question about *teswin?*"

"You been drinking *teswin* already and you only been here one-two days?"

"I kind of like it."

"That's our religious drink you kind of like. The BIA can't say nothing 'cause it's religious freedom. That's our beverage. Personally, I always preferred two six-packs better'n *teswin,* but now I stubbed my toe like everybody else, I won the Battle like not so many does, I got elected President, I try to stay away except for once in a while when I chug a little *teswin* on a religious event. What did you fight?"

"Fight, sir?"

"We here all fight the battle of the bottle and not many win. What did you fight? What's your beverage?"

"Other troubles."

"Want to fight me, Mr. Mary? You won't know me till you fight me. That's a firm belief we have."

Merian did not reply hastily. He was not considering the President's proposal; he was considering how to answer it. He was also waiting because they seemed to prefer slow-spoken folks around here. He hoped to learn quickly how to speak slowly. He ran through the elements of his present life before choosing words, which, if they were not the correct words, giving off the correct

103

tone, could lead to ending the investigation and a trip to a hospital far away, if he was lucky. There was Susan far away, there was Arnie Schultz. There were Sandra and Claudia nearer at hand, his brother in San Francisco. There was Hawkfeather, who also wanted to fight, who also believed it was how to know each other, and was at the age when the craziness ran loose with no interference from judgment. Rage was a preferred beverage for Hawkfeather. And now here was the President, suddenly alert in his chair, who had won the battle of the bottle but lost many other battles. He was waiting for a simple answer.

"There are better things I can do for you, Mr. President, than fighting. I can tell your story. I don't mean to show off, but I'm better at that than, uh, gladiation. Isn't the story about your Nation something you'd like told?"

The President moved the coffee can with its snuffed butts like insects burrowing into the sand. He moved it from the right to his left on the desk. "You think you will tell it correct like it should be told?"

"No. Journalists don't. But I'll do a partial telling, the best I can."

"Gladiation. Is that a language they talk?"

"No. I got nervous, Mr. President."

"That's good." For the first time his face seemed to slide off its accustomed tracks, sleepy to sullen, and something like a grin opened across the wide large yellow teeth. "I learned a language here, too." He stopped. He let the smile exhaust itself, drift away like the blowing grit. He was himself again. "I am now speaking explanation to you, mister." The President of the Nation uttered in a low recovered-alcoholic monotone: "What we have here is an interface with the BIA. We can't deal with their language, which is the software they use to top off the damned conquest."

"You were trained in computers, sir?" asked Merian.

"Self-trained. The fuckers don't know how to deal with the Enemy People's needs."

"You've worked at it? At computers?"

"They think I'm BIA issue. They run this vocational shit on

us. They think I can't do input, outgo. They want us to live on surplus." He spat out the sticky word "surplus" and the V.J. imagined orange blocks of cheese, boxes of wormy grain, pasty hunks of animals.

"There's call for computer people just now," Merian said.

"Software and mainframe, that's it. And shit lines running payrolls or fulfillments. But I'm into robots," the monotone continued. "I'd like to work so I don't have to work. This job of President I got elected for, it should ought to be full time. You drink from the Putah Creek around here and a few hours later you'll get the idea what I think of the BIA. You'll prefer being some kind of spirit with no body."

The V.J. applied a little redskin silence against the sudden torrent. The President of the Nation had a knack for keeping him off balance. This may have proven a political asset in the field of presidentiality.

"Where we live, *sir,* not like where you Anglo peoples live, the dawn is colder than the dark. Harder to see the sun come up than sit through the night. In the dark hours there is drinking and killing, but in the day there is only sickness. You understand my meaning?"

"No," said the V.J., "though your words are precise."

The President smiled again. Knife, fist, or bottle was not strictly necessary. He liked showing he was both smarter and crazier than they thought. Like Geronimo, he wanted to be a winner; but unlike Geronimo, he wasn't intending to lose. Like any modern President, he had the gift of a forked tongue.

"Jesus was a really terrific figure," said Jarls Coyote, making a European gesture he must have learned from daytime television, kissing the tips of his fingers, flicking his brown hand rapidly outward, indicating marvelous tastiness. "So was John F. Kennedy. And Burt Reynolds. All your gods are terrific, they got cheerismo, but we prefer our own. It may not be so rich, but the Great Spirit belongs to The Enemy. Like the fried cornbread is ours. And the *teswin.* It suits our bellies, mister."

"Those are not my gods," Merian said. "Not even one of three."

"You worship yourself?" the President asked. He was no longer in a fighting mood. Was that just cold coffee he was sipping? He was mellow. He was curious. He was making a friendly inquiry.

"I leave the question open. Worship isn't a part of my routine."

The President examined the lined and sun-creased face, the incipient accumulation of looser, not yet really loose, skin around Merian's jaw, and stated quietly, "You will pardon me, please. You look like a man in need of a little something. Perhaps worship might help. Profound respect does the trick."

"So I've been told," said Merian, "by several ladies."

"Ah! And you drink, also?"

"No."

"Man, you get a lot of no-sleep nights when you think some female would give you peace and she don't. Man, you are worse than I think."

Merian sighed. "I agree with you there, Mr. President. All religions are complicated, aren't they?"

Together they fell into silence. Piety called for this. With a nod Jarls Coyote passed Merian his mug with the cold coffee, but Merian shrugged and shook his head. The President got over the slight. They were joined by fraternity, or perhaps only by a pact of understanding, a nonbelligerency notice. Jarls took another sip. He cleared his throat. "We need..." and then cleared his throat again. "We need a communicator for the Great Spirit Religion. Prophets we got, shamans and medicine men galore, but what we need in our Table of Organization is a Great Communicator, somebody to tell our top ancestral truths in the form of lies that the outside world can appreciate. What I'm thinking: three-year contract, escalators, and the chance to get in on the ground fucking floor of an ancient credo. Interested?"

"I've always been free-lance," said Merian, "although I have a job. I know that's a contradiction. I work on a long leash."

"You'd have responsibility for a journal, the *Quarterly Review of the Great Spirit,* hopefully appearing every month, plus Great Spirit Publishing and Enemy Books—we haven't done our first one yet, if you don't count the pamphlet we ran off on the Nation's Gestetner machine, my inaugural address to the Elders, how I won the Battle of the Bottle plus the election—plus eventually a bunch of other stuff. The backlog of a rich oral tradition. You'd be asked to train a staff of Stony Apache communicators. There's a whole new generation coming up that don't fight the bottle. It fights the battle of the book. They read, they write, they punch keys, they are patriotic fucking braves. If chickenshit religions like Jehovah's Witnesses, Oral Roberts, that there Armstrong in Arkansas or some other eastern state can do it, why can't we? We got a genuine product here, Philip."

"I'm sure. It's time-tested."

"That's the kind of communication skill we need, to come up with an underline like that. *Time*-tested. So will you ride? We'll have a *teswin*—you want to call it firewater you can—and a corn-bread ceremony to mark the signing of the deal, all fringe benefits, health, pension plan, dependent allowance guaranteed by the Bureau of Indian Fucking Affairs, which is an Equal Opportunity Exploiter."

"I have no dependents, Jarls."

"So much the better for you, Ralph."

Merian took full advantage of this moment of correct first-name communion. He applied a little silence and let it soak. He was learning the Way, even as the President was practicing his talent for Anglo babble. Merian said nothing, but aimed a bolt of silent insight straight at the Native American hustler lounging there with his sand-filled coffee can and his murk-filled coffee mug that might have had a splash of *teswin* sprinkled in there someplace. What Merian was thinking: Poor as they are, with these grants and lands, their tax relief and unspent bonds held by Tempe National, they can finance Danny Grand's film. They can do other things. In unity there is strength, and in disunity there is also strength.

The President seemed to read his mind.

"You take them trailers," he said, "and you knock the wheels off so they set right down in the dirt, and you put up fences and stuff, you talk to the bankers, you got to talk to the BIA first, man—you can't do shit without you hassle the BIA—you get the papers through fucking Washington and the lawyers—and you ain't got land anymore. You ain't got streams and grazing. You ain't got mountains and trails. You got..." He leaned forward and gave Merian black slits of eyes. This was a smile through the *teswin* peephole. "...You got *real estate*. We got everything we need but honor. You see why we understand Danny Grand? You see why we need an explainer?"

Merian thanked him for the offer of employment and for his time. Begging his permission, he would visit the Nation and get some sense of its daily life. That's how journalism works, he explained; PR is something like that, too.

The President nodded. He looked bored. He wanted to do the dismissing around here. He didn't stand when Merian stood; he stuck a long wooden match into the sand-filled coffee can as if he were skewering something.

He wasn't finished yet. As Merian reached the door, he called out, "Friends, right?" and stood, and said, "Wait a sec."

Merian stopped. The President was short even for a Stony Apache. His broad sloping shoulders and powerful arms made him look immovable, a cinder-block square, though perhaps he felt himself at a disadvantage, looking up toward the visiting Anglo. His standing was a demonstration of trust and feeling. "Let me ask you something I never asked no white eyes before. This is kind of a personal question. You help me kill Danny if he rip us off? I hope this isn't too personal."

"You must be kidding," Merian said.

"I know how hard it is for a show-biz personality to meet people. So he rip us off, he won't want to meet us. You know there could be a little problem here. But I figure you ask him for an interview, a personality can't refuse. And I go along like an assistant, maybe carry a tape. I do all the work, Ralph."

Merian tried to guess what the proper response might be.

"Too personal, Ralph?"

"I hope we both forget you ever said this, Mr. President."

Jarls Coyote sat back down and opened and shut the drawer of his desk. He gave Merian a glimpse of something steely, blue-white, and unmistakable. He had a whole collection of presidential toys. "You see how much I start to trust you," he said, "to ask a white eyes a thing like that. But Danny knows we are serious people, our word is our bond, and we go berserk."

"I hope he knows that."

"You tell him," said the President. "You make him know. Even if he some crazy Indian, too. You write the story like a serious person, Mister White Eyes Reporter, and you let him know. Here you go!"

He opened the drawer again. The pistol lay in full view. He reached in and handed Merian a ball-point pen imprinted: STONY APACHE NATION, Jarls Coyote, Pres.

"Souvenir of Christmas before it's Christmas," said the President. "Around here, hospitality knows no season."

He pressed the button that opened the door.

Merian stood in the road outside the Quonset entrance. He thought he could hear his own breathing reflected by the metal arch as he walked through, but then he was out on the mesa again. Down the road Wildcat was crying, "Wildcat! Wildcat!" A woman in a blue "Apache A-Go-Go" sweat shirt and gray woolen men's pants and high-topped black-and-white basketball shoes was holding two shopping bags and watching a group of kids. The kids dashed back and forth across the road; they were out of school. The woman was slow and they were swift. No Hawkfeather on the road; Merian felt blessed for that.

He strolled toward the Guest Hogan, keeping his eyes carefully unfocused. He wanted to be interrupted by no one friendly to an Anglo visitor. He had things to get organized. He was considering what he had just heard and the requirements of his trade. President Jarls Coyote had made a few problems for him. The journalist must be alert and available, he believed, but also alert to betrayal by sympathy. He was not a moralist, but not an engine of communication to run amok, either. So what was he? Those weren't all the possibilities, of course.

He was not *not* a judge. He wished Susan were waiting for him at the Guest Hogan, not exactly waiting, having her own things to do, but available for conversation, for him to tell her his pieces of the truth, for her to do the same. He was lonely and distracted. Jarls Coyote had subtracted a certain confidence and self-sufficiency from him.

Arnie Schultz would not surprise him if he described Jarls Coyote's last proposal—another joke, another proof for Arnie—but he couldn't predict how Susan would react. How could he learn from either of them, since they didn't know what he knew? They weren't here with the grit continually blowing, scratching the eyes, itching the conjunctiva, and they would never meet Jarls Coyote except through his words and their prejudices, his prejudices and words, what he chose to see and hear. They didn't know Hawkfeather, they didn't know Sandra and Claudia, they didn't even know Wildcat. Neither did he. But he could taste this dry wind off the high desert that was hot and cold and hot again.

Susan might have a special view about Claudia and Sandra, of course.

His friends could not, even if he told them, feel the weight on him of Hawkfeather's arms and the President's sloping shoulders. He was in this thing alone, where he had always liked to be. Using lonely evenings in cement-block motels and the help of screw-top wine to do his five or ten thousand words—doing dizzy, doing earnest, even doing book-length—he had never before been slowed down by a war or revolution. A mere American dollar scam would not stop the propositions and paragraphs around here.

Sandra and Claudia just knew he'd feel alert after a shower. He used a fine-needle spray, then a thick beam, then needles again. Hot soapy water sluiced off the grime; cold water swept

110

away evil fatigue and conscience, making Merian young, as a shower always did, as he was not, icy needles of water being the fountain of youth with minimal suffering and at his convenience. A few gasps and grunts were a small price to pay.

The young women pounded at his door as if he were hiding in a dorm room, late for the game. "Hi hi hi!" cried nut-brown Sandra. "We don't just want to know how you're making out in general—"

Nut-brown Claudia liked good cheer and was smiling.

". . . we really want to take you to the ceremony. You haven't visited any secret Native American initiation rites lately, have you?"

Claudia was tickled by Sandra's wit.

"You probably shouldn't be with us at this ceremony out on the vast desert, but then again you should, right? No white man has ever seen it since the Gray Line tour bus stopped coming."

Claudia poked her friend and finally, herself, spoke up: "Just put on your feathers and headdress and tend to shout at the appropriate time."

"When in doubt, you can yell 'How,'" said Sandra.

"And we'll show you," Claudia finished, "how."

And they bent over with tears of laughter, slapping each other's hands in the approved South Side manner. Then they straightened up and pulled at their denim shirts. Claudia explained with sudden sobriety and earnestness, "This thin air up here gives everybody moods. Even Jarls sometimes has like his period coming on, you notice?"

"We're glad to see you from the outside world is all, Mr. Journalistic," said Sandra. "It gets lonely out here deep into anthropology. We sneaked a cup of *teswin* already to get up the courage."

Merian believed they needed no help besides each other, but how girlish of them to say so. It might be unnecessary to tell them he was already involved with a woman; their courage was complete already. It wasn't his Anglo cheerismo, it was their loneliness—he understood about that. They were fighting that battle. Sometimes a fit of facetiousness helps.

"I was just going to make a call to my lady friend," he said.

Claudia did a face at Sandra. So this shambling old reporter was trying to tell them something.

"What kind of perverts are we, that we interface with a person's oral declaration of fidelity?" Sandra asked.

"We're the new generation of socioanthropologists, just doing good is all," said Claudia. "There's a phone outside in the street, but someone ripped off the box."

"I can call later."

"Enough of these excuses, Mr. Journalistic."

Sandra drove like a maniac in the little green Spider, skidding through the restless blowing grit. They were climbing from seven thousand feet, going higher, Merian bent and crouched on the jump seat. He was somewhat powered by *teswin* and so was Claudia.

The ceremony took place miles up a canyon in a little clearing lit by fires, with a roof of green branches precariously intermeshed overhead. There were flickers and lickings in the sky as the swift dark replaced the mountain glow of sunset. Women, shaded from the sky glow under blankets wrapped around blue jeans, attended to fires and pots. Corn bread was being fried on open grills, then stacked in piles on newspapers, and then would be fried again when it came time to eat. An old man, uncle to the girl being honored, inducted into the flow of history on the occasion of her first menstruation, took Merian by the hand and brought him into a teepee. He drank from the cup that was held to his lips. Sandra and Claudia were left outside.

The girl and her mate (present? future? symbolic?), a boy with face chalked white, were dancing. They would dance for four nights. The drummer sat at the entrance to the teepee. His eyes were closed; he could drum in his sleep. The old man held the cup to his mouth again. It was a hot and peppery high-proof something. The old uncle jostled Merian into some dancing steps, and then chanted and clapped his hands, pushing Merian again to start him when he resisted. Merian felt huge, clumsy, and strangely content. He danced like a bear. He was not in his own life. He was a tourist elsewhere. He had left his own life behind, aside, he didn't have to think about the future. He didn't mind thinking about his present embarrassment. He was here, dancing, following orders.

A thick arm suddenly spun Merian around, out of the teepee, as he said, "Hey!" and a voice urgently hissed at him, "What you doing here, Mister White Eyes?"

It was Hawkfeather. Off balance, Merian held to the arm a moment. He struggled to awaken and find words. "Same thing you are. I was invited."

"That ain't why I'm here," Hawkfeather said.

"Don't surprise me like that, kid."

"You don't like to be touched, do you, mister? I *belong* here, what you doing? You got business here, mister?"

And then Hawkfeather disappeared into the darkness of the teepee, where the dancers were still dancing, the white-faced boy marked by chalk for death, the girl celebrating that she could now be considered a woman by the boy marked for death. She was marked for life. Why was she dancing with a boy who was smeared, doomed? Did Hawkfeather see the white chalk on Merian's face? And he might also have asked why Merian was trying to dance in the Apache fashion. It would have been a good question. It was what he preferred for Hawkfeather to ask. What was he doing and dancing here?

Hawkfeather knew what Hawkfeather was doing. He meant to smear his own face against the Anglo face. He was at war, and the enemy was supposed to be Merian. The enemy Hawkfeather had in mind didn't like the prospect at all. The boy was just a boy, but the V.J. was just another man whose face would get its chalk in due course, without needing the help of Hawkfeather.

Dear Arnie, Merian thought, this is not what we had in mind. Dear Susan, he thought, I don't know what I have in mind.

"Dear Mr. Merian," Claudia was saying, firelight flickering in her face, crumbs of fried corn bread clinging to her lips, "too much *teswin* are fattening..."

"Is," said Sandra, "it's definitely *is* fattening, Claudia."

"... and too many shots of penicillin, you know what I mean?"

"So assuming," said Sandra, "none of us is too fat or infected at the moment—and we're not, are you?—we'd like to visit you at your hogan away from home in about an hour. That gives you a chance to prepare yourself with a good long shower, getting all the fried grease off your fine old eastern college bod."

"Alumnus," said Merian.

"As recipients of information," said Sandra, "we want to share with you. We've had it out between ourselves and decided to share. We want to make the great leap from researchers to informants. Do ancient time-tested Apache hospitality more-rays fit into your scheme of things, Mr. Merian?"

Merian did not hurry at the invitation. For one thing, it had some of the form of information with the content left undefined. If they meant what they seemed to mean, he wasn't sure they really meant it. He listened to the ceremonial drums. To him it sounded too slow and regular, without the erratic excitement of bongos at Grant's Tomb on Riverside Drive. The pulse was ominously soothing, like the hookup in an acute cardiac ward.

He ate a slice of double-fried corn bread, a sticky crisp, hot and salty. He noted President Jarls Coyote standing with his arms folded across his chest, an Indian in a future Danny Grand movie, victorious over the battle of the bottle, brooding, scowling, deep-chested, dramatic. Yet it was not merely a portrait. He was lost in his own nation. Merian could not translate this sadness into the kinds of melancholy familiar to him—abulia, passivity, anomie, angst, longing for he knew not what, weltschmerz, the blues. They had their own sadness, these Indians, compounded of grit and silence, a staring voiceless rage. There was a devastation from history, a flood with no ebbing. They had gone under. They gave him the creeps, as Claudia and Sandra had probably been given the creeps. He believed the young women were nicer than they let on, just trying to rally against the Indian spirits among whom they dwelled.

As the night chill settled over them, seeping into the hollows, and he felt the dirt in the seams of his face, at the roots of his hair, he remembered a dream. He had been lying next to Susan, her body long and fair, his hands sliding and climbing. His head was close to hers. Tears of praise and joy were falling from his eyes; what he would not allow, of course, in real life. It was cozy and nice and a dream. The real tears in his eyes came of the grit, the steady blowing, the brutalized eyelid membranes.

The need for redeeming love must be beaten down. That's what causes the pain of moving from early boyishness to grown-up boyishness. The need for friendship and sex may be permitted, with a less acute piercing. A person then frees himself to get on with what's left in life—work and watching it go by. If you're lucky, you might have a revival of that pang-filled adolescent infatuation in love for your children. Or most often, as in all love, if you're unlucky you have it, with all its sorrows.

Merian didn't know about any of this for sure. He had noticed himself and other people. He had also had a wife he liked. When they cared for each other, which she did not seem to remember, they had thought of having a child.

A woman chooses a fellow, at least for a time, but why should a child give him a better run, when the child never chose him for father, might even prefer to be an orphan? Ralph Merian's brother, Chaz, in San Francisco, no doubt preferred not to have a brother.

The happy love of a woman and the love of children are miracles, and although many believe in miracles, others know how rare they are. The Veteran Journalist was one of those. He had grown cautious. He wasn't ready for pets, alcohol, or treating his own body in the Singles way as his only true lover, just as he was still a tail-dragger on the subjects of UFOs, permanent peace in the Middle East, and a steady, unremarkably content companion. Before finding Susan, the course of true love had not responded well to his investigations. When he had admired the chic style and unhealthy skin of a girl from Paris on a program of dissipation in Manhattan—the French equivalent of the Junior Year Abroad—he knew he wasn't ready. He only had a Learner's Permit. "Eet ees groovy New York," the girl had said. "A-vair-ay wan spik Frange, almos'."

She was a bijou. She was more fun than the punk *(punque)* he picked up in the line of duty, as usual, at the Blue Night Café (descent by recently returned war correspondent into depths of New Wave scene; human interest plus tragic waste, a Sunday magazine one-pager). "This dude was gonna rape me," the New Wave lady confided, "till I said, 'Hey, man, that's my *body* you're fuckin' with.' So he paused to take that thought in. He was gonna reason it through his head, you know, but I'm not into reasoning, especially when I kick him in the—pow! a karate!—balls. More than ten words of disputation is my limit, man."

"I'm not going to argue with you, Mzz."

"You," she said sweetly, "my softwear tells me, Hey, this dude is a gentleman! Brains plus verbalization skills plus consideration for a woman's inner feelings."

"You do me too much credit," Merian had murmured, lowering his eyes.

As a reporter, he often met the kind of journalist who always found himself in the wrong place. As a seeker of love, he had been that kind of lover. Wrong place, wrong time, wrong good-natured lady.

"You got a bathroom here?" Sandra asked.

"Why are you asking that?"

"We use it?" said Claudia.

Pushing and shoving, giggling, the two of them pulled the plastic curtain around the commode and shower territory. In a moment the steam began to rise. Merian considered what he was in for.

116

This claustrophobic voyage with Sandra and Claudia was a lazy old habit, wasn't it? A former habit, as when he had been floating without a port, without Susan Pollet. He remembered the green-skinned French girl and the vinyl punk, and missed Susan. And was not sure at all about the quality of his longing. Making love with Susan was a return to a different past, when he was part of a woman, and to the future, when he would be a mere scattering of earth and air. Poor lady, this was too heavy a program for a pale rosy intelligent person who thought he said too much and yet managed to be too much silent.

Merian rubbed a hand over his itching eyelids. You tell a kid not to do that, but a grown man does it anyway. Once he went picking through the rubble of a bombed-out drugstore in Beirut for opthalmic ointment and found mostly tubes of contraceptive jelly, foam, and cream, the remedies no one cared to loot. La Pharmacie du Pont Alexandre Premier it was.

Merian had studied the art of letting go of love. Holding on was too easy; everyone can do it. He gave it up as much as he could. He used to blame the woman for not causing him to love her more. He sulked, he grew irritable. Now he knew whose fault it was—that's progress, that's an improvement—but when he got really good, he wouldn't blame anyone. Not any body or soul. *No one.*

So now, wasn't this peculiar? Without any reason, unless a lunar curve of forehead, sweetness of skin, monkey grasp of hand against his, were reasons Merian found himself in that state of greed that is something like love. Not so painful as a deformed spine, nor so distracting as alcoholism, but it was like them in its inconvenience. When he tasted Susan's breath (but this had occurred with the breath of others), when she breathed him in (as other women had also done), the important matters seemed unimportant. His routines were impaired. This was severe about Susan Pollet.

Arnie Schultz and Ralph Merian had learned how to thread their way through the inaccessible. This is what Chaz had not learned, still lost in the maze. First a person defines the thrill that seems to make everything whole, then pursues the truth, gives it a shapely five or ten thousand words, makes everything complete. But when a person can do that, he can't necessarily do the same thing with a woman. She doesn't solve herself in five or ten thousand words, or in the case of a major war or revolution, a series of pieces to be rounded off into a nice quick in-depth instant book.

Too many solutions, he thought. Not enough problems.

There was a tumult here. The V.J. was uncomfortable. Noisy print did not bring that soft breath and skin smelling like petals and understanding heart that he longed for (he didn't need it, he did without it, he was okay just longing for it). And could the woman who strolled by his side in Port-au-Prince, in London, and on Riverside Drive and let her flanks touch his, send him off willingly to the Green Revolution of Qaddafi's Libya or to muck around in the film investments of the Stony Apaches? Well, he was here, wasn't he? Maybe it was the V.J. himself who thought of saddling up a home desk and riding it for the final while in his life. Susan never asked him to give up the discomforts in which he had bathed so long. He was doing what lazy explainers do, blaming the facts instead of finding better facts.

While philosophy ran its course and Sandra and Claudia finished their entertaining shower together, Ralph Merian looked for the hall toilet. He flushed. Nothing happened. He lifted the back lid and saw that the miniature metal derrick, the rubber plunger, the floating metal ball, all the parts were gone. Instead, a copy of his book, *Coups and Countercoups: Third World A-flame,* had been placed inside, soaking up the rusty wet.

The kid Hawkfeather seemed to want to bother him.

He retrieved the drowned book. He filled the plastic waste-basket with water from the sink and washed down the commode. Patient improvisation was the answer to harassment by Hawk-feather. A better occupation than philosophy, he decided.

Sandra and Claudia had been chirping softly together in the shower space. Now they joined Merian in his silence. As the two social workers sped down the road of life, sometimes snug in the little shared Fiat Spider, they chattered and laughed, but now they let themselves be oppressed by Merian's lack of conversation. Dullness could be a way of life, too. Sacrifice required a deep resolve. They had checked on each other's state of mind; they would not flinch. This was interesting. They stood in the near-center of the room, or the center of the part that did not include the bed, and they switched their tails like animals in a lair. This way lies escape, this way comes the light, this way I stand. This was sort of fun.

Merian admired their animal wariness, their human youthful courage. Merian thought about whether he had any friends and whether Susan and Arnie should be counted as friends just because, in his peculiar way, he cared for them, and he thought about why these women were waiting for him, slightly impatiently waiting, in the middle of his cinder-block room at the Stony Apache Guest Hogan.

"Anyway, since we're going together," Sandra said.

"Going *steady*," Claudia said, "isn't that what you used to say? Your generation? Steady?"

"Going unsteadily," said Sandra. *"Teswin* makes me smart, if it's only a teeny hit."

"Going unsteady with this here person," said Claudia, and the two young women slapped hands, merry with each other, swift in merriment.

They would have to include the V.J. in their joy or he would just shovel them out. The dust of the day, the dirt, the winds, the grinding sun, the heat, the lowering clouds, the noise of pickup trucks, the grit blowing, the sudden harsh dry chill when night fell—the utter featureless darkness on a night of low parched clouds, like this one—made it easy for Merian to think of drink rather than sex. Everyone had been caked with a film of dirt and sweat; only the young guests were clean with their temporary soapy freshness. When he thought of embracing someone, he thought of air-conditioned rooms, humming quiet, a shower first,

119

a bath with the lady. Those were proper remedies. "Well?" Claudia asked.

Not that Sandra was in a hurry.

Fortunately, plenty of hot rusty water came with the deluxe rooms in the Nation's Guest Hogan. Fortunately, the volunteers from Chicago and Winnetka understood his feelings in the matter of daintiness, had similar feelings themselves, due to hygienic rearing. Other feelings might apply later, when you really get to know a person or persons. Unfortunately, the shower was small and narrow for three, but fortunately again, none of them minded the crowding. They worked at it, two do-gooders scrubbing down a visitor to an Apache nation. Will wonders ever cease.

"Intimacy at our age," remarked Sandra, working a snubby fistful of soap between the V.J.'s buttocks, where lurked the tickles, "this kind of closeness has all sorts of echoes from childhood. We need it from our fathers and mothers. From Mom and Dad at the same time. Isn't a threesome the most natural form of lovemaking? Stop tightening up like that, Ralph. Isn't the triangle the most favorite image after the circle?"

"Not just mother, father, and child," said Claudia, "it's also father, son, and holy female ghost, it's also a triad symbol among the Apaches."

"Fertility I'll bet," shrewdly guessed the V.J. "Hey. Careful."

"But you better not," Sandra said. "You had one?"

"One?"

"One vasectomy."

"None," said Merian.

Claudia whipped a little packet out of the pocket of her jeans skirt, which hung over a chair. "Never mind, I take responsibility for my actions."

Sandra looked dubious, worried; she sniffed at Merian, showing him where to have a vasectomy. The young women were toweling and blotting.

"I'll get to him in time," Claudia said. "Ooh, that big thing. You're a worrier, Sandie. Trust me."

"It's not so big. Haven't we seen bigger around here?"

"It's all in the head, darling—look at it blush when we talk about it."

Merian hoped they wouldn't get to quarreling over him. Not now, not in the air-conditioned room with incipient relaxation on the path ahead. He didn't even want debate. He preferred coziness. "Trust her," he said softly to Sandra.

"Just relax," said Sandra. "You're the one who's nervous. Considering you're an older man, you're supposed to be calm. Didn't your generation say 'cool'?"

"I was out of the country then," said Merian.

This pummeling was no lavish intimacy, this wetted giggly funning with two grad students who knew the Stony Apache people had been betrayed, oppressed, and demolished, but still had their pride and other scraps. Claudia and Sandra were of the generation that named a place in Arizona the Third World. For Claudia and Sandra, Third-World sympathies were now at work. They licked and puffed at the wrong recipient of aid. But why should that recipient complain, even if he was only oppressed by himself?

"You're one of us," gasped Sandra.

"You're part of the process," whispered Claudia. *"But I think— don't you?—Hawkfeather is peeking through the window."*

Merian jumped up and both of them giggled. "Gave you a noodge there, didn't we?" Sandra asked.

"In the books it's called a frisson," said Claudia. "That was our plan."

"Come back, come back!" cried Sandra. "Come back here at once!"

Slick with saliva and sweat, erect and dumbfounded, Merian pulled at the raddled window shade until it began to split off its roller. He prayed that keen Indian eyes could not see through coated paper hanging crazily over pitted, fly-specked glass. Clau-

121

dia came to take him gently by the finger. She led him away. He returned to what they were doing.

Maybe Hawkfeather wasn't charting his lope hither and yon across the room. The bed was in a *teswin* time zone. Sandra stretched and pulled at a leg, kneaded his thighs, rolled him onto his stomach, then flipped him back with a touch of her hand. How clever of Sandra. Something oriental or elsewhere going on here—another continent at work. Claudia also explored the secrets of the lever. She pressed him. They made him jump, they eased him wetly. Forgetfulness was part of the plan. This was amazing. He had to admire the two graduate students. Claudia squeezed her eyes shut, peeked to see if Merian was still alive. So this too is how I am, he decided. But he was not devoid of shame. He disapproved of their little jokes—the idea of Hawkfeather crouched at the window. The kid was too young for that sort of thing.

Sandra remarked, "Isn't it best like this? Aren't we pals?" She pushed a strand of damp hair away from her eyes. She gleamed up at him. She returned to Claudia and Merian before anyone could answer. He guessed it was just a way of saying hello to those present.

Susan was different, and that's an old story. One thing had nothing to do with the other. Sandra, Claudia, and Merian were merely co-researchers. They were merely restless. They were passing a long evening. They were serving the problem of insomnia in a way recommended by many songs for getting through the night. The night up here was a humming buzzing footnote to real life. That steady remorseless wind jerked at the loose building. It wasn't even an entire, complete, enclosed night. And then it was over. At nearly two o'clock, when the graduate students were gone, slipped into the little green Spider and rattling off, Merian looked out at the yellow desert moon.

He tried to decide whether gymnastics with a couple of energetic Chicago-area graduate students might be a form of twin betrayal of Susan. He preferred to think not. For one thing, he wasn't ready to define infidelity, although most people thought they knew what it was. What about the daydreams of those people, the hidden boredoms, their funhouse nightmares? Secondly, did he owe something to Susan that he had insisted was not possible?

In a cinder-block structure amid a nighttime sandstorm, a panic of longing contracted him. He was in a state of not being himself—an old alibi. *Teswin*, altitude, fatigue, and temptation. Also distractedness. These were some of the older, feebler excuses, and he didn't like them even now.

He thought he might sleep off his dismay.

Probably most people, even Arnie Schultz, would not consider his aerobic exercises with the Chicago-area social workers a legitimate answer to the problem of grit blowing and scratching. It was not a form of tribute to Susan.

Try reversing the situation. Merian would not credit her with fanatic devotion to him if she permitted some stranger to console her loneliness, lick and stroke her at the end of an amiable evening. What was that lurch in his belly? Bile and sickness are a means of transferring information about jealousy. If it were two giggling strangers, his stomach would feel no easier.

At his age he had better not pretend to justice. When he made lists of questions with obvious answers, it usually meant he was on the wrong track to start with.

When in doubt, brush the teeth and pay good attention to the gums. He stood at the sink mirror and did so.

Merian was beginning to have seams in his face where the skin had worn from too much sun, years, an accumulation of questions with self-justifying answers. It darkened with age. Later might come a graying, circulation problems, but during this healthy interim, there were ripe mottles and blotches and a leathery toughness. His life had been put in order for the last run. His dentist congratulated him on periodontal hygiene. It was pink in there. He had one friend, Arnie, who listened with his head tilted, favoring the bad eye, and grinned at his lies. Arnie enjoyed him

123

and Merian liked Arnie. They might even be friends if Arnie were not his editor, keeping tabs on the property. Well, they were friends anyway.

He also had a brother, Chaz, in San Francisco, whom he never saw. Chaz had his own troubles. Since he was here in Arizona, he should go on to San Francisco but would not.

Merian had also loved several women. Would he have loved them if he did not stiffen at night, keeping himself awake? It wasn't just that curved magnetic yearning that suggested curling up, sniffing, and cuddling with someone and murmuring a path into sleep together.

Hungers led to others. Is that the same as affection?

A gritty storm of middle-of-the-night questions afflicted him. This had happened before. He didn't recall finding any good answers on the previous occasions, either. He rinsed his toothbrush carefully and set it in the notch provided for that purpose. No sense in overdoing matters. He had done all the brushing recommended, there was a satisfactory tingle, and he didn't have the answers.

He stood at the window and held the broken shade away. No Claudia and Sandra anymore, no certifiable evidence; it was as if that cheerful clatter had never been. Yet he was sleepy, so they had existed. No Hawkfeather, either.

Warily he searched the darkness, his eyes gradually settling on skylit forms and colors. The blowing had settled a bit, but the night clouds were still moving west across the moon. Someone had done a Sitting Bull and Custer mural in spray paint on the building adjoining the Guest Hogan. Custer wore his familiar long yellow hair and the expression of Judas. The building looked like another infantry company headquarters. There were overflowing GI cans beneath General Custer's blond pageboy, swastikas in his eyes. Sitting on a horse opposite him, Mr. Bull looked inscrutable to Merian, but that was definitely a cream-colored halo behind his head. Christianity even penetrated the struggle between the Anglo general and the Ancient Belief of the Apache hero. Everywhere, Merian thought; it doesn't seem to miss. Nothing was moving on the ground except the stiff branches of scrub bushes. Wind.

Merian tried to consider what Claudia and Sandra should now be doing with themselves. Sleeping, he earnestly hoped, silent, and breathing softly and contentedly. He wished that much for them and more. Sleeping, but not in each other's arms. That was not up to him to decide. It's easier to do unto others than to do unto oneself. He did not know how to do unto himself and Susan, so dear, so frightening to him; needful and brave she was—how could both of these things be true? How did he let this thing happen that he had managed against so long, so cleverly?

Dear. Dearest.

Dust in the air made the moon yellow.

He was astonished to find his lips moving in consideration of air and silence as he stood lifting a broken shade in the middle of the night, this consideration of the night, the past, the diminishing future—mere air, mere wind and desert—as if he were a lonely, lonely, very lonely tired old man.

He was not that yet. He would have to wait awhile. But perhaps he was now ready for sleep.

The next day, with one of those abrupt changes of direction in the high desert, the hot dry wind snapped off and the morning began with a gust of sleet, changing to snow, a light snow dusting the dust, a white silting over the look of dirt-hard things. And then the sun came out and took it all back. Even the denim stains of wet were gone by noon, except for jagged patches on the mountains.

It was like a miracle blizzard in Manhattan, everything clean for a moment, and in the next moment, impossible to believe.

Today also brought a Special Offer, not to be repeated. Merian was in the Guest Hogan coffeehouse, hugging his mug and wondering if he should ask again about the scrambled eggs—probably

125

not. Hawkfeather burst through the door, dramatically critical of Merian's presence on earth, and said, *"This."*

He shoved a piece of paper into Merian's hand. "Not now. When you're by yourself."

The young man turned his back. He stared out the window at the slow morning parade outside, people huddled against the wind, going or just waiting. Hawkfeather was using his fingernail to scrape at flyspecks on the glass. He meant that Merian was now alone and should read. Merian unfolded the slip of paper.

When I go home
I am far far away

When I circle in the sky
Not home either

When I am I
I am nobody

When I am nobody
I am home.

—Hawkfeather

The eggs came. They were crumbled and brown. The cook had forgotten, then scraped them out of a frying pan. The woman watched a moment to see if Merian would comment. When he didn't, she left and returned with a dish of corn grits and set it down without a word. Merian took her cue—do all this in pantomime as a shadow play—and showed her his empty cup. He moved it an inch toward the edge of the formica tabletop.

Hawkfeather turned back to him. "Sit a minute, please," Merian said. "Ask the lady for some coffee. You might have better luck than I do. Signal, do they have juice? Would you like some toast?"

"You read it," the boy said.

"Yes. It's . . . I'm not a poet. I used to think I was. It's, uh, enigmatic."

"I wrote it myself."

"I know you did. I'm impressed."

"Not hydromatic, automatic, or any matic."

"Please tell me what's on your mind," Merian said. "When I was your age—what is it, twenty-two? twenty-four?—there were so many things on my mind I couldn't explain anything. My brother was like that, too. I was rushing around to figure it out. I still am. So I was enigmatic, too."

"You look at the painting?"

Hawkfeather must have seen him at the window during the night. The mural on the opposite wall was the only painting he'd seen, wasn't it? "Sitting Bull and General Custer?" Merian asked.

"He wasn't no general. When I do a badness to a woman," Hawkfeather said, "I think of Colonel Custer and Sitting Bull. I bet you didn't."

Merian was grateful for the crumbs of egg. He concentrated on keeping scorchlings on his fork. He busied himself with getting brown bits to his mouth. A few home fries had found their way into the mixture. "Which one," he asked slowly, "which one do you think of, Custer or Sitting Bull?"

"I'm the one who wins. I'm the Chief. If I rape a woman, that's who I am." He looked straight into Merian's face. "If I rape a boy, I'm Custer."

"Have you ever—anyone?" Merian asked.

In a monotone Hawkfeather said, "I'm only twenty."

"So this is just theory?"

"You thought I was older. I got plans; makes me look older."

"Do you want to talk some more about your poem? Is that part of your plan?"

The kid was easier now. His shifts of mood were a way of taking control and he was pleased that he had it. "My plan is for people to pay attention," he said. "That piece of paper is just something I wrote."

127

"Okay. You may proceed."

Hawkfeather stretched out his legs under the table. They were heavy legs in caked blue jeans. "Listen, gramps," he said, "I got this surefire Anglo idea."

"That's nice, but I hope it's not mugging or purse snatching, son."

"You think I don't know brutality's not where it's at anymore? I keep in touch. They tested me and I'm not some stupid Indian. Didn't the President tell you? He promised. So what I'd like is this Wienerwald franchise. Extra-long weenies made from pure pork plus all meat and a little extender. The President and me got this idea, he was suppose to tell you. Now how about you back us—you know, like a little reparations to the folks that found this great land of ours. We found it first. For gormet cousine we could use our own Native American buffaloes, hand-shot by authentic braves in native costume, and call them buffaleenies, gramps, at a few pieces of silver more."

"Son, you are not making friends with the prospective backer with this gramps shit."

"Okay, dads, I'm sorry. Like we finished a battle to the death and dignity, now it's treaty time. I learn all about modern pale-person's crappy ways from those horny social girls from Chigago, you know?"

Merian's eyebrows shot up and over. So this was the good ladies' game, too. His eyebrows asked, but his voice kept the peace. Hawkfeather was on a run of explanation, little flecks at the corners of his mouth. A jam of clogged words was breaking loose.

"Got me a little piece of my reparation, and it weren't no scalp but it sure was pink and hairy, man. Naturally that ain't what I want from you. What I naturally want from you is both the bucks and the mature old-folks guidance, okay? It's a surefire fighting chance. It's a certainteed maybe winner. Will you make a deal for it?"

"You're running some jive on me, Mr. Hawkfeather."

128

"I'm a quick learn. We got the teevee here, we got the outdoor movies sometimes on the back of the Red Hogan, we get most of the shows one way or the other. Cassettes, man. Before the army I went to school sometimes. Is it a deal?"

Merian stared. Was the kid just messing with him or was he serious? Probably both. Was he asking something or was he just shucking for the joy of confusion? No doubt both. Was there a threat, a plea? Yes. And a love-me look in Hawkfeather's eye, an angry thrust to his head on the powerful neck, forearms, and bulges under his white T-shirt. Arthritis complications if he lived long enough.

Merian heard a burring whine in the air, some machine working across the way. No, that wasn't it. He was listening to anger in himself. "I'm just a journalist," he said. "I work for a salary or a payment. I'm not a banker, pal. It's not my line. You're the guys that are bankrolling Danny Grand."

"You don't get it? You growing forgetful, due to the wear and tear? *All* palefaces is bankers, dad."

"Then this old paleface is something else, Hawkfeather."

Hawkfeather looked at the clever sticky flies walking upside down on the ceiling, he looked at the edge of the stove and the grill visible in the kitchen, he looked at Merian, and then he looked at nothing at all. His eyes went sleepy, seeking a solution in his resources of somnolence. He considered into his depths. At last he found something.

He made a little productive cough. It wasn't much, but it would do. He gathered himself and spat into the dust on the linoleum floor. He watched the lifelike curl of worm form and crumble. It was a living blister of spit dust. It seemed to grow and die. Merian and Hawkfeather admired it together.

"Gramps," said Hawkfeather, "that's what they're all worth, B of IA, Bureau of Indian Assholes, white girls from Chicago with hard little titties and pink snatch, and so-called reporters use their fucking driving license to get out of any little trouble they get into."

He spat again, a splatter of pimples in the dust near Merian's foot. He had a repertory for this, it seemed.

Merian watched the boy carefully. "You been studying that teevee real hard, haven't you?" he asked. "I guess you've been practicing."

He had seen kids like this in Beirut, Teheran, and Angola. There were kids like this in Europe, too. There were kids doing this style elsewhere in the U.S. The love of a good woman, supposing a person got involved in such, might just as easily lead to a kid like this, couldn't it? But what Merian felt was not discouragement; it was not even fear. What he felt was willingness to avoid letting this kid lead him outside to a quarrel that might end with a careening pickup and a knife. He didn't even want it to end with the simpler resolution of a bloody face here and now. The V.J. had only lost one tooth in his whole life up to this point, and even that one wasn't his best experience.

So what he felt after all was discouragement.

The boy winked. "My idea was also a special extra-short weenie for folks on a diet."

"Tempting," said Merian. "You're a thinking person."

"Bet you're on a diet."

"I watch it, that's all."

"I say live and die, mister. So far I ain't gotten around to it, but that's the choice. For other people it's live *or* die. And for me, mister, for *me*"—he made a karate chop at the empty air, his brown arms bulging with the impact of nothing—"for me it's gonna be the same damn thing. Now come on!" he suddenly said, and shoved Merian. "Come on, fight! It's time now!"

"We're friends, Hawkfeather."

"I'm waiting for you!" He was crouching. He had raised his fists from a boxer's crouch, but then he undid his belt and Merian saw why. He slipped off the knife and let it slide clattering to the floor. The belt undone, he was waiting and dangerously trembling.

The cook was scraping the frying pan.

130

"I'm your friend. I'm an older man. I'm old enough to be your father. I read your poem," Merian said.

Hawkfeather spat in his face, watching for only a second, then turned his back, walking away, leaving the knife in the dirt. Merian did not move. Presently he took his handkerchief and wiped his mouth and cheeks. The stuff seemed to have a kind of foam in it.

Ralph Merian stood at the airstrip with his hands around a plastic cup of machine bouillon, waiting for the Christianaire charter plane to finish, like an insect, its impatient tour of the valley. The same pilot leaned out, nodded, and said, "You're going out now." Judging from his face, the past few days had not seen much of a revival of fundamental religion. He didn't come down off the Beechcraft.

Merian saw no place to leave the cup. He carried it aboard, along with ski bag and Olivetti Lettera 32. He didn't expect anyone to see him off and there was no one. Not Hawkfeather, not Claudia or Sandra, not Jarls Coyote, not Wildcat. Not even Mr. Kramer, his fellow Anglo. The motor changed its pitch and the plane started its run. They were off the ground. The land stretched with its coppery and blue tints at the mountains, layers of mesas like shelves as they rose swiftly through the valley. He looked back and down, and there it was again—the swift green Fiat Spider racing to the airstrip with the two of them waving merrily good-bye. It looked from this height as if Sandra was driving, somehow standing and steering, and Claudia blowing kisses into the thin air. If they were late for this event, they must have been late on purpose. Merian gave them credit for planning everything, even their improvisations.

Coppery and blue tints of mesa and mountains, and then a thin green woods along a stream, and blue skies with firm, sun-absorbing chameleon clouds. It was a land to dream in. But what were the dreams anybody dreamt out here?

They were already halfway to the Phoenix Airport. It was time to stop thinking about the ravines full of wrecked cars and his friends of the past few days. *We're rich, we got fried corn bread for our ceremonies, we're good buddies of Danny Grand,* the President had said, and he ought to know. He had won the battle of the bottle and would surely win in arm wrestling, too, at any high-level international meeting of the arms.

"We may be rich for Indians, but not people. We're not what you'd call satisfactory off."

That was in his notes. Jarls Coyote also said that.

Suicide rate thirty times the national average. In his research from before he arrived.

Rumors, he thought, and the rumors of rumors. They don't kill themselves; they go to the great happy hunting ground in the sky. They were terrific in Korea and Vietnam. That wasn't suicide; that was patriotism.

The Veteran Journalist frequently felt panic before he began to organize his material. He told himself this was now his useful panic. He would hide in his room for a few days and sort through his notes, type them up, ransack the jottings, and find an architecture. It's been done before. This panic is something like stage fright, he supposed; nothing to worry about.

A smell of Band-Aids and candy wrappers vibrated off the cracked vinyl seat in the Beechcraft. Merian pressed his face to the plexiglas. He understood why tourists like to take snapshots. The shot snapped off is a lie whose memory they treasure, a moment with none of the smells, hungers, and loneliness, the boredoms and anxieties of travel—just someone or a tree or a sunset smiles into the camera. Hawkfeather hunched his shoulder muscles. Jarls Coyote looks away and stubs his butt out in the sand of the coffee can.

The snapshot does not report what he was intending about spite and Anglos, winning the battle of the bottle, losing elsewhere. Wildcat's mouth is hilariously open forever in a laugh, not a howl. Claudia and Sandra ride their green Fiat Spider, hair streaming, teeth gleaming, brown-skinned maidens greeting the paleface friend.

Merian remembered that the same bikini-clad girl with dark skin and perfect teeth that had never bitten into anything less grateful than a mango or a man, and she had promissory eyes, besides, came out of the surf on the tourist folder advertising the Kapalua Bay in Maui, Bora-Bora in Tahiti, and—a miracle of ecumenism—a new condo development on the troubled frontier between Santa Monica and Venice, California. (According to the V.J.'s sources, she lived with a Mexican silversmith near the boardwalk in Venice.)

In the air the road like starlight flashed away from the Nation of the Stony Apaches.

5

O N THE CHARTER back to Phoenix, and then in the taco western, happy-hacienda, contemporary franchise mission Phoenix airport, where it was roundup time for leather and black string neckties containing Indian magic signs, fish or deer, or Anglo ones with silver dollars, and then on the flight to New York, Merian experienced his familiar exhilaration of escape. He postponed worrying about the story; he would get to that later. On airplanes his will was strong. There was the pleasure of escape into trouble and the different one of escape from it. Merian would be willing to stipulate, for Susan or Arnie or anyone else who chose to make a case, that he was peculiar. ("Almost as crazy as a photographer," he had said to her, "and if you knew the people at Magnum and Black Star as I do, that's a real confession.")

What was better for a journalist doing his job than sensory overload? Clear choices. Ample material plus no need to think.

Gathering thought was a softer and less taxing procedure, a job of mere classification. Judgment required no dangerous nosiness. The next step before retirement was the shame of punditry. Merian preferred to leave that to the fatter-assed ones with permanent desks and word processors.

So nice of the airline to provide an empty seat next to him. Tray above lap with lunch while he recalled Red Power of a few years ago and considered Hawkfeather today. A steward—male, mustached, beautiful—offered him a drink. He chose beer and thought of President Jarls Coyote's battle of the bottle. In the normal course of events, he put the tray and the empty beer on the empty seat and went to pee, and while he regarded this task, he recalled Sandra and Claudia, absently, peacefully. None of it really applied to anyone or anything specific anymore, did it? He was high in the ozone above history, where he was always comfortable, wasn't he?

Then why this? This jitter and shake was what happened to other men, nervous about a job, nervous about a woman, nervous about traveling, nervous about the past and future, with chicken nerves and without a chicken's excuses. Anxiety was a mistake other people made, not the V.J. It did no good, it was like jealousy, accomplished nothing, it was a waste of time.

So this queasy shame, as if he had escaped alone on the only lifeboat, couldn't be an anxiety attack. It must be something else. Maybe Arnie could help him with the word for it.

He might have checked in with his brother, Chaz, in San Francisco, whom he hadn't seen in years—now there was a champion of anxiety—but he didn't. One of these days something would take him west again.

It wouldn't have done any good to give Hawkfeather money. What the kid needed only the past could offer, and one of Merian's hopes about the past was that it was over, although he guessed it wasn't always.

Can't write the story. How could he tell Arnie Schultz? Arnie would throw himself back in his chair and let out a short amazed chuckle and say this was a first, old man. The V.J. agreed. So little was asked of a journalist that he could always do the little piece or corner that sufficed. This was a first. Everything was partial and incomplete; the V.J. had always been able to be partial and incomplete with the best of them. Now what? Can't write the story, so now what?

From Kennedy (he corrected history: *Idlewild* Airport), he took a cab directly to the News-Press Building. It might be considered a humorous act. At least it amused him in his jet-lagged state to catch Arnie with surprising and irritating news at the end of his day, late, after any normal person's hours, when he especially appreciated surprise and irritation. Just as if there were a deadline rush, Merian bustled in, leaving his duffle and Olivetti with the blue-coated ethnic at the elevator. Arnie Schultz and Ralph Merian were about the only laborers in this high-rise salt mine who remembered the old days, before bomb threats and crazies trying to break into the news by breaking into the newsrooms. In the good old days the crazies were all lovable bores. They shuffled in off the street and sat patiently in greasy chairs, waiting to see if anyone wanted to hear their stories. A copyboy might be sent out to listen. Still another pensioner who got police calls on his tooth fillings. And now the copypersons were too busy; an ethnic security in blue coped with the speed freaks.

Red sand from the Stony Apache Nation made Merian's scalp itch a little back here in Manhattan. A veteran journalist learns to endure and prevail (William Faulkner's Nobel verbs) while in need of a shampoo. Everything must come in good order. First self-abnegation, then clean hair.

The smell of air conditioning floated through the News-Press Building like the smell of a lie from the mouth of a Respected Senior Official on Air Force One. It cooled things nicely. Ralph Merian could wash himself in this smell just by walking through it, so many times had he carried a text toward Arnie on its way to the word processors and computers, and before that to the "girls" (now Executive Assistants) who sometimes met his eyes with a smile, a cooling air-conditioned smile, because he was one of the paper's stars and needed, or if he didn't need, he *deserved,* this radiant cooling by ambitious young women. Some things evolve, but don't change. It was the treatment they offered because they had their womanly pride and their ambition. And it was the treatment he deserved because he had his firm foundation of not needing more out of life than work except during those eccentric middles of the night, when the lights from the windows across the way made him think people were awake and chatting, having a cup or a glass of something and a conversation, maybe repeating a conversation they had had before, just cozy together, easy with each other. Then, at those times, he used to wish he had asked for the telephone number of the executive assistant with the radiant blue ambition in her eye but it was too late to call anyone. And now he would call Susan, wouldn't he?

Usually it was part of the deal. A person had these moments and the other person said now, may I have your company now, please. He wasn't sure this was part of his deal with Susan. That was for love, and Susan allowed it. But Ralph Merian was not programmed for that solution.

He was explaining to Arnie about the Stony Apaches and Danny Grand. He wasn't explaining. "I can't do it, Arnie. It makes no sense and right now neither do I. I'm not going to do it."

"Are you gone silly?" Arnie asked. "You're my miracle workhorse boy. This never happens to you."

"It happened," said Merian.

"I don't accept that explanation."

"Accept it."

Arnie lowered the demand and shame decibels. He drummed fingers. He shrugged as if he could go along with anything. Then he said, "You're tired; anybody can see that. Just tired is written all over your ugly face. Take a few days and then type up your notes. Come in and use the word processor, they take the ache out of it. Hell, get drunk and just give *me* your notes, Ralphie."

"Tired, right."

"That's all it is, Ralph."

"Can't, Arnie. No."

Arnie raised his hand, wait, wait; held him with the gesture; patted the air. "Wait. Let's talk."

"Danny Grand is not the story. This story is not the story. I have to take a no. You want me to give back expenses?"

"Oh, shit." Arnie looked troubled. A journalist makes an insane, irrational, drum out of the corps and rip off his epaulet offer like that, he must be cracking up, down, and across. Feeling his way, Arnie said, "Maybe it wasn't really the right—" But then decided kindness would be unkind when a friend allowed himself to tumble into stupid self-indulgence. Arnie didn't have to decide on taking no foolishness from the closest thing he had to a friend—it was his character to edit hard. He narrowed his eyes with a bad-smell squint, intending anger and meanness, intending to communicate these helps to his old pal. He may even have felt something like betrayal. "Get your life straight, mister. This is shit and it has got to cease."

"You owe me a little patience, buddy."

"All you want. No question. What I said I say with infinite patience. When I say this shit has got to cease I say it with the angelic sweetness of my deepest nature. So now that I've done all I can, what do you do for yourself?"

From where he sat, Arnie looked out the forty-fourth-floor window. A corner office and forty-four floors off the street, with a view of the World Trade Center and of not looking into his friend's eyes. He added: "Merian, let me tell you something. Don't think a woman can help you. I think a woman can't save anyone, that's my personal view and opinion. Not anyone and not you. Of course, I never had soul-to-soul dealings with Florence Nightingale or Joan of Arc or the divorced English mother of one. But I remember even the enemas my sainted mother used to give me—those were the days when women really wanted to help—didn't help. I'm still stuck with my own digestion. So Ralph, don't put this on her."

"I don't. She's not my mother, Arnie."

"Just don't, Ralph, okay?"

"You've got it wrong."

"How I've got it is irrelevant. That's not part of the modern deal, Ralphie. It's how you've got it that counts."

"I'm back," Merian told her by telelphone.

"You said you'd be back by now and you're sort of reliable. Why aren't you here?"

"Something's wrong."

"What's the matter?"

"My stomach. My head. Let me get my innards in shape first."

"Oh, dear, you're sick? Can't I take care of you?"

"I'm all right, I'm just—" He let the empty fuzzing of the telephone finish his sentence. On the electronic bundle they could hear the busy chirp of other voices settling things, arranging things. The voices of Susan Pollet and Ralph Merian were not among those electronically bundled voices. He said at last, "Don't be angry. This is a favor to you. I don't want you to smell my breath."

"You're lying. I'm not mad. Everybody's breath smells."

"You have a right to get sore at me. Just give me a little time. I really don't feel right. Just give me a day or two."

"Take three. Take what you need, okay?"

"Okay," he said, and therefore it was time to say good-bye, and they didn't say it yet.

"You want to put me on hold?" she asked finally. He didn't answer. "I'm on hold then. You pressed the button."

"Just give me a chance to get organized."

"Get. You said that already. You got it. Get, hang up, go."

Merian stopped between assignments in his one-room bunker on Riverside Drive at West Seventy-ninth Street in Manhattan, and sometimes finished off the work there, and sometimes merely hid, tarrying, doing nothing, before he flew someplace else. The room had a tall marble fireplace; those brown Italian swirls were creamy and previous; it was a fine space from someone's house, sliced up, cut off from the rest of the building, kitchenette added, bathroom improved, and he had bought into gracious living at a lucky time. Not a sitting room in anyone's granite house anymore, it was the V.J.'s home away from any other home. A double ceiling. No bear hibernated in a nicer cave.

He slept on the Castro Convertible. He typed at the long desk made of a flush door held firmly by its own weight on filing cases. The Contemporary Style section of no magazine or newspaper would ever do a feature on this Journalist's Hideaway Studio. An absolute lack of potted plants to water, but scraps of paper money and glinting coins left over from various travels lay in a liberated Fort-de-France Meridien ashtray near the closet. Subway tokens, too, including some that were no longer operative, with holes in them, souvenirs of a historical epoch that had vanished while he was away.

The custodian left his mail, mostly junk, in a box kept for that purpose near the door, and when Merian returned to New York for a while and started to go through it, he seldom got to the bottom. There might be five-year-old personal letters there, but usually he managed to fish out the bills, so his credit was not cut off. He left unopened Christmas cards with stamps that no longer provided first-class postage. Maybe somebody's kid someday would like his stamps. Once every year or two there was a note from his brother, Chaz, in San Francisco. "Dear Ralph: Less crazy now, hope you same. Chaz."

Thank God for high ceilings in this monk's luxury cell. The thing that defined it best was plenty of airspace above but not much ground-level room for more than one person, unless it was a floating person. The V.J. liked to keep the clutter and litter clean and dusted; he arranged for this to be done even in his absence by the custodian's invalid wife, whenever she had a good day. The precarious ecological balance of his Villa Solo was such that a single tube of lipstick would tip it toward overload. Even the suspicion of extra tubes or jars brought drastic risks. Every environmental study on a female presence had indicated problems. He could put up with Syrian plainclothesmen outside his door, but not a hair dryer in his bathroom. Merian's ability to change hibernation and loitering requirements was limited. The large, high-ceilinged room with the unused Italian marble fireplace was his secret weapon.

When he got the place, he thought it would be a convenient refuge. It had become the closest thing he knew to home, family, the world of nonwar and unrevolution.

Two people in such a life would be like three people making love. One too many.

He slept. A person who studies sleeping alone can even learn to do that very nicely.

In the morning, upon rising, Merian brushed his gums. He hummed a little Ommm between familiar morning moves. He studied himself in the mirror, enjoyed the crispness of rinsed toothpaste on his tongue, in his mouth, Ommm, and thought what a pity it was that now a person had to eat and dirty such a nice clean mouth. But of course just a few minutes farther down the line, a person would have breakfast. And although he could then brush again, and in fact by all rights *should* brush and floss again, he might get involved in something else and that's how life is. The white zone is not for loading and unloading only.

Merian stood at the mirror with his nice clean mouth and trimmed off a few hairs. He saved such housekeeping for New York, for being home in Manhattan, although it took just a moment. Making up his mind about it took longer. Last year he had bought a little set of scissors and clippers in one of those tourist shlock shops on Fifth Avenue. The leatherette case said "New York World's Fare"—manufactured before the days when the great leap into high technology and correct spelling had come to Japan. There, crane neck, peek, clip, examine, the job was definitely done, Ommm, and would probably stay done for this furlough in New York. He didn't want to grow tusks and stray whiskers in his age, and sit perched by the sea like an old walrus. Arnie, for example, had long teeth and unnoticed (by Arnie) long hairs. Arnie had definitely gone periodontal on him.

Now nonsugar wheat'n'bran cereal from the Nature's Own Mother Earth Aquarian Age Very Little Cancer-Causing Preserv. Added box, banana sliced over it in a little accordion flourish, raisins falling like dead flies on the banana, and then a half cup of instant nonfat powdered bachelor milk, which he formulated on the spot. Good. Not so bad. Another stroke of genius by the master breakfast chef. Traveling, Merian mostly ate eggs for breakfast, because that's what you can usually get, except in French-speaking countries, but at home he liked this all-American low-cholesterol repast. Then instant no-fuss coffee from El Salvador, instant espresso luxury from a gay munchie shop on Columbus, the Gor-May Bo-Tique, with more bachelor powder stirred into it, buffering the kick but not cooling it. Oh, good. Whoever said a fellow needed a loving hand to help him with breakfast, when there were creative food persons galore on the outside and his own considerate hands on the inside? Here, by his own concoction, lay plenty of protein, plus very little fuss or mess; and here, wrapping his taste buds around it with positive enjoyment and relish, sat a man who was the sole support of a poor orphan child—himself. He sat and he stirred and he cleaned up. Unlike Arnie, he didn't put his bowl in the refrigerator so that, without washing it, he could use it again tomorrow. He wiped off the whole grain debris with a wet newspaper and hung the bowl upside down in the dish drainer. To dry. To be clean tomorrow, except for a sanitary hint of newsprint. Merian had standards.

Now consider the morning and the problems thereunto appended. Try, for example, looking outside. The knocking of the radiators had beckoned, but Merian was absorbed in his homely preparations. He was shriven, shorn, fed, and ready to meet the new day from safe on the inside of it.

Through the steam on the windows he saw a sudden white light blasting through the morning—new-fallen snow—and the traffic on Riverside Drive pumping through the trails cut by earlier traffic. Now why hadn't he noticed that right away? A glorious sight it was—too busy at the hairs in his nose, were you, V.J.? He wiped a porthole through the steam with his hand. A pair of watchcapped black corner boys was strolling and kicking the soft clots of wet; "Hey man whatcha say?" if they happened to glance up and catch sight of him.

Whenever he returned, Merian relearned the New York habit of never meeting eyes. A person had to be as wary as an animal at a watering hole, looking out for predators at the edges of vision while he lives as he must. A cop car slowed down, grumbling in ruts of slush that were beginning to turn gray already at the edges. The snow kickers called to the cops, "Hey man, snow! Whatcha say?"

This time the cops didn't leap out and say, *Against the wall! Spread!*

The white zone is not for loading and unloading only. A cockroach paused nervously on Merian's shoe, resting and watching, waving little filamented brown legs, considering whether there might be something nourishing here, such as anything but boric acid. Merian flexed his toes (this was a test) and it scampered. It had no intention to sting him—it lacked sting capacity; it dashed into a crack with hurt feelings, like a scorned pet that wouldn't come out again until coaxed. Merian admired the nervous intelligence of New York cockroaches, who had smarts like their distant cousins up the evolutionary scale, although despite his admiration, he occasionally spooned boric acid into cracks, especially if these subtenants dared to use his telephone as a nest. Once, back from Beirut, he had to take apart the machinery to get them out; this violated his territory. He left the red and yellow and green wires exposed, the boot off the phone, to let them know there was no hiding place here. There was a limit to squatters camping in a person's equipment. Otherwise, live and let live.

When he was gone, they were there. He did not go so far in his treaty with them as to provide food for the refugees. He was not the United Nations.

Merian sat in his oversized room in New York, remembering New York, absorbing the hum of the city through his pores, that hum that made him hum right back in the morning as he struggled

144

out of sleep. Sitting there at his typewriter. He was trying to remember President Jarls Coyote and Hawkfeather and the Stony Apaches after all. He was trying to carry himself back to the Nation while an urban creature explored his mountainous shoe, a volcanic range of leather and glue and hedges of stitching, and then rushed into its cave until danger subsided. Somehow in history it had learned about the dangers that lurk for itself and its kind. It had learned respect.

For Merian, who was also a part of history, who even made some effort to fill out the immigration forms required by history, very little of his life was anything personal about himself. Life got personal for other people, usually the non white-eyed ones whose wars and revolutions occupied him now and then. He was a technician. He seldom looked in mirrors; today was an exception—seldom means sometimes. Usually he knew he was twenty-seven years old. A respected senior official had informed him during a background briefing, not for attribution. He also knew he had been practicing the trade of journalist for twenty-seven years. This raised a purely arithmetical question. He disliked to doubt the word of a respected senior official, although he knew they were all liars. He preferred not to look in mirrors because he might find a stranger there, a thicker-faced boy than the lean dark sharp-nosed one who discovered he had a knack for putting facts in order and then jangling them until they were pathetic or funny or a little of both. This was not a purely arithmetical answer.

For Ralph Merian, veteran journalist, history was scarred by the disappearance of clacking typewriters in the newspaper offices back home. They had word processors now. He had liked the old sharp clack; it was one of those sounds—ball into mitt, blade on ice—which set his appetites going. His ankles wanted to move. He was still a sprinter on ice and on paper. Now those sharp friendly impatient sounds seemed to have vanished from his life. People poked at keys and studied ice-green letters on ice-blue screens. Overhead, the blind blinking of fluorescent lighting tubes, cataract tubes. It used to be bulbs they had, green shades or no shades, sometimes even a lamp on the desk of a great prima donna. Now people smoked less. People were less fat. People around him grew younger—that was history for you. They treated him with respect; he was a star, maybe a prima donna—more history caused by the trivial fact of survival. He used to write for newspapers and magazines; now he "worked in media."

Oh, history isn't bunk, but it's not all that terrific, either.

Maybe, with thoughts like these pinching at him, he was no place in his body or soul twenty-seven anymore. But he was sure he could still sprint when he had to and when he really wanted to.

What rescued history for the V.J., and perhaps even made him still seem twenty-seven years old to himself—often! not now!—besides his good ankles when he was in a hurry, his swift taking in of things when the griefs around him caused things to jump, was that he still found it all very interesting. That's sure a bland gray word, "interesting," which he would only use in his heart of hearts, not when he was trying to fit matters into a piece that ticked like a watch. He wasn't sure he had enough room in his jangling, data-stuffed brain to find something simple, such as love, interesting. Well, yes, interesting it was, but distracting. The spaciousness of it. The silences of it. He wasn't sure he could jangle it into shape and make it run smoothly. So therein lay the problem for Susan Pollet and Ralph Merian.

In the history of these matters, Merian knew, you mustn't shake and jangle and expect innards to tick swiftly and run smoothly. So perhaps the prudent person, faced with such a difficulty, just runs for his life. Or perhaps he just stops. He might even learn to follow correct procedures, as other people do.

And just when a fellow understands all this pretty well, it gets to be too late. That's history for you. Often it's about being too late. History asks correct procedures of a person, but asks nothing of itself. A vain self-centered entity with no sense of the alternatives left behind—that's history.

Merian felt himself slyly coarsened during his own little span on earth by the easy exercise of a talent like that of a guitar plucker's. He could carry a tune and remember the words. His fingers put the lyrics to the music. He used what he saw and heard, neatly, amusingly, pathetically, so that to some readers it seemed a priestly calling, giving understanding, putting them in touch with trouble, suffering, and the usual resolutions in more trouble and suffering. For others, not him, the trade of journalism seemed to be difficult. He often apologized about this, but for him, like a born musician, it was just something he could do without thinking. He was an idiot savant. He was a conga drummer in the park; like a ghetto kid jiving instead of going to school or working. Perhaps a high calling should require sacrifice. When he felt good, he thought his jiving and happy teasing of the material squeezed juice out of the rinds and wasn't all bad.

Now, with Hawkfeather, for example, his rapid naming no longer seemed to be enough. It merely made the time pass, which the time would do well enough without his help. There had been women to pass the time with; now there was Susan. He wanted to share the distress and grief that everyone knew and hardly anyone could tell. And he didn't want to share it. He wanted not another wail or complaint, but the truth. And he didn't want it. What was that black sleep into which the great Indian civilization had fallen? Hawkfeather was a child born into the senility of genius. Could a Hawkfeather rescue himself, could anyone help him? What was that black sleep into which lovers fall? Susan clutched him and he wordlessly pinched like a cancer until she said, "Don't! It hurts. You hurt! I love you!"

There was a pinching wrath in love too.

But since he had done an easier thing with words so long, how could Merian, now that his mind and body were surely running down, how could he consider these ordinary hard needs of races or of himself? With pride in craft, he had given up the pursuit of largeness beyond himself. Teasing with his friend Arnie, all that trust and joking, was as far as he went toward some permanent link with another. How could he now abandon a working system that was leading him straight and without pain into his old age? In favor of a system that would lead him roundabout, with many griefs, to the same goal?

Susan was asking a lot. Merian himself was asking too much. Even Arnie and Hawkfeather seemed to ask it, although they admitted, didn't they? The answer was out of the question.

He didn't want to work this morning. The coffee was too strong or not strong enough. His alertness stirred and went with a rush. He should have a physical exam one of these years. He would close his eyes on the couch a few minutes. He pulled his Indian rug over his shoulders and tucked it around his cold feet. He slept.

For the first time in years Merian dreamt about his father. He had stopped these dreams by the time the old man died in the nursing home in off-ramp city near John F. Kennedy Airport. It had become too sad to dream about him, it did no work, it was an inappropriate procedure, and just as he commanded himself to loose the torrent of words on a job, he had commanded himself to stem the nighttime bleeding. The last times he saw his father, the old editor didn't even recognize him; called him Boy, as if he were carrying copy; and then said, "Where is that young man?" Merian asked, "Which young man?" and his father said, "That young man who used to come to see me. I used to call him Son."

Whether it was ministrokes, as the doctors said, or something else in the passages of the brain, accumulation of fluids, stagnation and backup of circulation, whatever it was, whatever the medical mushmouths drew out of their great wisdom, could not be determined with precision until autopsy. "One can guess," a doctor said. Doctors can. Anyone else could, also; this is a free country. Could someone tell him where his father's soul had gone?

Merian refused the authorization to autopsy when the telephone call came, and said to Chaz, "To hell with science." Chaz, who liked to think he was still an engineer, screamed at Ralph, "You never cared! Weren't interested!" But Ralph assumed this was just because they were both upset. Maybe even Chaz was upset this time within the perimeters of the normal. He listened to Chaz and said, "Well, it's done now."

Chaz wasn't rational and therefore the duty of an elder brother to explain fully did not apply. Although information was his business, he saw no reason to cut and slice at pieces of his father's brain when the old man was gone. Cranial tissue? Fibroid ganglia? To hell with that. The old man had been gone for years. The old man's tissue was gone forever now.

And suddenly one morning Ralph Merian, who wondered if his own brain was drying up, who couldn't seem to get down to his story about the Stony Apache Nation, had a dream about Ralph Merian, Sr. The old editor was walking out onto a shallow spit, hard sand, at one of the seaside resorts to which they had gone when Merian was a child. Without Chaz, the baby; just the two of them. It must have been New Jersey. At some boardwalk Captain's Table—not yet the Ye Olde Salt Fish'n'Fries or Surf'n'Brew—they had eaten steamed clams with butter—lots of shells, piles of shells, glorious light reflected off silvery buckets, and the boy remembered himself greedy for the new taste, something grown-up in the complication of eating those wriggly little twists of garlic and butter and salt, remembered and tasted that boyish greed. . . . But now his father was just walking out into the sea as the saucer of shore deepened. Merian ran after him, taking his arm and saying, You can't go that way, Dad. You can't go there. You can't go yet, Dad.

I want to go. And the old man stretched and tried to shake the boy's arm free and strained toward the open sea.

Not yet, Dad. I want you back. You can't go yet, Dad. I still need you.

* * *

He blinked awake from this unrefreshing morning nap.

It would make more practical personal sense to dream about Chaz in San Francisco. After all, there could still be something to do with the living.

It would make more sense to dream of Susan. He still needed the all-out sleep of love. How he held her, dug his face into her, sank with her. He was developing this uneasy nonsleep, a dimmed and fretful passing of the time, which he would prefer to think came of loneliness, not age, but perhaps it was both. In one case or the other, regrettable. He would prefer other. Still, he preferred to burrow his head into a back, a shoulder, a breast, to sink with someone. No, with Susan, to sink with Susan, not someone.

That wasn't a mere detail. The Left and the Right in Guatemala might turn out to be a detail. The Radical Socialists and the Socialist Radicals, the Christian Democrats and the other details were mere killers in wars here and there. Why should he care about Hawkfeather's future? What was he to Hawkfeather and Hawkfeather to him? A woman's scent in his nose—Susan's smell—was what the old liar really required.

He also had strict obligations.

6

TO STRETCH AND breathe between his bouts of sitting with alert motionless expectation in front of the type-writer, to climb out of that Stony Apache Nation lodged in his head, Merian put on his boots, clattered down the stairway, out the locked front door of the stone monument on Riverside Drive, and sauntered up West Seventy-second Street—not a care in the world!—past the dark hulks of hotels near Broadway, the side-walk bazaars of all-night outdoor fruit stands, Cuban and Haitian revolutionary parlors upstairs, along with the chess gaming rooms and exercise emporiums for gay and straight and maybe, and then down to Columbus, which was now Singles-on-Avon. He poked the ground with his feet while the Stony Apache Nation ripened someplace above his sinuses. He had watched this Hispanic and Irish avenue of bars and bodegas and shoe repairs give way to surplus and safari and glassed-in cafés; Harrington's gone, To-maso the Shoeman gone—cappucino and quiche infestation had come to Columbus. The sexually alert and ambitious had found a new playground. It was a powerful national impulse. Each time he returned from an elsewhere, intending to find himself home, the street took a new turn toward the nervous emporium, the country cute; and the strolling same-sex couples, the window-shopping different-sex couples, were all of them strangers to him. To them he was also a foreigner. They didn't mind too much if a person was male or female—old was the thing not done.

The people of the street ten years ago had been strangers to him, but they were the strangers he knew. He was at home among them. These new strangers made him feel like a tourist in his only neighborhood, forlorn at their celebration, left out of their extended-run musical play. Although some bearded codgers with cascades of white down their chins, Dutch schoolboy caps on their heads, skinnied and dapper, strolled with girls or boys— the codgers were, many of them, even older than Merian—he felt they had landed from another world, the Planet Boutique which orbited around Manhattan.

A workman in Ralph Lauren French Workman's Bib Overalls looked up from his honest labor of refinishing a New York City School System desk and chair, bolted together with honest bolts, and cast a winsome workman's smile in Merian's direction. "You're a cute brunette," he said. "Do you have a home to go to after I get off work?"

The workman must have noticed that Merian was loafing, possibly in need of companionship. It was all his fault. "I'm too old for you," he said, smiling.

That was a mistake. "I'm looking for a father," the honest workman confessed. He had nothing to hide. "Father figure, anyway. You'll do, dads."

Much as Merian loved the smell of sanded wood, lacquer, and varnish, just now he needed exercise rather than gossip with a proletarian craftsfellow with a solid grounding in a men's group.

Columbus only discovered America, but now America was discovering Columbus Avenue, where Lifestyle was the way of life. The various anonymities of New York, even the new, revised, unisexual Columbus, appended to the television production studios and Lincoln Center, and also attached to the bakeries and delicatessens of West Seventy-second Street, enabled Merian to go into a kind of sleep when he paced the neighborhood between assignments or between attacks against the litter on his desk. The city gave other people shifty eyes, the jitters. For Merian, it was neither real life nor vacation, it was not where his heart dwelled— only his nonportable typewriter waited there, an old industrial-duty Royal manual, which he could hit like a punching bag, and the high-ceilinged room with the marble fireplace, in which a person could hide, or even, hardly bent at all, be incinerated, should that come to mind as the resolution to a difficult assignment. It hadn't yet been necessary, although Merian sometimes burnt drafts and false starts in the fireplace, and suffered the results—ash smells in his lair.

Strolling alone in Manhattan, Merian puzzled over things. Did he need help or improvement, as for example Susan could help or improve him? Or should he merely sink into the way he was, since he had been that way so long? Or an optional variable to feed into the process: Accepting the way he was might mean he *really* needed Susan to help and improve him.

There were other possibilities. A friend in . . . was it Rabat? Jerusalem? No, it couldn't have been Jerusalem. And he couldn't remember the friend at all, but he recalled the accented voice, Hebrew or Arabic, and with a French education in the precise message: "It should be every man's ambition to be his own doctor."

That's a clever thing to say, given everyone's suspicion of the arts of curing, but a chap really can't do everything. He can't gracefully bury himself, for example, and he shouldn't be in the business of grieving for himself. "When the world meets the self, give the world its due." Now there was a more practical counsel.

Jean-Guy Archambault, that's who it was that said it, West African correspondent from *l'Express*. And it was in Dakar at the time of the attempted coup in Gambia, halted with the help of Senegalese troops. *"La Gambie"* Jean-Guy called it; everything is French to a Frenchman.

Probably Jean-Guy would think the American journalist's feeling about Susan was French, too, since romance is French, but this was not the flirtation and festival with which Merian had learned to entertain himself. He was like a Detroit auto manufacturer going through a difficult time. The model change wasn't in the product but in himself. He might like to run the same model changes forever, but he had fallen into unnecessary complication. He understood why love was called the friendly enemy, or if it wasn't, why it should be.

The usual six-month warranty on Merian's romances had already expired. In the past his love affairs, when the romance went out of warranty, depended on interruption and distraction, and were renewed after some restorative visit to Khambasa or the Falklands, so that both parties concerned could be a little older and fresher and lonelier and willing to race the well-known roads again. Sheila was now married and happy, Lydia was now married and unhappy, Joanna was now unmarried and noncommunicating; his accomplices had proceeded to more normal paths, like normal people. They might see no reason not to meet their old friend the V.J. for a drink, should it fit into their schedules. And no reason, either, to make any effort to fit it into their schedules.

In love there was no guarantee against user's malfunction. The manufacturer was not at fault. Just as Merian wrote articles, not books, he also did little lyrical sad love affairs, not marriages. A collection of pieces is no more a book than a collection of love affairs is a family. He had friends who did marriages, but usually they didn't do them very well. Merian was not smug about avoiding the taking of chances on love, "the full catastrophe," even though loss seemed to be the predictable result. Usually it was. His survey was not complete. He had been told there was a town in Nebraska where people remained happily married. Or maybe it was just called Grand Union for political reasons.

154

Yet again Merian had sought out that early glow, when he woke in the middle of the night, she woke too, and this gazing into eyes, those smiles, those touches and the clasping of hands, how the circulation of blood gave the pleasure of a long warm undertow, and then that renewed sleep of babylike contentment. Susan and Merian had awakened like that. Isn't it a promise? Doesn't it mean more than a cozily interrupted night? She did it for him; he seemed to do it for her—at least she said so. In such a condition, one believes the other party.

In such a condition the two parties are resolved on trust and truth. It's an odd modern state for persons to find themselves, himself and herself, in. It's even grammatically difficult. It always seemed a miracle, not to be compared with anything, anyone, even any history. Just now it was not yet faded, and that was a further wonder. The law had been breached by a lady with pale blue shadows under her eyes where the man had crinkled pouches and too much sunburn.

Maybe start blaming her for his difficulties with the Stony Apache Nation and Danny Grand. Oh, fella, next comes quavering voice and watery eyes and a cardigan sweater. Don't blame Susan for these changes.

Chaz seemed to blame his big brother, Ralph, for his troubles. When Ralph heard from Chaz, it was usually what he heard. Merian had learned to avoid that way, and incidentally, not to blame another for his pleasures, either. Then why did Susan's pale bright hair, high temple, the way her pale bright hair clung to her head, upset all his plans just to proceed as before, with no plan at all, just comfortably going along? Trying to think about the Stony Apaches, Merian found himself thinking about this head, this hair, this pale blue fatigue under the eyes, the hair floating and clinging, when it was time to put matters of texture away. His habit of replacing woman with work was an experienced one. It was no excuse that Susan was different; such excuses were not acceptable. All women were sweet and different, or fun, sharp, challenging, and different, or patient and different.

155

"That's the bugaboo," Susan once said, using the word incorrectly. She meant that some things were nice, unexplainable and menacing.

"Bugaboo is not what it is," he said. "What it is is that I care for you."

"Tell me," she said.

He was not telling her. He was walking on Columbus and uttering imaginary reassurances that were more like a debate; he was mumbling like an old man who was some kind of bugaboo because he longed for her, he admired her, he pitied her for choosing him. He did not want to give her any power over him.

This shit, thought the V.J., as he had thought under bombardment years ago in his first war, when he was very young, this shit has got to cease. Long ago he had discovered that, for him, harmony consisted in the absence of personal troubles and the presence of immediately engrossing public ones. How clever of him to find the war and revolution trade, how clever to let the years merely roll over him, leaving him older but unkilled—how clever!—and in a state of truce that often felt like peace.

Now there was real danger. The color was fair and blue-shadowed and pink in sun or pleasure, and the eyes were sweet and welcoming, as was the mouth, and the temperament was not so mild as it seemed. Who could have thought such weapons might succeed? They didn't even intend to menace him.

"Asshole, I'll kill you," said a voice in the street throng.

"No you won't," Merian said, violating all the rules of street survival by entering the man's system, looking him in the inflamed amphetamine eyes, and replying to him. Perhaps this local commentator was just learning West Side English and needed practice.

Merian knew an insomniac Polish journalist who studied English in the middle of the night by talking with the overseas operator for Poland, who could usually translate the idioms that gave him trouble. The street speed freak was used to crowds that parted before his closed fist. He raised it at Merian, and Merian continued to smile at him, thinking the chap would sleep better if he stayed away from coffee and methedrine, thinking the look in his eye was the crazed hurt of Hawkfeather. Then Merian wondered if he should take his hand and hold it like a father with a child, as he had thought of doing with Hawkfeather—no, that would be going too far—and then suddenly, while he considered his options, the man stepped off the curb and darted through traffic to the other side of Columbus. Why, he was afraid of Merian!

He was wearing a short jeans jacket and—the jacket flapped as he ran—no shirt. Bluish flesh showed as he hopped and dodged in his speed rage. Merian would have followed the Standard Procedure for Street Crazies (don't look, keep moving) if he had known there was no shirt under the jacket.

If he was so cool and brave, why couldn't he reckon with Susan, like some average person of medium forthrightness?

Merian just nicely threaded his way through the clusters of distraction shoppers. They might buy a funny napkin holder, or a book, or an espresso (pronounced expresso)—they might be out to buy a purchase—or they might strike up a friendship with a member of the opposing or the nonopposing sex, or they might head home in the company of failure to find what they wanted. Not often. As long as they were still moving, as long as they had a vague idea about desire, they weren't finished. Merian hoped the same was true for him.

A waiter was passing the slow period between meals out on the sidewalk with a new customer, both of them sunning a little with the help of the radiance of the building, hands around their mugs of coffee. They were in a mood to make new friends. "You ought to come in for dinner and try our french-fried zucchini," the waiter advised. He was rotating slightly in his green and yellow Zucchiniland apron. "People come to Zucchiniland for a rest from that de Laurentis phony foodstuffs. They get tired of quiche, stuffed cross-ant, pot-tay, just one quiche after another. They generally make a festive occasion of our french-fried product, if you know what I mean."

"I think I do."

"Well, it's not just the zucchini alone, it's a sauce—"

"Sounds good to me."

"It's a whole way of life."

Merian lost the rest of this courtship in the turmoil of Columbus. It was a violation of the law of human nature and adjustment to go from the Stony Apache Nation to Columbus Avenue on the West Side of Manhattan in one day.

He saw Sandra and Claudia at the glassed window of a sidewalk café, "La Folia, Est. 1981." He saw two girls who looked like Sandra and Claudia. They were not Sandra and Claudia. The dry pinching of his nose in the high awful wind of Arizona was still what he knew for sure. He hurried back up West Seventy-ninth Street to try to think about Danny Grand, Jarls Coyote, and Hawkfeather.

Leaning up and down the slight slopes of Manhattan island, he hurried home to the comfort of his typewriter; his high Italian marble fireplace, in which a fugitive could hide; his scattered books and unread magazines and newspapers; his privacy. If he could fret about Susan at the other desk, the one he used for paying bills—the little tight table—he might get the job done.

There was a way in life beyond distraction. That was only Susan's opinion. It was her procedure through the years. All he had to do was believe her. All he had to do was make up his own mind and hope she hadn't decided to cut her losses, a man who moped instead of one who drank. All he had to do was what he didn't think he could do.

Maybe, besides, he could tell the story of the Stony Apaches in a way that made sense for him and for the others out there.

7

SINCE HE WAS having such trouble getting the Stony Apaches into some sort of coherence, he thought he should do what he always told young reporters to do. Stop working. You can't see the highway if you stare at the headlights. Look away for a while, look at the darkness. Stop squinting and straining, don't give yourself piles. Then come back to the problem barreling down the road.

In the meantime, of course, collisions are possible. And it's hard to live both blithe and worried.

What was best for him just now was to look at Susan awhile. He hoped she would not chase him off, although it occurred to him that he was a bore. He was prepared to be told to come back when he was more interesting. The ideal man was not a hairy, lower-lip-sucking old journalist who couldn't put his notes in order on the subject of wasting a Native American treasury and therefore went calling.

He took a taxi this time, not the crosstown bus. There was a little panic in that Checker, not blitheness, as the swain proceeded without flowers.

If Susan was a friend of his (he had one of those cab drivers who breathed in regular curses, needing fucks and shits and cock-suckers to get the air into his lungs), she should want to hear about President Jarls Coyote, Hawkfeather, Wildcat—at least he hoped so—but perhaps not about the non-Indian young social workers from Chicago. He was planning what to tell her, how much to tell her, so as not to bore her, confuse her, anger her, send her away. It would not be a grown-up and correct procedure to tell her the entire story; please omit the young women from Chicago, for example, a matter that just sifts without shadow through the mind. Already, far from the Nation, the Stony Apaches had begun that process he knew from other places of becoming distant, strange, articulated and mediated by abstraction, like the wars of outer space that he would never have to cover.

Usually he put the uncanny swift fading to use, forcing him into an immediate recounting. It would not be a correct procedure, either, to let her take it personally when he said he was in this funny condition about the story.

He always did the story. This was a first for him. He always came up with something.

The cab driver's lips stopped moving as he studied the bills Merian lay in dirty strips across his hand. The driver was used to being the crazy one around here. He had his medallion; here was his turf for mumbling. He looked at the money and then at his passenger's mouth. Merian's lips were rehearsing a greeting to Susan.

He rang, she answered, he skipped the elevator and ran up three flights, he pushed open the door. "Something came up," he said. "I'm not writing it."

"Hullo," she said. "Say hullo, kiss first. Then talk."

"It didn't used to bother me when I couldn't make sense of what I was explaining. I didn't have to understand things, only seem to. Now it bothers me."

"Maybe that's a good step, Ralph?"

He stopped and his voice was hoarse. "If you say that, you don't understand anything at all about my trade. You think those London *Times* teams get to instant depth, writing every other chapter like they do? You think they do it different in England?"

She looked at him carefully until he dropped his angry stare. She could wait. She was pretty good at that. She was not so much looking at him as examining him; a weary specimen he was. She saw no good justification. She didn't see a lover returning but a man being rude. "We're going to have a quarrel," she stated, "aren't we? Would you like to quarrel or would you prefer just to turn around and try visiting me again tomorrow? Would you like to telephone tomorrow and ask if I might happen to be free for dinner and make an engagement with me? Would you like to try behaving with consideration for someone else— I don't care what troubles you have—just think of someone else? Would you?"

She was pushing him backward and out.

The door was shut. He put down his coat. He sat there, leaning against the door in her hallway, until she might choose to open it again. Then, of course, he would apologize.

His head was against his coat, his coat against the door. The Stony Apaches and not doing his work had worn him out. The accumulation piled over him while he said to himself he would just wait awhile. He fell asleep in the hallway, so that when she opened the door in the morning, too early for the newspaper, his body fell toward her, and there was first a shriek and then laughter and he woke up to her laughing.

"Did you know I was there?" he asked.

"Of course I knew. Notice no curlers in my hair? But I wasn't going to let you in until you asked nicely and said you were sorry."

"I didn't."

"Well, you're in now. And you mean to apologize, don't you?"

"I do," he said. "After a wonderful rest in your luxurious hallway I feel so much better."

"Now tell me about the Reservation."

"It's called a Nation," he said, "and that's only the beginning of the trouble. I guess I'll write it after all."

She stared at him in dismay and amazement. What manner of American was this? Was he used to sleeping in strange doorways where the paperboy might stumble over his body? Might not another tenant grow curious and disturb his rest? Although he hadn't even been under fire this time, unless her disapproval was fire, he was ready to try to explain. The professional explainer unleashed himself.

She tugged. "First get reacquainted," she said. "First reconciliation." She pulled at his belt. "First this, dearest. Later that."

Other considerations were postponed for a while.

Then she proposed sending him home to do his job. "You say there's this awful fraud going on with Donnie Grand."

"Danny," he said. "It's stupid and complicated."

"That's your job to sort it out. Wipe your nose, my dear, take another shower, drop your fidgets, get to work."

"Normally I don't fidget. I never do. Having no doubts has made me an efficient contraption."

She said warningly, "I don't want any blame for your fidgets. The contraption works on its own. That's what you told me. I think you had better not have any fidgets on my behalf."

"What I mean is, I drop my conscience."

"Doesn't that always make you feel alert and braver?"

"It has to be done without shame."

With her lips pressed tight and her eyes half shut, as if looking inward to discover why she was growing angry, Susan said, "Do I have to put up with this? I won't put up with this."

"What's the matter?"

"Do you realize I'm rather, oh, caseworn, my dear? I can put up with your American *musing*. I can even put up with your, uh, your great sympathy with yourself. But—" And her eyes were wide on his now, and not doubting herself, and not fooling around. "But there's a limit."

"This is what I am, Susan," he said. "This is what I want from you. Can you take it?"

She put out the fire with laughter, with giggles. "You haven't told me what you want, Ralph. You haven't thought to mention it. And besides, I'm not sure I want to hear it. I haven't told you what *I* want, Ralph."

He looked at her, waiting.

"Doesn't my example help, Ralph? How I have no shame— me, a well-brought-up young, or recently young anyway, English person?"

"It does help, Susan."

"If we can do such things together, fresh in my memory at the moment, and I'm such a respectable person, then surely at the least you can do your job—"

"Are we lying to each other?"

"Mr. Ralph, do you wish me to grow impatient again? Am I harmful to you? Are your vital fluids intact?"

"No. Yes. My brain has turned to guacamole. I'm sorry."

"Oh, are you silly."

"I humbly," he said, "regret my foolishness."

"That's much better. That makes up for every crime."

It was nice to laugh. It was not so bad to be easy. He explained what guacamole was. He would see her tomorrow, and by that time he would be well started on sorting out his notes. Surely it was possible to imitate order in the jottings and scribbles. If a person asserts order, he might even cause it to happen.

"Enough talk, dear, no more fussing. When you say there's this awful fraud going on with Donny or Dannie whatever Grand I think that means you have to start typing, then you line up the pages; we do this sort of thing in serious academic research, too—no reason on earth you can't be serious and diligent and line up the pages like me, is there?—now come on, don't answer, I've forgotten the sounds you make in a rut, they're well-orchestrated, too—don't answer, get moving, Ralph, *get*—"

And she pushed him out the door. She waved to him from her window. She put her hand to her breast and huffed to say she was out of breath with so much talking.

He stood in the street, feeling like a guitarist in purple velour pants, except that he was not a guitarist, wore no purple velour, and didn't know how to serenade. She was smiling and waving as if she understood how he felt. How he felt was that he hoped a cab would stop right away and conclude this tender moment.

He also felt good because he had felt so bad; sometimes that's a fineness coming up suddenly into light and air, as when he began to do, really do, the work he had abandoned hope of doing. The need to get the job done was screwed into his brain as tight as a lug nut. He would do it! The stubborn sloth fell out of his body; it was washing away on tides of coffee exhilaration; he was tight and flagrant again, like a boy, in the morning crosstown traffic moving and banking nicely through Central Park.

Could love equal this? Could sex, even? This euphoria of the body running before the fleet ideas in his head? He would not look for answers just now; to be on his way was enough.

And what about kindness and generosity? None of such distractions in his thrills of self. The manic pleasure that he took in morose poking about in corners had kept his heart and mind occupied since he was a boy. Is that what health is?

Never mind, by God. Now he'd just do it.

Out of the park, heading west, with a silent cabbie this time, Merian considered the adolescents of Beirut, driving around day and night and randomly shooting their weapons into the air, sometimes shooting the next customer on the street whose eyebrows happened to displease them. Or Hawkfeather, poking through a desert slum, looking for ambulatory trouble. Merian was different, wasn't he, wandering the world with his Olivetti Lettera 32, which tended to stick and rust? But usually he could write with it anyplace—on windowledges, on airplane seats, or on his lap—pinning leaders of their struggling people and teenage killers to copy paper, indiscriminate as anyone.

164

The boys of Beirut just shot off their jism. Hawkfeather was enraged by history; he wasn't prowling only because of the itch in his crotch. And naming the things they did was Merian's job. Stick with that answer, he told himself, if the questioning gets tough.

In urban guerrilla civilization the acids of gunpowder and fear were wearing against the soul. Chemical fatigue set in ahead of metal fatigue. The body looked threadworn even if intact; within, the brain was feeling less grief—a mercy the world offers the aging and tired. Sometimes a key fits more easily into a lock polished by rough use.

Yet when Merian considered his possibilities, his capillaries still flooded with blood, desire bloomed and clotted; he had hopes, and he told himself to seize the delights sometimes offered in life. Susan gave him a chance. He would not be young again, but he could be a person like others, wanting what he did not have, running the risks of trying to take what he wanted, maybe getting it.

He overtipped the cabbie and, to the amazement of all experts in the field, got thanked.

The front door of his building on Riverside Drive was stuck ajar. A rolled newpaper lay between the door and the jamb, as if someone had just gone out to spit or play the alternate-side street parking game and was coming right back and had forgotten his key. Well, that meant Merian didn't have to use his key, either. But in New York people aren't supposed to leave the front entrance unlocked.

Merian came down into the real world, which does not always include doormen, off his crosstown flight of euphoria and reso- lution. He was not yet threatened, but it was time to pay attention.

He entered and sniffed. An animal has the instinct to smell danger, which is the correct procedure for an animal, although a mere human being such as Ralph Merian had smelled so many bad smells that he couldn't really sniff it anymore, not always.

He felt his nose at work anyway; it twitched. Dry radiator air. Dust from a carpet worn to the brown threads, which were occasionally scraped by the custodian's broom. That door was never left ajar.

Slowly, listening, Merian walked one flight up the stairway, stopping every few steps. He kept thinking he heard someone. His breath was heavy, as if he had been running. What did he hope to hear—a prowler prowling? Or hope to smell—a burglar burgling? He heard the creak of the building, his own steps, the velocity of the city outside. He saw wood, plaster, a stack of newspapers at the incinerator, one dead light bulb, then one live one. He smelled dust and grit.

In emergency, everything comes into focus. A person becomes a devoted witness. Butterfly subscription forms from a magazine carried by someone since the custodian last took his broom here. Merian stopped again. The furry hum of the city was like a disconnect signal bundled to other people's conversations. He had tattered thoughts about the meaning of his life. Was that fear? As a young paratrooper, he never bothered with such things. Watchfulness should be the only procedure—that dustball, that light bulb, that funny business with the rolled-up newspaper at the front door of the building.

Which had been propped open by person or persons unknown and it didn't seem right. And Merian's whiff of anticipation turned out to be a correct judgment. His door in the hallway was also ajar.

He stood there a moment, staring at the slit of light coming through. His own daylight was leaking into the hallway. No doubt he should just turn, walk briskly away, avoid the daylight, call the police from elsewhere. But it was his door, and however lightly he camped in this place, it was his air and floor and desk and radio inside. The files and papers were his.

He would have preferred to change the immediate future course of things. He would have preferred to turn the room inside out, like a sweater, and shake out the lint. It didn't seem like another normal Riverside Drive burglary in process. He would very much have preferred to understand what was going on. Why would a burglar already inside a building prop open the front door? That was incorrect. A person can get out without any difficulty, once he is in. The trouble was supposed to be getting in. Did this burglar have any real on-the-job experience at the burgling trade?

Merian wound himself up like a spring in the hallway and then uncoiled and kicked the door all the way open. It smashed against the plaster. Hawkfeather stood in the middle of the floor, lounging there with a smile of welcome. "What the devil!" Merian said.

"No devil, just some red Indian come to visit and powwow," Hawkfeather said.

"What goddammit you doing here!"

"Returning our hospitality to you," Hawkfeather said. "You're not like other Anglos, are you? You don't like to owe people things and never pay them back, do you? So now you can pay me back for what you're taking from the Nation."

Merian glanced at the cardboard box on his desk. Hawkfeather had emptied out the notes, airline schedules, receipts, Merian's debris from his stay with the Stony Apaches. There was a heap piled near his typewriter. No sense in all that yet, unless Hawkfeather was quicker than Merian to see it.

"Tell me what I owe you," Merian said.

"Sit down, mister, please. We have to talk standing up like this? What you owe our Nation, not me. Ain't you making a living off our dumbness? How we stupid red Injuns give money to some maybe one-eighth Cherokee or something because he said on television, poor baby, he wants to make a movie and them Hollywood Jews won't give him the money so we do? Maybe two million of tribal funds?"

"I think you understand the story. Maybe you should write it. You've been paying attention."

"I been researching, Mister White Eyes. How poor we are, I been tasting that, and you making a living off it, how you do that. So I kind of like to make a living, also, like you do. So I heard about that individual initiative everybody call it; they say leave the *reservation*, like they call our Nation, and learn a profession or trade, sir. . . ."

Merian made a little nod at Hawkfeather to ask permission to sit. He did so, and stretched his legs out, arching his back and presenting his belly toward Hawkfeather. He needed to stretch, to level out his spirits, and to offer an attitude of nonquarrel. *Patience* and *wait*, he was thinking. He had enjoyed this kind of stretching in a chair in Beirut after a surprise bombing nearby. The statement of ease by the body made it true. In Beirut he had felt lucky; it was another of his lucky bombings—he happened to be not where the bomb was. In the Congo, now Zaire, it only happened the next day that he could stretch like a good cat and hear his neck crack a little, soothingly. History helps.

But just now his arms and legs still felt tight, too tight; there was a muscle flicking at his right calf. All this turmoil on Riverside Drive in Manhattan amounted to mere conversation. The threat, if any, was only in his mind. It was nothing to get upset about, unless a person happened to dislike his door being pried open, a crazy kid working stupid maneuvers on him, spilling his papers out on the table, a few of them kicked onto the floor—a person should get used to that sort of thing.

The nice young Indian intruder, off the silent desert preserve, no longer not crackling twigs underfoot in the forest, came to study how to talk a whole heck of a lot, how to waste himself the way the white eyes do.

At this juncture in the history of conflict between native Americans and less native ones, perhaps the Anglo person should just properly listen and say, "Uh-huh, uh-huh," like a patient good fellow. It seemed appropriate. Close reading of *Hiawatha* many years ago had not prepared Ralph Merian for this new association. He didn't know the Great Spirit personally. Listening and saying "Uh-huh" seemed like another correct procedure, especially when the Native American person had advantages on him of age, weight, protein concentration, and carelessness with life. Merian's acute peripheral vision—walls, fireplace, *New York Times* under the desk, paper-thin dead insect of some sort on the floor, stranded out of the oasis of the shower—was fading. The furry adrenaline buzz in his ears was diminishing. The calm he preached to himself was coming to be. He kept an eye on Hawkfeather, studying his mouth for when he might pause in his rapid chatter, and then saying, "Uh-huh. Uh-huh." Ralph Merian was developing into a nice patient person whose life has slightly caved in and whose house has been slightly broken into. And who doesn't want worse.

Hawkfeather talked. No dissension from Merian, who stretched his legs, arched his back, revved down, listened.

Hawkfeather explained how he was getting in touch with his people, both those alive and those in the great hunting ground, emissaries to the Great Spirit. He hoped to take on some of a medicine man's powers without all the horseshit. If he couldn't do the buffaleenie stand with Merian, a traditional Apache fast-food operation with franchise possibilities, okay, he had some fallback positions. For example, to live without eating. It was scientific. The *National Enquirer* filled in the scientific details. If a man willed that chlorophyll stuff into his bone marrow, like the plants do, he could synthesize nourishment-type food from the air with the help of the good mountain sun. There was plenty of sun, plenty of air. No limit on that; you don't need no investment. Breatharianism. If they franchised it, they could find a snappier name—McBreath, McBreathburgers—those were mere details.

To do it best, you needed a shot of Mohawk Brandy, Hawkfeather always found. Not every time you took a meal in gulps of air—your nice evening dinner while you stood out there looking at the setting sun, inhale, exhale, think breathing thoughts—but sometimes it was better; it was what the traditional Indian medicine men call a catalyst. Cats were known to the ancient Aztec people, also. Now Anglo science has ripped off catalysts, no credit given, of course, that's the white-eyes way....

"You hear me now?"

"Doing nothing but listening."

Hawkfeather stopped a moment. He wanted to make certain

of Merian's attention. It also gave his breath time for nourishment.

Sometimes, of course, when a person finds the secret of living on air, which Native Americans have been studying for thousands of years now in their open-to-the-sky laboratories, you get to eat flat corn bread without ruining everything. It was a taste treat. In fact, the best. At a ceremony, where it's not food so much as spiritual nourishment. And then you go straight back to air, sun, and water to cure the headache some people get from fried grease. Water was also important, but it shouldn't have mites, bugs, and runoff in it. That just confuses things. Plants can use shitty water, but human chlorophyll is more spiritual.

"Uh-huh."

"Personally, I'll just rest at a table, sipping Mohawk Brandy," said Hawkfeather. "Sleep on my elbows, you know? Then I'll step out and take a shot of sun. That's all. I don't crap more'n a plant does."

"You'll be pure," Merian said.

"That's the story." He paused. "It's not too complicated, but you don't believe, I can tell, and that's why your civilization is gonna blow itself up. No neutron bomb can touch a chlorophyll person, mister."

"I have a brother in San Francisco with great ideas, too," Merian said.

"I bet he's not an Indian." Hawkfeather stared. He didn't take to criticism, but he recognized it. When a person goes to all this trouble to break into someone's house just as an educational and informational venture, he doesn't have to deal with criticism besides. He said, "That's how they teach us things, on-the-job training, watching people do it—in your case writing the journalism, in my case breathing. Also doing my breathing around here in New York City I can kind of like oversee how you write about us, man. Us native Americans got a way of doing two things at once, like we do Christian and we also do Great Spirit. We do European and we do Asian. We do Bering Strait and

Tijuana. We do quietness. We do drink-a-lot. You gonna try to call the police?"

"No."

"While you do, I wreck the place, plus I wreck you."

"I said I wasn't planning that."

"Come back if I have to. Might mess up a little right now anyway, man, what we movie mongols call a preview of coming attractions."

"Yours is the choice. I'd try to stop you." Merian felt he owed him a personal comment, since they had been friends now for almost two weeks. "Off the Nation, pal, you sure do run on. Does the Breath Franchise allow for a dose of speed, too?"

Hawkfeather's solemn brown face opened in another smile. He stuck out his thick slab of hand. "Yours is the choice, man. Know any Anglo girl friends for me? Ain't that a fair exchange for the secrets of breathing air?"

Merian was taking it easier at last. This was a change from butting his head against the typewriter. "So you can drain off some of that adverse energy, Hawkfeather?"

"Just what I was planning. A adverse energy drain. Since I'm young, I can drain my adverse energy maybe three-four times a night. I don't suppose you old white eyes can do that."

Merian rubbed his face. "I remember, though, and you know what? I'm not willing to go back to those days."

"Yours," said Hawkfeather, rubbing his own face in sympathetic imitation, "yours is not the choice, doctor."

Merian sighed and said aloud, maybe just to change the subject, "Why don't I leave and get the police?"

Hawkfeather shook his head slowly, as if Merian was being stupid, which he was, going back to foolishness. "And like I say, I could stay awhile and rip the place apart, all that stuff of yours. Didn't I mention I could do that? I ain't bad, but I don't think I'm what you call rational—do you? And if they ever found me, which they wouldn't—they gonna look for some crazy Injun you picked up on your travels, like you bachelors do?—they gonna say lovers' quarrel, won't they, being smart New York police and all, isn't that right?"

Merian couldn't answer all his questions. Hawkfeather was full of questions today.

"Don't really care about this stuff. Don't live here, only park between jobs. Where I travel is where my home is."

Hawkfeather extended his hand again. "Me too," he said. "Listen, Mister White Eyes Journalist, let me park here also. I'm between jobs, like you tell me. Let me hang in awhile, okay? Just like double park, keep the flasher going, till I get straight, okay?"

There was a black look in his eyes, dangerous, in danger, the breath gone out of it, and Merian pitied him more than he feared him. Merian valued his own life less than he should. With age, a person should treasure what is left, but sometimes a person gets to feeling worn about things. Hawkfeather aroused his curiosity. He didn't have a son of his own to do this. "Stay here tonight," he said. "We'll talk. I wouldn't mind a little company. Then tomorrow I'll give you some money for a hotel. I've got some work to do eventually. Pay by the week—it's not too much— you look for a sign that says 'residential hotel,' and then maybe you won't love New York and you'll want to go home. You got a ticket?"

Hawkfeather shrugged. Merian was making a peculiar white-eyes assumption, planning so far ahead, as if a person might want to go back.

"We don't sleep on street corners in New York."

"Yes we do. Take a look around," Hawkfeather said.

"That's not what I said. I mean you're not meant to."

"Say it more clear so I can hear you."

"If I give you money, what'll you do with it?"

"Treat myself."

Merian studied the young man. "Do you know what you want from me?"

Hawkfeather's slow solemn grin. The eyes glinting, black, and expressionless. "I get what I want, man," he said.

This was not responsive. It was Hawkfeather's habit to answer his own question and not the one asked. Merian wasn't sure he liked the young man or his manners, but Merian had his own peculiar habits for following a line of inquiry. "Then stay in town and have a little vacation from all your plans," he said. "See if you can use this New York air, sort of like a breatharian casserole. Talking to an informative person like you would be a great pleasure."

"Research, like those anthropologists keep coming from the universities and the BIA, eat off us."

"Do you think I'm one of those? I might like to listen to you, that's all."

"That's all, man? Even if I take something you don't want to give me in trade?"

Merian wondered what that might be. "One of my problems is there's not too many things I really and truly do want, pal. At your age it might be a little strange to hear somebody could end up not wanting enough and maybe prefer it like that. Maybe I don't make sense to you."

"You have a right to your opinion, mister." He considered a moment longer. "Mister Merian."

Hawkfeather had achieved a style the Veteran Journalist had also noticed among Iranians, Pakistanis, East Indians, Arabs, and some Africans. They could be Oxford or Sorbonne graduates, with cards printed in many languages and on both sides, and rolled umbrellas in the proper climes, and then if it suited a purpose, they could go native or bush or desert, some variety of Proud 'n' Ancient, all in an instant. It was a game they played with the colonizers. They had freed themselves, and now they tipped the former folks off balance. Probably Merian shouldn't have been surprised to find this talent on home ground. He decided to leave the game if possible, and asked, "What do you want from me? We know each other a little now, but I don't really know anything at all about you, Hawkfeather—"

"That's a pretty good gain, ain't it?"

"Tell me what you want."

Hawkfeather's face crumpled in thick folds of laughter without sound. An avalanche rippled down his cheeks; the miracle caused no damage. He knew how to laugh. The face wrinkles, mouth twists, and reddish-brown skin shows temporary fissures. He just didn't choose to make any sounds. Then he stopped laughing. The silence of his laughter ended. "Help me, mister," he said. "I'm lost here. I don't know what to do next."

"I don't know, either." This was dangerous. Merian knew it was a dangerous thing to hear.

"Truth is, I can't live off air yet, mister. I ain't got the chlorophyll."

"None of us do, Hawkfeather. Lighten up. Not lucky enough to be a plant."

"But I can be a rock, man, and don't you forget it. Don't even need to breathe. Far as I'm concerned, don't need *anybody* to breathe."

8

MERIAN AND HAWKFEATHER came to an agreement. When the V.J. put his cranial meat word processor into the work mode, he was accustomed to moving. The head began to stutter, the arms began to twitch. The thinking was done, the feeling could come another day—now was the time for all good fingers to come to the aid of Command Central. Rapid on the keys, branched directly into the nervous system, Merian sought to bypass brain and heart at this juncture. It was a knack he had. The biology might be a little off, but whoever said a V.J. was obliged to obey his biology, when nobody else did? He could be civilized and irrational like everybody else.

The facts flew into place, perhaps even into the right ones. Later, he might caret in a few more. And what he had lived through or passed over—sometimes that too was not irrelevant.

Breaking up with a wife during the Christmas season while a commitment on two parts on Central America came due; there was one case where a mood of thoughtful irony did not originate in Costa Rica, struggling little democracy, gallant little President, maybe Robert Vesco in charge. Arnie liked the piece, said it had "resonance," didn't know why. Merian thought he was guilty of Joseph Conrad murk—anopheles mosquitoes and offshore banks—not his fault, but if Arnie was satisfied, who was Ralph Merian to complain when his life seemed, temporarily, over? Often he seemed to have to deal with the world while his own world was in trouble: when his father died, also when the old guy was still alive. And now here was Hawkfeather, who couldn't turn into one of his serious problems unless he let it happen. Merian decided to take control here, not be a victim, and get the thing done.

"Think of this," Hawkfeather was saying. He was a little uneasy. For some reason he did not hold all Merian's attention. He had not had the experience of a journalist boiling to let go at the typewriter. "Think of it as a treaty."

"Think of your people," Merian answered. It was time to clean him out of the work space on Riverside Drive. "You are Noble. Consider that."

"Bullshit. Lower than niggers."

"Say black, please. Say something measured."

"Dogshit."

"That only measures a little heap. Try something else."

"You try smartass, Mister White Eyes, you put yourself in jeopardy of a fist in the face or a cutting—"

"Hawkfeather, buddy, you've been reading. I like that word 'jeopardy.' You've been here reading in my books a couple of days now. That BIA school can't be too bad."

Hawkfeather felt a little more comfortable. Discussion meant he had called his friend away from whatever else was on his mind. He liked having a person's attention. "Junior college in Albuquerque," he said, "was worse. They got a grant to train us so we can fill out gas-station credit slips, write dayroom reports in the service, press down hard for carbon copies. You know, man, Higher Education for the people that does the shit work till they get those other robots on line. But us Injuns ain't as trainable as the Chicanos and the, oh, yeah, what you call 'em, blacks."

"Hawkfeather," Merian said, sighing, "you are a disgrace to your proud and ancient people."

"Like most folks," Hawkfeather said.

That's his aim, Merian decided. He was reviewing the discussion in his head as it went along. He liked to write down his notes later, using the gift of partial recall. It was almost work. He sighed again. When he wanted to get things really going, he stopped stewing about them. He said, considering only how to make his intentions get through to the lad—he said crisply, "I know you're at the age when what you want matters, not what I want, but here's the deal."

"You gonna pay me off?"

"I don't owe you, pal. I'm going to make a little loan."

"I don't have to pay you back?"

"You really take being Third World seriously, don't you? Let's call it a loan so your pride'll feel better."

"My pride feels fine, White Eyes." He left off the Mister.

"Terrific," Merian said. "So wipe your nose and clean your armpits, there's a Native American Center down west of Times Square, maybe Ninth or Tenth Avenue, you must have kin down there, here's a little stake." He lay the money on the table. He went on talking while Hawkfeather picked it up; better that the lad not be too embarrassed. He wasn't embarrassed, of course. But it was important to keep momentum going until it just rolled out the door, not quite sure what had hit it, which was a journalist needing his privacy to get his job done.

Merian waited till the money was in Hawkfeather's jeans. Then he ventured a little shove, a little colonizer's severity: "You weren't my host on your Nation, pal. I'm not your host here. I don't want you messing around me; I got work to do. Maybe later I'll find you a little more—"

"Already found it. In the drawer with your socks."

Best to treat this as perfectly normal houseguest manners. It was only petty cash—stamps, tips, delivery-boy money, money for postage due. Oh, yes, plus a hundred-dollar bill for mugger's money. Some foreign paper and coins—did he expropriate them, too?

"Okay, okay now. And I don't want to find you around here anymore. I want you *out,* pal. Listen to me: My place here isn't part of your Nation." He studied Hawkfeather across the small stretch of rug. The lad was beginning to bother him. The lad could give him a good beating. If he had a knife, which he no doubt had, the lad could kill him.

He didn't think this would occur just now. These sighs that kept heaving up from his chest were more like yawns. He decided to finish his thought. "Get out. Get out pronto. You grabbed yourself a little stake—okay. Try to pay a little attention, Hawkfeather, because no matter how it seems, I don't have great resources of patience."

The lad said nothing. The lad did not move on him.

Then nice, obedient, and also with more money in his pants than he absolutely needed for the day's fun, Hawkfeather departed. Merian took only a moment to look in his sock drawer. The hundred-dollar bill *and* the foreign currency but no socks were missing. Well, maybe Hawkfeather was planning on a casual lunch, wearing sandals.

Merian didn't even think about changing the locks on his door. For the moment, he only thought about getting to work.

When he said *Wipe your nose* to the lad, wasn't that what Susan had said to him?

Medium-long ago, when Ralph Merian had only tended to a half-dozen wars and revolutions, he was enjoying a lively young woman who worked in television. She was as pretty and skinny as a dancer, too skinny, of course, and with teeth slightly irregular, which made her look like a misunderstood child. She had no interest in fixing teeth, moving to on-camera behavior. It was partly the mysterious lack of ambition in her, combined with great skinny energy, that pleased Merian. And when she danced signals as an assistant director, sharp elbows askew, beckoning and flailing behind the rolling apparatus, that little bug in her hair, she was pure delight to watch. Her name, as Merian recalled without any effort—this was a pleasure, this occasional sharpness of his mind—was Valerie.

Valerie and Merian had met when the paper asked him to do eight minutes on the local CBS outlet, promoting his Dominican Republic series. Arnie said he needed to do it because Americans are intrinsically, basically, fundamentally, stubbornly, passionately—this is the most essential fact about Americans which de Tocqueville, despite all his wisdom, never discovered—totally uninterested in anything that happens in Santo Domingo.

"Gotcha," Merian had said. Although he wrote better than de Tocqueville—so Arnie devoutly assured him—he could not overcome the basic problem without offering his mug to the noon chat show on the local CBS outlet. Merian said yuck; Arnie said granted; and Merian submitted to the ordeal because there was a firm foundation of passivity and agreeability in his character.

Whereupon, on a dumb CBS local outlet chat show, he was rewarded for sometimes doing whatever Arnie asked. Fiddling with the snap-on mike, dancing three cameras about him, Valerie appeared, feathery gleams of sweat in the teevee lights, smells of nervous health, crooked-teeth little-girl smiles: "Oh, Mr. Merian, don't worry about where you put your hands, but try not to cross your legs too high; it looks kind of less handsome on camera. Here, let me just tuck this little guy behind your shirt."

He felt her busy little fingers on the little electronic guy, tucking it behind his shirt.

Which proved that a firm foundation of passivity and agreeability and letting Arnie send him on foolish errands sometimes paid off.

Later that week, over their second breakfast, Valerie shared her philosophy with him. "I salute producers, but I don't salute ad agencies."

She made tough distinctions. "I used to go to bed with people, but now I've got to like the person. Do you think it's a new phase in my life? Am I getting old?"

"I've had so many phases," Merian said, "I've gone right past them."

"I guess your friend Arnie never hit on you for sex."

"No, but for dinner. That can be worse sometimes."

"You like him, don't you?"

"He's my best friend."

Valerie grew pensive. "I'm going to have to get through this phase all by myself. You're no help."

"I'm sorry."

"You're nice though. Guys have feelings, too, I've always said that. But I get kind of lonely for the days when all I wanted was to go from assistant director to floor director and then the sky's the limit. Things were simpler then. Do you like me?"

He held her hand and smiled and she didn't repeat the question. Not yet.

The spring came and impatience began to set in. Valerie was a rising young person who didn't like to be stymied. Merian returned from a little trip, a little job, and after the appropriate greeting, nice as it always was, a whole long evening of greeting, she asked, "Am I reducing this to pure emotion? Because I sure wouldn't want to do that, like so many old women do. I'm not even twenty-seven!"

"You're twenty-six."

"That's what I said! No wonder you make me feel shitty, not cute, although I've always been able to do cute pretty good—"

He reached to grab and hug her. "You're delicious, Valerie, you are definitely cute. And smart. And nice. And you make bad decisions sometimes."

She looked at him with a cunning smile. "Don't assume," she said.

They were not ready for a serious quarrel. They still had a few months to run.

Then, a few months later, in the usual course of such matters, the path of untrue love not running any more smoothly than the path of true love, Merian and Valerie were quarreling. Now what was it about again? Whatever they said it was about, it was about how Merian enjoyed her but didn't want anything more than to continue admiring her crooked teeth, lively arms and legs, enjoying her; and despite her terrific performance as a high-tension adolescent career woman, Valerie really wanted a nest in a highrise on the East Side, with the two of them saving up for couch, kitchen equipment, automobile, and eventually a weekend place in Sag Harbor or one of the Hamptons. Enjoyment wasn't central in her life plans, although she was so young that she didn't realize this. She just bit her cuticles and knew things were almost great. She thought it would double her pleasure, double her fun, to play permanent house with an already veteran journalist with half a career behind him. She was so intrinsically sweet-smelling that Merian forgave her smoking although he had given it up. She did not take his sacrifice into consideration—the blitheness of youth!

First she tried to keep the tone proper to a citizen of the Lincoln Center electronic media village, while expressing her needs, her frustrations, her not yet abandoned expectation, her anger. "You have the Midas touch, goddammit—you change everything to mufflers."

"Oh, come on, Valerie. I really like you."

He was remembering the quick tuckings of her fingers, fitting the little microphone out of sight between the second and third buttons of his shirt, and they had just met, and she was patting down the jitters of the noon-hour talk show before a studio audience of shoppers taking a break. He was remembering her with wonder and fondness. How she called everything and everybody, human or electronic, "guy"—"this little guy." How even something very personal and individual to him was his little guy. "Oh, I like this sweet little guy of yours."

And meantime, while he was wasting his strength in pleasant recollection, she was fussing and scrambling tearfully around and over the furniture as they suffered an argument honored by time and history, polished by hundreds of thousands of couples through the ages; perhaps millions. *"You don't really love me!"*

When she wept and despaired, her elbows darted, it was almost the way she directed three cameras.

"I sort of do."

She did not take this into consideration. "You don't care!"

"I do."

"Sort of! That's all you care!"

So after all she did hear him.

Merian could have gone along with the quarrel. He could have ridden with it until she worked it out in her mind and gave him up. Women usually made this decision about him, and afterward liked him better for it, and carried a small store of contempt for him into eternity. Merian could live with that. It was better than hurting a person.

But one afternoon, he was banging away at his story—it happened just by chance to be a follow-up on the occasion of their first meeting, the American disposal of President Juan Bosch in the Dominican Republic, and Merian had been away talking again with both Bosch and William Attwood, the American ambassador, who had, according to Bosch, betrayed him—and it was an interesting backgrounder, even if it wasn't de Tocqueville's thing. . . . Merian was trying to recall the atmosphere of the tanks and the gun-toters and the Gulf & Western functionaries in the streets of Santo Domingo, and the fluctuations in the price of sugar (the commodities market had been an interesting place for a few days), and also to describe the rage and hurt of the deposed president, who was also a distinguished historian and even a poet, with distinguished, tightly curled white hair—he almost called him "a distinguished-looking Latin guy," but of course didn't— when Valerie came banging and bustling at the door of the Galahad Hotel on Lexington Avenue in the East Fifties (now gone, of course, redeveloped), where Merian used to rent a room for an office.

Valerie brought something to add to their previous conversation. She had continued the dialogue in her head, without Merian, which tends to make it less of a dialogue. His imaginary responses infuriated her (she probably had the general line down pretty accurately) and so she had come to quarrel. That's a worthy purpose. It was moving forward all morning, all by herself, and now she had enough of rehearsal. She banged on the door. Room-service love spat in a hotel with a gay health club downstairs and space to rent cheaply, on a temporary basis, no lease, until the building came down in a shower of dusty speculation in just a few months—no overnight sleeping. What a person did with a lover here had to be done before bedtime. At least that was the agreement with the rental people.

Merian opened the door and Valerie hurled herself at him. "I'm working!" he said.

"And another thing about the way you are, you crud—"

And he threw her back into the hall, slammed the door, shouted through clenched teeth, "It's over! I was working! It's over! Get out!"

And it was over. And he went on with the backgrounder, which because he was an unreliable formulator to order turned into an examination of the whole tawdry Dominican episode—a mini-Vietnam, an extension of the Bay of Pigs, a precursor and a harking back—and it got him a Double Trenchcoat Award from the Overseas Press Club. The prize included his choice of Burberry, plus a one-week bar credit sufficient to wreck six Irish livers. Several ruddy-faced colleagues told him he should have had a Pulitzer (Arnie said he was nominated; so what?), but when he stood up for the ceremony in the building across from the public library and the needle park on Forty-second Street, Valerie and regrets came to mind. He thanked "the young woman who patiently let me work when she had more important things to discuss, such as why I wasn't willing to discuss the things she wanted to discuss while I was running this series past the deadline."

Laughter. Nice Valerie, who wasn't patient at all, who had already married an anchorman (local show), a bar mitzvahed Puerto Rican guy who had gotten the job on a rare combo of bouffant hair and ethnicity. He was the answer both to Geraldo

Rivera and Valerie's dreams—nice Valerie, who deserved better than the non-Geraldo Rivera, better than Ralph Merian, better than what appeared in the studio for her at the right time.

Maybe, in the grand scheme of things, where no one remembers Juan Bosch, the distinguished historian, poet, and deposed president, Merian should have allowed Valerie her quarrel, settled things differently, not pushed a sweet person out his office door in a tantrum over interruption at work.

Because, in the grand scheme of things, no one needs last year's Double Trenchcoat Award and a possible Pulitzer. And Valerie was a decent craving young woman with a skinny lively craving body and smelled sweet despite her smoking. Except that Merian didn't crave what Valerie craved.

Did she still?

She used to. How could Merian know about now? Only older fellows begin to live in the past and present all mixed up.

After Merian's father had finally died, he thought consolingly (whom was he consoling?), and said aloud to his mother, "Well, now we can remember him as he was before he got sick."

The old lady turned away from him, saying, "What makes you this way, son? You were a kind boy."

She died nine months later. Over tea one afternoon she told him she would soon "pass on" and, because he used to be a kind boy, he resisted telling her that euphemisms for "die" don't help at all. She held his hand and he studied her brown lumps, the blue scatter of veins, the soft boniness, the terrain of this woman's hand, which was so different from any other woman's hand he had held. Probably what had to do with her rapid decline and passing on: a son like Ralph, a son like Chaz, and then not even a husband. It was too much for her.

At her bedside, watching her go, he burst out suddenly, "Ma! I'm here with you! Do you know?"

And a deep sound rattled up through the slumber, the coma, the fluid-filled lungs—not his mother's voice at all, but his father's, the old bastard's grumble inhabiting her now, just as he had fed on her in their life together—

"Do you hear me, Ma?"

That death voice called out to him from her chest: *"Ralph. Ralph. Ralph."*

When his father died, Merian had been working on a border fight in Bolivia. Che Guevara's murder took precedence over the ordinary loss of a father afflicted with Parkinsonism plus a whole series of small strokes. But when his mother died, he was with her. So he was not consistent. But then he went south again to finish the story about some CIA shenanigans in Panama.

Yet he dreamed the same dream with each death. His father was marching out to sea on a sandspit, sinking slowly, half in sand, half in water, and Ralph followed, rushing after, splashing and struggling in the ocean, saying, *Don't go, don't go yet,* and his father answered impatiently, shaking Ralph's hand off the soft old flesh, *Want to go right now.*

And then nine months later, as if one death conceived another, it was his mother's turn, and he dreamed she was walking through still waters toward the horizon and he was following. *Ma. Don't. Not yet.*

He woke in the mornings. He wrote his pieces. They were not up to his standard during this period. He was having the wrong dreams for good work. He couldn't push his mother and father through the door as he had pushed Valerie. But he did the job anyway.

So with a normal quota of middle-aged distraction already behind him, who the devil could suggest that a mere Hawkfeather might stop him from working? "Whatever blocks my path only redoubles my determination to get through"—probably some nineteenth-century mumbler of pithy remarks said this. Merian would not dream about Hawkfeather, he would not think about Hawkfeather, he would give him a few bucks and not get agitated about his stealing a few more, he would shut the door behind the lad as he had shut it behind his father, his mother, his wife, Valerie. He would decide about Susan when it was right to decide.

He might grind his teeth a little instead of dreaming. The dentist had said to try self-hypnosis, think "No grinding before sleep," but he preferred to think of the cold and hot high mesa where the Stony Apaches threw away their money on Danny Grand. No antitooth-grinding mantras for the V.J. Somebody around here had to do the work of the world.

He did not dream about Hawkfeather walking out to sea.

He locked himself in for a brainstorming few days of nothing but scrambling his fingers into the machine.

Arnie could be proud of him.

Why, shit, Ralph Merian could be proud of himself. The V.J. still had his stuff. He remained adequate. "Burnout" is just another word in media shuck.

Four days later, he had a first draft. Two more days and it was ready for editing. He thought he might share the nice news with Susan and Arnie.

9

A RNIE TELEPHONED WITH good news for him. Something terrific had come up, "a little swerve in the routine like you wouldn't believe, fella—it's the sort of thing makes life worth living."

"What?" Merian asked.

"I'd do it myself, put on my chaps, whatever they are, and boots and strap on the old credit cards..."

"What?" Merian said.

"...only I'm too busy not living, just editing instead, fella..."

"What," Merian said, "or I'll hang up on you, Arnie."

It turned out to be those Stony Apaches—great that he'd gotten a draft out of himself (fella)—but here was an opportunity with time value and a person can't miss it. Alamo Oxman, the oil billionaire and molybdenum speculator with a shape on him like an office coke machine, said he would talk to someone from the *News-Press* and Syndicate. He wanted to get his true story out.

187

It must have been a stage in his diet spansule. He wanted the people to know what a fine conniving Texas boyo he was. "Strike," said Arnie, "while the irony is hot."

"Danny Grand has no time value?"

"Didn't you say you have a draft? You want to let me see it? Let it ripen a couple three days, who knows, you might change a word'll get you some big national award from the America Needs Indians Foundation."

And yet both Arnie and Ralph managed to tell themselves each piece of work was essential, as today's hunger is critical at mealtime, when it was only the latest piece of work that really seemed to matter. Oxman's availability was crucial today. Maybe Merian needed a few days away, doing something easy like a Texas bull billionaire. Arnie said, "Go explore," and Merian put the construction site rock on his Stony Apache papers and hoped that Hawkfeather would stay away. On second thought, he hid the draft in the most back part of his closet, where he kept the overcoat for the Soviet Union in winter, and he put it in the oversized pockets he had had sewn in that overcoat for lugging his notes around and not leaving them in hotel rooms. He asked the custodian not to let any young Indians borrow his apartment in his absence.

The paper arranged the meeting in Dallas with Alamo Oxman. the computer set up a nice hotel, room with a view of quiet air conditioning, and a library of tasseled instructions about Elegante Dining á la Français, All-Nite Coffee Shoppe, The Heart & Ribs of Dallas Room, the Cobbled Shopping Arcade. There was also a history of the hotel chain, bound in leatherette like the Bible. ("In the Beginning was the Hilton...") To prepare for his hour with the overweight billionaire the next morning, Merian took a prime-rib dinner the night before, read the background stuff by the glow of red candlelight and cherry cobbler at his table, limited himself to one glass of Soave. The cherry cobbler came with the prime-rib special. Merian broke the crust to avoid reproach from the waiter.

Oxman hated the press. Arnie assured Merian he would be an

entertainment. That was an assumption. Oxman might prove to be a vibrant revelation about the nature of his family which supported some oil and metal lobbyists in Washington, plus one religious cause, a church whose chief tenet was that black people are descended from a marriage between Cain and a dusky field girl named Rebecca Rabinowitz. This was also an unproven assumption. The First Church of Jesus the Supremecist (look up exact name in Oxman files). Merian hoped for a surprise, but wasn't sure he would find one.

The V.J. was used to dealing with chiefs of empires for which his world-renowned newspaper would have been just a rinky-dink investment if only their bankers could get their hands on it, a mere detail that so far seemed to stop them. He expected short shrift from the pious three-hundred-pound heir, but he hoped for a response—this is not the same as an answer—to a short list of questions. He had a list on paper and a shorter one in his head, if that seemed the way to go.

Slowing down past the Southland Life Building, the cabbie told him they didn't hate Lyndon Baines so much anymore for his betrayal of the real Texas on behalf of those Reds in Austin. Merian knew enough not to mention John F. Kennedy. A billboard said PROBLEM DRINKERS MUST WANT HELP? NOT TRUE! ASK JESUS! The driver told him to be sure now to visit Old City Park "'cause you look like a boy interested in bygone era. They got some of the best bygone era in the world you wouldn't necessarily know we got in Dallas. Want me to come round later, drive you there for a tour?"

"I'm here on business," Merian said.

The driver fixed his gaze on Merian by staring into his rearview mirror. "You don't look like one of those eastern boys here on business. If you're not oil or construction, you textile? If you not money, you're no banker man, you here on monkey business? Cause I got some of that, too."

Thinking fast, Merian said, "Teacher."

The cab slid into a little breezeway. "Here y'are, perfessor. You lyin' to me, but that's your business. You know Mr. Oxman, the big one, got a office in this little old building?"

There was a smell of chlorine in the elevator leading to the Executive Office on the sixth floor of the Oxman Building, a pool smell, clean and more chemical than pleasant. The smell of Third-World soap was like this. Merian sniffed and recalled a girl's hair in Beirut, a thoughtful person who liked swimming for the oceanic privacy of it, liked doing her laps in the American University pool before she visited him. She believed that swimming in a pool left her hair clean. Merian didn't have the heart to disabuse her of this touching simple faith.

Alamo Oxman, also a man of strong conviction, relied on the germ-killing qualities of chlorine in his elevator. Some people left sweat traces and he liked to be immune to them. Security guards were particularly bad sweat people, yet he couldn't do without them; hence this elevator solution.

The slim blond guard in green twill, riding up with Merian, asked his pardon as he patted his pockets, then opened the door to Oxman's office with a courteous "Sir?" Alamo Oxman sat high in a barber chair behind a French Provincial desk. Dense beer and coffee rings lay in nondesigner patterns on the lacquered wood, superimposing an evidence of contemporary civilization like a palimpsest upon older cabinetry, from a time when refreshment didn't come in cans. As Merian entered, Oxman made a little sound, neither hiccup nor grunt, but with some of the qualities of both, indicating that he might have stood up, given a hundred and fifty pounds less; then again, the expression on his face, an extinct volcano of a face, said, he might not. "You like to talk?" Oxman asked. "You got a hot Dallas hour, that's fifty minutes, so it's you talk or I talk, pick your druthers."

Merian got right to it. The Baran Oil Field in Libya had been nationalized away from Oxman Oil by Qaddafi, but management contracts ensured a continued flow to the Free World and maybe even a smidgen of profit. Now the profit was being squeezed. Merian and the *News-Press* hoped to put a few rumors to rest. Was there sabotage of the oil fields? Was Oxman trying to buy Qaddafi, or kill him, or make a new deal, or some combination

190

of the preceding? Since Occidental worked things out, why were the Oxmans having such trouble?

"The Oxmans is me, Alamo. My brother does the horses, women, and says he's president of the shipping—that's what he gives out."

"The Oxman group. Could the question stand with that stipulation?"

"You sound like a fucking kike lawyer, mister."

Normally Merian didn't enjoy business stories. However, since oil had escalated the connections between killing and money, even he found the oil wars and revolutions generated enough pep to keep a person awake. Alamo Oxman, three hundred pounds of person, very little of it devoted to wide innocent eyes, seeming to peep at Merian through pinholes in his eyelids, now worked the lids apart and described how the Jewish conspiracy tried to deprive him of a regular flow into his refineries. He had water on his lungs. When he paused to wheeze, the V.J. was able to ask, "The Jews, sir, work for Qaddafi?"

"Ain't much of this known." Oxman hawked something into a handkerchief and stuck it into a French Provincial drawer for future study. "I can only conjecture a reckon, but let me tell you this, buddy boy, I didn't get prosperous being wrong. Sure Daddy left me a li'l nest egg, but Alamo sat on them. I'm right here like I been right ninety-two percent. You prefer a whole-wheat brownie and an orange from mah lunch basket? Ain't hardly got no appetite these days, being fucked over like they do by the snot-noses. You know how much Neiman Marcus charge for a toothbrush you can pick up in Walgreen's for thirty-nine centavos?"

Sharing Alamo Oxman's lunch basket was exactly the refreshment the V.J. had in mind. So kind of the billionaire, but he didn't want to take the time to chew just now. Would he care to answer a few more questions?

Nope, not exactly. Merian's reluctance to partake of the chow turned Oxman wary. Instead of giving Merian answers without any cause to do so, he would care and prefer to recount once again how the family had achieved its three-generation rise into deserved eminence, following the lines described in the authorized family biography, bought, paid for, and issued as a public service by the Book Depository Press. All who tithed to the Church of One Howling-Mad Jesus got their copies along with the quarterly computer readout on what they owed the Lord, regular adjustments for inflation.

Now Merian didn't have to look up the Church. Had it right there in his notes.

Oxman spoke in a Texas duck-shoot, don't-care-if-you-hear-me, six-pack accent until he got on the subject of the North, the East, money, and Jews. It didn't take long. The accent remained the same except for the don't care if you hear me; loud enough, the voice was also clear enough, like a full-channel station operating from Laredo across the plains. There was a lovable little-boy smile that occasionally serrated the beef of his face. This was a sign that he was adding 'niggahs' to his repertoire; 'niggahs' or a joke or both. His teeth were tiny for a coke-machine-sized man. Maybe they were an optical illusion based on total scale.

"We kind of famous in Texas and yonder," the molybdenum and oil bulk allowed as how, showing his baby teeth. "The Panhandle, Oklahoma, wherever. Some of them broker firms know us, too. And the chickenshit Congress back East in Washington with all them collud preachers and smart Jew lawyers. But we overcome. That's the family's trademark—We Shall Overcome—because they cain't keep us down. You got to squash a Oxman good, and then I'll rise anyway. On that mineral question, they infringed our freedom pretty fair, but we wiggle out, dint we?" The attempt to produce a corner in the molybdenum market had squeezed Oxman, and the memory of it seemed to clear his lungs. The commodities exchange speeded up his breathing. "Someday, I got nothing better to do, I'm gonna dictate me a little bitty 'nother book. No, scratch that. A *big* little bitty book."

"I'll be the first to read it, sir."

"But I'll have to be crippled sick to write it, shit my time away like that, pull up my dress and show 'em what I got. I got the usual. What else I got, they don't know, 'cause I got it better, am I right?"

"Your success is the proof, sir."

"You better believe it. I hope you call me sir like that because you know better'n not to."

Merian tried to take him back to the more current issue. How about Muammar al-Qaddafi? Did he have any thoughts about doing business in Libya in the future?

"I have a dream. Gonna get me a smart New York liar or two, gonna pile it on, gonna get what's mine and what's right, like we Oxmans always do...."

"Always" came out something like "alluz." Oxman offered Marian a cold beer from the white foam ice chest underneath the desk. When he opened his own Coors, flipping the top with an expert thumb, he took half the contents in one gulp and then fit the can neatly into the mark from a previous can. Alamo Oxman was in a mood these days to be careful, precise, and accurate.

"Them whiskey dents in your head, mister? You got some sickness in you?"

How nice of the tycoon to ask. "I'm just tired, Mr. Oxman. Been traveling a lot."

"Stay home in Dallas and enjoy all you can stand. I don't know why people alluz tend to go wandering."

"I live in New York."

"And here I was trying to forget that fack about you. Here I was trying to act nice, offer you the proffered hand of friendship. Your twenty minutes more'n a hour's up, mister."

The security guard studied Merian through a pale thick fringe of sleepy lash as he escorted him to the elevator. He had a bug in his ear, just like a presidential guard. Wouldn't want to be carrying away any souvenir pens or ashtrays from Alamo Oxman's office. Merian wondered if the bug was connected to anything or just ear decor for a pretty security guard.

The smell of chlorine in the elevator going down was stronger. It must have been freshly squirted to overcome whatever New York germs Merian had tracked in.

The guard rode down with him and made a little half salute in farewell. "Now you enjoy our city," he said. "But it sure get cold out there at night."

"I thought this was a warm climate."

"You heard of John Kennedy? Sometime it get really cold out there."

So here was the romance of journalism, leading to the long distance wire with no new developments, the wrong time zone with no sleep in view, the hotel prime rib consumed by the stiff face of no companionship. Killing time is not an unpunished murder. Merian's exasperation and jitters ill behooved a distinguished veteran. Rougher climates than Dallas, static-blotted telexes and blackouts, distracted him from the normal journalist's blues. He was better at war than at creepy tycoons, better at revolution than at a city that went to its deserved country-western rest at night.

No revelations for Arnie or the world about Alamo Oxman. A staff of skilled accountants might dig something up, but the paper wasn't geared for that job.

The V.J. thought of getting a night flight the hell out of Dallas– Fort Worth, go anyplace else where he really wanted to be, but he was too irritated by his wild goose chase to inflict himself on Susan. He didn't want to inflict himself on himself, either. Arnie should have known, since he said aloud it would probably be futile, that it wasn't worth the trouble to poke through the layers of fat in order to try to reach the inner heart of the real Alamo Oxman. And now Merian had to take a night flight or stay in Dallas till morning. Not a fair choice.

Another prime rib "with our *au jus* sauce" in the hotel dining room to ease off the memory of the orange and brownie he didn't accept from Oxman's lunchbag. A double Scotch although this V.j. was not one of those hard-drinking v.j.'s who burn out at forty-five or earlier from too much of, among other things, drinking. Whatever was right.

As a special favor to the lonely salesman, the waiter put two little flags in a glass on Merian's table, the Lone Star Republic of Texas and the U.S. of A. He could tell Merian was in need. "Would you like some extra *au jus* sauce on the side?"

Here is how Susan seemed to be different from other women for Ralph Merian. He had always been able to forget his woman, if he happened to have one, during the hours of work. He would look at the world; he would look at his notes; he would think about these matters with a focus that was like lovemaking, but no tristesse afterward. And then afterward came the search for distraction with whatever happened to be available. He set out from the hotel if necessary. But Susan was like a buzz of hangover in his mind while he did other things, even pressing against the fat tycoon. He could feel her calm wary dry hands on him. He could feel her lips. He could feel her care.

What was worse, he cared about her and it got in the way.

In the wintry Dallas dusk, the sky yellow and failing, twister weather, he wished to be elsewhere, he wished to be someone else. It was the martini hour for those who used martinis. Maybe he should have. He wanted something only she could give him. He had believed in multiple options. He was not content with this failure of his system.

The elevator took him up to his room. A tiny Cambodian girl in a red tasseled Philip Morris midget suit worked the buttons and studied him without expression. She had seen this American condition before. It was merely a lonely man.

Merian was not alone in his room. A mint on his yellow pillow and the red button on his telephone was pulsing. A message, that's company. But Susan would wait for him to call. Who else? Maybe Arnie had some further clever idea that would keep him here in the Hilton for a day or two, or send him to another Hilton, because contemporary readers had the right to know, for an informed public is the bastion of, sure thing, and the tree of liberty must be watered by the ink of patriots. Maybe Arnie wanted to test some theory about Susan and him.

It was a Veterans Administration psychiatrist in San Francisco, area code 415, and he got through right away. "Doctor Alexandra Michalski here. Thank you so much for calling."

"I'm returning your call, Doctor. Is it about my brother?"

"Charles. Lately Charles has gotten somewhat... It might be helpful for you to visit Charles. Charles is no longer interfacing as well as we had hoped. We believe it isn't Charles's medication that is causing some concern about his possible, uh... and Charles is resisting hospitalization. In the present climate of adversary litigation there are lawyers who would... but in our staff's opinion I believe he is definitely pre... pree..."

"Pre what?"

"Pre-harm himself, we hypothesize. That's a consensus of my thought. But we can't just institutionalize Charles."

"Why not?"

"Mr. Merian, do you want to try to commit Charles?" The doctor seemed to think she had made a joke; her laughter filled his head in a room of the Dallas Hilton. "Charles is rational. Charles may be as rational as you and I."

Merian thought this over. "Maybe more so," he said.

"Dat's-a da trobble," she said. She was a VA doctor, stuck in a bureaucracy, but also safe there, all things considered, with the freedom of rules and routines surrounding her, not too bad a kind of freedom when you think about it—think of the paperwork other doctors go through—and she was also a fun-lover with a sense of what goes over big in clinic lounges. The routines of dealing with suicidal heroes of extinct wars required distraction. Boredom is the great enemy even in the most fascinating, highly paid, and prestigious forms of service to the community. She didn't mind sharing her jokes with a member of the immediate family.

"You're Italian, Doctor?" Merian asked.

"Polish-American is my ethnic persuasion, but I like to use my all-purpose accent to break the tension in situations like Charles. There's an analyst in LA, Reikian, *Theodore* Reikian, wrote the book on humor and I attended the seminar. The important factor is ego strength and defusing anxiety. I find it gets sixty, seventy percent results in some situations like these with the nearest responsible kin of Charles."

Merian began to revise his view of Dr. Michalski. From no view at all he now had a fuzzy one. Little came through the telephone except that he wasn't sure this Polish-American prankster was taking good care of his brother. "I'm sure jokes are productive," he said. "Chaz likes jokes. Okay, I'll come have a visit with him."

"That's entirely up to you, of course."

"I said I'm coming. I'm in Dallas now."

"It's a situation," she said. "I understand you're the journalist Ralph Merian. I think I used to read you when I had the time, didn't I?"

Merian kept the peace. He had no way of judging what she used to read in her spare time.

"It was very interesting, I think—concise. Maybe you should write about situations like Charles and the problems we face in this modern world of today, Ralph, with all the malpractice harassment suits that drive idealistic medical personnel uppa da wall."

Ralph Merian did not stop to consider the inconveniences of visiting his brother, because if he did so, he would postpone calling him, and then, because he was a responsible person, a fully grown elder brother of an orphan, he would go anyway. It was like the IRS, one of those stomach-churning pleasures of citizenship. Better to do the return early than to dread and dread and wait until it was too late and it got even more complicated.

He telephoned. His brother said, *"Who?"* and he answered, "Your brother," said Chaz said, *"Ralph?"* and he said, "You got any others?" and added, "Did I get you up?" and Chaz started to laugh through his cigaret wheeze as if this were one of their private childhood jokes. Well, in fact, Ralph used to bother him about sleeping so much.

"I never sleep unless I'm knocked out," Chaz said. "Yeah,

you caught me coming up from the knockout area. I been working on fixing the radio."

Merian said he had business in San Francisco, a story, an interview, something about oil and the Oxmans—when he lied, he preferred to keep a connection with the truth—and he would just like to catch up with his only and favorite brother.

"Oxmans who?" Chaz asked. "I don't read the papers. Take time to do what?"

Merian said he would be there the next day. He didn't wait to see if Chaz would invite him to camp out with him. He didn't expect to be met at the airport. He would call from the St. Francis Hotel.

"My place is kind of grungy or I'd ask you to stay here, but I don't even want you to see it if you can afford to stay at the St. Francis. Call me if they haven't disconnected my phone yet. But the radio works good now. Those slow vacuum-tube jobs ran okay in the durable department."

He was still doing a slow wheezy laugh when they hung up. So why did Dr. Michalski say he was depressed?

What durable radio?

The space-age fairground modules of Dallas–Fort Worth Airport weren't so bad. The plump tube of a Boeing 747 wasn't so bad. The blinking hubbub of San Francisco International Unfinished wasn't so bad. There are more important things in life; a fellow can learn to pass the time in thinking, for example.

Whenever possible, the V.J. took his ease, especially after arrival hassle. He specialized in wrinkled clothes and a ski bag with a long loop. Even when the shells were coming in, he liked to shower if the hot water was working, as it sometimes surprisingly did—no one else using it, he guessed—and stretch out, flex his back, the Official V.J. Unwinding Exercises. If the hotel was under direct fire, he had been known to do his back exercises on the floor of the shelter or among the panicked rats in the basement that now belonged to one liberation movement or another.

This was not the case at the St. Francis Hotel on Union Square in San Francisco. He did his back flexes while telephoning Chaz to confirm their fraternal summit meeting. He liked the black-and-gold decor of the St. Francis: black for the hearts of bankers, he thought, gold for the mining and railroad fortunes. But of course it was just some traditional splendid decorating motif. The Fleur de Lys wallpaper did not prove that Joan of Arc had received her marching orders here.

Chaz had been too busy to clean up his place, finishing a little wiring on that Zenith mother. He would prefer meeting and greeting his brother at the Black Sun Tavern on Castro Street; now let's set a time for this rare consultation—"try not to be bugged by the Swish Alps."

"Are you trying to tell me something?" Merian asked.

"Aren't you a star reporter, Ralph? Think of it as research for a guerrilla war that hasn't broken out yet. The turnstile at Castro and Market," he said, "won't let you out of BART, that's the underground—you call it the subway—if you have more than a twenty-eight-inch waist. Those Four-Wheel Drive People roar around with their Oregon and Colorado licenses and don't fight with them. Those buggers picked up their high ideals from Macho Man. You'll pass the White Swallow Bar—get it?—and keep on walking. You can get arrested for following too closely. Then there's the Hibernia Bank, we call it the Hibernia Beach, all the boys with their shirts off, their lean muscled tummies, and brother, if you see a kid with his pinkie in another kid's bellybutton, just assume they are engaged."

"Are you trying to tell me something?" Merian repeated.

"Persistent little buggerer, aren't you?" Chaz asked, laughing, and hung up. His emphysema had gotten worse.

Merian assumed his brother would be there, as promised. If not, he would go look for him at home.

When he did an interview or a background piece, Merian liked

199

to turn up early, stroll through the streets, touch the walls, furniture, security arrangements, traffic, poke the things, and breathe
the air of the place. He arrived at the corner of Market and Castro
by cab, therefore aboveground, avoiding turnstiles, half an hour
early, and walked up the little slope toward the Black Sun Tavern.
The frozen yogurt shops, Moorish theater, temples of drink and
sociability, theme fast foods, calzone, sushi, and pizza, Italian
and Japanese and piped-in Des Moines hamburgers, the no-hip
lads on the street whose jobs allowed them to devote twenty-four
hours a day to improving their social lives, the paperweight and
track-lighting shops, the clothing museums with the jeans on
mannequins backward in the windows, the bathhouses and Nau-
tilus workouts, the short-order snack windows, were all part of
an international civilization that had reached the East and West
sides of Manhattan, plus the Village, and also Picadilly, Saint-
Germain-des Près, and cozy back streets in Beirut, Amsterdam,
Copenhagen, and Stockholm. What was on the mind of his brother?
To astonish him? If so, he had a ways to go.

At the doorway of a Frogurt chapel, a black guy in fringy blue
jean cutoffs popped halfway out, murmuring his mantra, "Weed?
Coke? Speed?"

Merian said, "Narc? Snitch?"

The black guy was a muscle man, as if he had been working
out in a high-security yard for, say, five to seven years. He had
tight little hairs on his calves, even on his knees, where normally
the hair gets rubbed off. He squinted up red conjunctival eyes
and stared at this joker. "Lighten up, brother," he said. "Weed,
coke, speed, answer the question."

These streets, Merian decided, must be safer than people think.

It had been so long since he had seen Chaz—a couple of years
now—he wondered if maybe there would be one of those telltale
blank instants when a brother isn't sure he recognizes his only
brother. And suddenly Merian felt a yawning in his belly, like a
heart weakness further down, the sort of feeling that does no
work, like jealousy, like an attack of dysentery, for which there
is very little favorable to be said. So far he had not been able to

eliminate these moments. He remembered a Biafran doctor screaming at a child with kwashiorkor who had been sitting up a moment ago (about 4:00 PM, 3 May 1969), then had crumpled in the dust of the hospital yard at Ihiala. *Don't die! You cannot die!"* the doctor shrieked. But the child could and did. Over the years Ralph Merian had been spending his inventory of feeling in combat against grief. He was digging in the reserve tank and someday he would run on empty. *Chaz, be saved. Chaz, don't fail us both.*

The Biafran doctor wore wire-rimmed specs, red dust on the lenses, lips pouting and red eyes, like the ones of the recently friendly neighborhood pharmaceutical peddler; but the Biafran was in charge of an outdoor ward of huge-eyed, swollen-bellied, starving children. Those kids were finished. The doctor's name, Ojukwu, indicated Ibo money—relatives at the top. He might have come out okay, practicing medicine again in Port Harcourt, or he might be working in Ghana or the Ivory Coast, or he might have been killed toward the end. Merian said good-bye to him on 23 May 1969, and would never see him again.

The point in war, including civil war and revolution, including civil strife, including even student riots, is not to get involved past working hours. You might want to confirm a detail, but then nurse your own glass. The V.J. was not sure how to apply this rule to a long-term, round-the-clock brother.

In front of the Black Sun a young man stood negligently lighting his mouth with a torch, then spitting flames. It made an acetylene whoosh as he performed his stunt. A person can get singed doing that, but the flame-spitter seemed to know his business; it's a distinguished tradition, one proud step up from geek. As Merian paused, the flame-spitter offered him a volcanic mouth to kiss. He blew him a cloud of fire. Merian declined.

"Hard to get, man, too old to play that game," said the flame-spitter. "Might end your day with *nada.*"

"Street buskers generally don't argue with the folks," Merian said.

"This is Frisco, man, where we do whatever's right. Flame's

the name—how about just a little hug? I give good hug. I dig seamy faces like yours and those liver spots you get from old age."

Flirtation seemed inappropriate. Merian was here on family business, not investigative reporting or discussion of the wear and tear on his outer wrappings. The busker was shrugging as Merian moved on, and blew a spiteful blast of fire into his wake.

"I'm a jet, I'm a vet, I go down in flames!" the man called after him. "Wanna go down on Flames, anybody fresh?"

Two Castro clones—short hair, short mustaches, short tempers, tight small asses, boots on one, Adidas on the other, red farmer handkerchiefs in the appropriate pockets, signaling some code Merian had not gotten clear—stopped to giggle at him. I'm old enough, he thought; to them I'm a shaggy gray wolf. They were video arcade heroes. He was not in their game.

Ralph Merian believed he could endure better fire than the flame-eater, work tougher in bad climates than these Castro cowboys; it was not a question, and their laughter did not eat out his belly. A girl in jeans, frilly white blouse, freshblush on the cheekbones, was wiggling to the music outside a disco. Since she wasn't throwing flames, kisses, or insults, he offered her a smile. It flew into the sunny dry afternoon air, uncaught by the lady. She wasn't accepting smiles today. She was concentrating on the twitches and jerks of her speedy bony body, making very small steps while she improved her tan.

A voice nearby was saying, "My productivity went up maybe a hundred percent since I took the Advocate Experience."

"That's good? That's good?" asked his friend.

"I give more blow jobs. I take more."

"That's good," said the friend.

"But now I got fucking herpes, first simplex and then duplex. So what's the plus sign here?"

"I can't answer that," said his friend. "The plus sign might be you haven't got AIDS. But I get a shot of how they're bound to find the cure this year, next year. There's too much at stake. I bet before they find it, it's gonna be too late for the bathhouses, man—the CIA is behind it, that's the shot I get—"

"I did the Advocate Experience so I could up my productivity and now I'm into plain old celibacy with another herper. For this I left Grand Rapids?"

"I don't know, did you?" his friend asked. The friend had his own problems; now he wanted a turn. Merian got off the street, where it was always Independence Day. A couple of quick steps past the bouncer's empty stool and he was sitting at a little curve of bar near the Black Sun's brown-tinted window, waiting for Chaz, smelling the used air in here. It was a chilled and conditioned version of the air that used to be held on sun porches by screens—so thick it couldn't get through the mesh where Chaz and Merian were wrestling or playing Monopoly or whispering together as their parents shouted at each other inside. The smell of ashtrays here was different. On that porch, they could also sniff the insect spray that Chaz used to say was the smell of the dead flies underfoot. Chaz was being funny. The used-air smell was moved and pumped back and forth by bodies, by fans. It could almost make a person homesick for the chlorine breath of Alamo Oxman's executive elevator.

The place was occupied by gentlemen with a quick afternoon wiggle and jump in mind, or if not for today, just a wiggle and a suggestion of a jump in front of an audience of sensitive, feeling, caring, like-minded male persons. There was recorded music for the occasion. The man next to Merian stared at a young person who was approaching him with a match folder held between two fingers.

"I got your note," the young man was saying.

"You like it?" the matchbook writer asked. He pushed against his plaid shirt with a high belly.

"You could of just trucked on over, you don't have to try to be an author of notes. But it's kind of cute. Old-fashion." The young man, up close, was not so young as he seemed. He was just skinny, but his act was young and teasing. "Why not cute note plus also one single red rose?"

"You're worth it, I'm sure, but I see no red roses for sale in here. I go looking on the street, I go losing my place in line for you—your name's Terry, isn't it?" The older man, belly worn high through no choice of his own, pushing up and down, was breathing deeply in pursuit of calm. These were crucial times in a person's life.

"Why me? You go out and come back with the flower and I'm not here, you give it to some other kid, your best regards. You might find some real chicken in here if you lose me."

"I like you is the reason."

"That's a good one. I like that one."

"I bet you chew with your mouth open and no teeth, Terry."

A decision was being arrived at. The young man smiled. "Hey! A compliment!" he said, sliding next to him. "So who told you my name is Terry?"

Nearby, a fellow was doing a funky soft-shoe routine in airline booties that said Qantas on them, plus a stencilled koala bear. The music was from the sixties, Richie Havens singing "High-Flying Bird." These were nostalgic gray wolves in this place, or maybe they were the ones who spent the money and brought in the chickens. A rice queen with a Japanese boy (maybe Chinese). A paunchy Civil Service cowhand with a fourteen-year-old runaway with zits and a San Antonio high school T-shirt (how does the Black Sun settle with the Alcoholic Beverages Board inspectors?). Merian had an appointment to meet his brother Charles among these simple honest souls who enjoyed their simple honest pleasures.

Now Johnnie Ray singing "Cry."

Now the Everly Brothers: "Wake Up, Little Susie."

For these folks it was a steady round of rhythm, nostalgia, poppers, and chickens. It might not be elevator music they were living by. It was *fast* elevator music, loud elevator music. For his brother's world Ralph Merian would have preferred the keening of Arabs and Greeks, the rhythm chanting of central Africans. This loony American clamor was not home to him.

Yet, as he waited among natives of a strange land, he was pleased that Chaz and he were finally visiting each other again.

204

They might have a good talk, tell a few of the old stories, check on the progress and the lack of progress of things. A coziness of anticipation washed through him. These family nostalgias were unpredictable; Merian sometimes felt them in new places—once a flood of longing for his mother in the Hotel Oloffson in Port-au-Prince, another time an epidemic of dreams of his father in Upper Volta, although he no longer even remembered the color of his father's eyes. He was here to see Chaz, Chaz would appear in a moment, he could check on the color of his eyes. Merian was contented.

The sun glinted through the amber glass, and outside on Castro, the boulevard of boys, it was forever springtime. Merian ordered an espresso and a brandy. The bartender, a mentholated lumberjack fresh from the redwood forests, asked without commas: "Coo-vwa-zay Remy Martin or Mohawk, sir? Napoleon is extra."

"Napoleon," said the V.J., and through the door came a person bearing down on him with smiling conviction—the family space between the front teeth—plumper than he recalled him to be, with a spongy nose, spongy orangish skin, a slack plumpness, and yet the boyishness was still there as he touched Merian's hand. "Chaz," Merian said.

"Ralph. Hey, Ralph. Let's move to a booth, okay? I'll take the coffee, you take the hard stuff, I'm not even supposed to touch it with my little finger and sniff."

They settled into a dark corner that smelled of colognes, aftershaves, disinfectants, and non-locker-room effluvia that didn't belong in a proper health club. This was not a health club. Men were dancing on a little platform near the jukebox. There were splinters of glass underfoot. They had to lean toward each other to be heard. Merian resolved not to complain when his brother lit a cigaret and began steadily blowing the smoke at him; this was part of the deal. Chaz said, "To answer a few basic questions right off: Doc says the emphysema is picking up steam, Doc says I might as well smoke since I'm not gonna stop anyway, Doc wants to know if I think I'm Jesus anymore but I say not, Doc says I got to stay on the Thorazine they tried lithium didn't help but I'm getting there anyway. It adds to the weight, Ralphie. Watery fat it gives me, I'm not my slim and lovely self. But I got your radio for you."

"Glad to see you, Chaz."

"The hell you are. Shit no you're not. And nobody calls me that anymore. It's Charlie around here."

"I'm closer to you than they are."

The orangish spongy face closed down for a moment. The eyes fell shut. "I guess so," he said. "That's part of it."

"You want me to call you Charlie?"

"Any damn thing you like, Ralphie. But I got your radio for you anyway. I should have fixed it before now and I been too busy is all. I never got it off my mind, Ralph, no matter how busy I got with my own stuff. I thought about it, just had to take the time to pick up a little solder, a little wire or two, couple of those old-fashioned vacuum tubes take a minute to warm up, Ralphie—"

"Hey!" Merian held up his hand. Chaz stopped at the command. Merian said, "What is this you're talking about?"

"Your little table-model Zenith, man..." He paused and sketched an invisible oval in the air with both hands. He twirled imaginary knobs. "Sort of his master's voice, you know? Only a postwar Zenith before the transistors and the printed circuits. I'm sorry I didn't do it before, but I been busy, plus when I thought I would have it done tomorrow, I was looking for you and you were, well, you wouldn't want to carry one of those big table models overseas with you—"

"Chaz, slow down, please."

"Slow down please slow down sleaze slow down you're in a pear tree."

"I don't know you when you're like this, Chaz."

The spongy nose wrinkled coyly at him. "Oh, that's a good one. Ooh, that's terrific. When I'm like this he doesn't know me. He can turn being a brother on or off like he always did."

Chaz gazed at the invisible judge above the sun on the wall to whom he offered testimony. Merian followed his gaze toward the crumple of vinyl that was the emblem of the Black Sun.

With a nonbrother, a fellow should just stand up at this point, pay the bill if he hadn't already, and get the hell out. Merian did not do this. With Chaz, he tried something very clear and precise, one step at a time. "Refresh my memory about the radio. You always had a good memory and I still have to write things down. The spiral notebook was invented for me. I run on three-by-five cards."

"My doc says I'm manic when I feel depressed, I go down when the world is just marvelous, but when was that? She thinks that makes sense and she gets paid for it. I always remember I was an engineer in the navy and I promised to fix your radio. I just got involved. Got myself committed that's a joke. I been looking for you for years, brother of mine, but you're never around. Supposing I still had your radio, how would I find you?"

"Chaz, what the hell? You remember the one we had in our room when we were kids, listened to Fred Allen and Jack Armstrong?"

"The All-American Boy? I wouldn't remember? You shitting your own kin, Ralphie?" For company their parents had given them twin beds. Separate rooms were out of the question, and besides, this meant they would be close friends in addition to brothers. When Ralph was the Lone Ranger, Chaz was Tonto. He liked to examine the innards of the radio to see if anything changed, anything lit up differently, when the announcer proclaimed that the Lone Ranger originated in Detroit, Michigan, Station WLW, and Ralph said pay attention to the story, not the radio. . . . "I told you I'd do it for you, just charge for the parts, if any, no labor, gratis, all that gratis of any charge, just as a kid brother and all. The Zenith. Nice little table model before they brought in FM to confuse the people."

Both Merians had a thin vein, like a misplaced hair, snaking across their foreheads. They were both sometimes explainers to excess. Kin they were. They each suffered from unquenched hope; perhaps Chaz didn't anymore. He was staring intently at Ralph's hands and his lips were pursed as if he were humming.

The Black Sun gave them too much other music, sexy bass juke-box boomings, to hear the low sounds Chaz was making. Ralph Merian kept telling himself to wait, see what his brother had in mind. "Why do you do like this?" Chaz asked, imitating a twitch-ing flight of bird wings, fingers leaping.

"Do I?"

"You caught the Parkinson or something in one of those tropical virus places, I think I read you were in Yemen?"

"No."

"What then?"

"Nervous, I guess. Maybe I'm trying to get your attention."

"You got it, Ralph. You got it all the time. Even when I don't see you. You got it."

Merian knew about that twitchiness in his hands. It was a caress in the noisy air that touched nobody. It was the desire to touch his brother.

"...so I didn't want to bring it in here because somebody'd just knock it over," Chaz was saying. "After all my trouble, didn't want to go having to fix it all over again when parts are so hard to find these days and the solder is probably full of cancer, Ralphie. So I left it home. But you can't pick up just now because my place is a pigpen—people do that. You were always the nice little housekeeper between us. Your side of the room, right?"

"Okay, Chaz."

"So another few minutes without your Zenith won't kill you."

Chaz was smiling and looking straight into his eyes and coldly enraged about the trouble Ralphie had put him to.

Gradually it came into focus. Ralph Merian wasn't sure at what point concentration on his brother and listening to what his brother was saying and remembering his brother and noting what the V.A. joker, Doctor Michalski, had to say about his brother all came together to bring back the giant wired mouth and ear, the shattered fruitwood cabinet, of the Zenith radio that Chaz had wanted to put back together just as he was diagnosed sick, di-agnosed from crazy kid to crazy person, from navy engineer to disabled veteran, moving fast into disrepair while he promised

208

to do this one little thing for his big brother to show how much he loved him.

Twenty years ago?

At least.

Chaz had taken that discharge from the navy, taken the shock treatment, taken the release from the hospital, taken the disability payment, moved from youth to the next time in a man's life, moved to San Francisco. Now here he was in the Black Sun Tavern on Castro Street, not wanting his only brother to see where he lived and how.

Merian would not have minded if Chaz lived with a man or boy who cared for him. Love was rare enough; no stipulations needed to be added; Ralph, the big brother, was living proof of that. But he was sure Chaz lived alone, too.

He would not have minded the papers, the dirty clothes, the splintered floors, the pieces of junk equipment like a forty-year-old who had scattered his toys near his bed—he expected them. He would not have minded sinking into a Goodwill chair like the one he too kept on Riverside Drive, and talking with his brother or not talking as the haze of the city settled into night and the wet clouds slid through the Golden Gate. If the radio didn't exist anymore, he could live with that. Susan and his own life in a space capsule, Hawkfeather, Jarls Coyote, the Stony Apaches, and doing his job had made Chaz not so strange to him. The craziness was right here in the family. He was ready to pay attention to his brother.

When Chaz got out of the navy, then out of the hospital, he took to another uniform, white shirts with short tab collars, shiny black pants, thin-soled DuPont Corfam shoes that he bought by mail with special prices for double pairs; he got a job as a utilities engineer at a level comfortably below his training and capacity as he adopted the YMCA loser's uniform. He stuck to the uniform. He didn't hold the job long. Disability money was enough to give him what he settled for. The clothes disguised a man who had briefly been the Savior of the World, now suffering from lack of recognition.

Friends and women cost money, comfort costs money, travel and strawberries and books cost money, so Chaz did without. He spent his monthly check on coffee, cigarets, and furnishings from Goodwill that don't wear out a person's financial resources. "I'm sufficient to my own," he said. The thickness of speech was supposed to be temporary, but it left him slowly, as if he were fond of the elegant formulations it forced upon him. "Electricity is my poetry," he said, which at the time only meant he was working for the utility company. He had gone into the power field after the double series of charges into his frontal lobes. It seemed a shame not to use all that electricity he had learned to store.

"Chaz," Merian asked, aware of his hands, keeping them still, ducking under the tides of oldies and newies, disco and reggae from the jukebox, a grand old Wurlitzer that gay rescue had brought out of some dusty warehouse, "Chaz, are things going okay?"

"That's a very question I can't rightly answer. As I stated to the committee of doctors when they asked if I'm Jesus, I'm not even a prophet anymore, I'm not a saint, I give you the very answer I gave them. I could be a sinner, but I'm not telling, Ralphie." Slyly he winked at his brother. The steady frown, the wrinkling of the brow with its orangish skin, the pinching of the orange lips, were mitigated by fraternal conspiracy looks. They used to be funny together. Chaz couldn't wink at the doctors. They used to have their own private jokes and routines. Chaz reached into his pocket and put a handful of silver on the table. They used to play coin games, chance and skill games, penny toss, but of course now he only wanted to pay for a round of anything his brother wished. The mouth was working to make an offer of hospitality. Merian resolved to go slow, ride with him.

"You're not sore at me?" Chaz asked. "It's been heavy on my mind. I know I was unprofessional all the way, Ralphie. Even with a brother, professionalism is called for. First of all, do a little simple tinker job like fix a radio, for a trained electrical engineer, work on weapons systems, big guns, night vision, infrared sights, Varo Manufacturing, apparently had a mind just as good as any sibling—no sweat it should be. And in these matters, secondly, *not* to do it when I said I would. It's a burden to me, Ralph. An obligation like this should not be laid on a troubled person who used to have the gift of prophecy until the VA hospital relieved him of it."

"We can still do anything we want to do," Ralph said. "It may be exaggeration, but that's how I try to live."

"You always had that thought, Ralphie."

"You're younger than I am. You could still get the jump on me, Chaz."

Chaz looked at him through the thickened orange mask. It was smooth and ageless and filled with pity. He was familiar with self-delusion. Bedside manners were not appropriate for a brother. Chaz sighed and gave Ralph a chance to do better, try again.

It was okay with both of them that two dancers in combat boots were clumping together nearby, but it was less okay when hips bumped against Ralph Merian, moving out of the boundaries of dance territory painted in a silver semicircle near the giant Wurlitzer, and that was more okay than the dancers making a point of it, making rhythmical hip bumps against a bystander fellow who was just enjoying an afternoon with his long-unvisited kid brother. Merian slid his chair away and stared through the neon murk at the rhythm boys. The stare was intended to make words unnecessary. The butch bumper, a Bekins Moving & Storage hunk with freshly wetted hair, grinned at him, as if he could be next to mix it up a little. Did Merian want a fist in the face and would Chaz stand by him if his brother started a stupid brawl in the Black Sun Tavern?

An electric smell surrounded them. It was the smell of Chaz over the telephone when they sometimes talked, a smell of wiring and electricity and memory. Here it was thicker, drink, crotches, cologne raised by body heat, but still that telephone presence of Chaz. There was acid in it, too. Maybe it was in the innards stench of a radio—batteries, tubes, heated rubber and filaments.

The words of Chaz flew and evaporated, yet he followed Ralph Merian wherever they went. Long ago, when they shared a room, it was the smell of his brother's bedclothes on Saturday morning when he slept until someone tipped the mattress over or squeezed a wet cold washcloth on the stubborn ten-year-old sleeper's face. Ralph did that.

His pilot light had blown out. There was also the smell of gas. Chaz reminded his brother of mechanical things not running very well, although he had always been clever with his hands, fixing wires and fuses and gears, the bicycles that his older brother bent. At Merian's age the sense of smell was supposed to fade.

"You're not sore I took so long? You sure?"

"Not at all, not at all."

"'Cause I thought maybe that's why you been avoiding me these years—a card on Christmas was the last time, Season's Greetings, wasn't it? I kept an eye out for you. I kind of resented you avoiding me like this, around all these corners of life where I looked for you, but I suppose you had a right, my being sick and neglecting the Zenith after I promised and you just couldn't face me, I suppose—"

"Not at all!"

"Well, it's not upfront of you, let me point that out," Chaz said. "It turns out I wasted a very lot of my time telling people I was the Savior when what good did it do? I don't tell people stuff that'll just waste my and their time anymore. Season's Greetings is good enough for me these days. Fellow says he'll fix it and then he goofs off completely, you really don't need that, do you, Ralph?"

Merian held up one hand, *stop*. Chaz was beginning to feel like a wall in front of him, growing perpendicular extensions like two more walls, and Merian could predict his becoming a set of walls, a box that just closed in and down and around him. "Chaz," he said, "it's really okay. Listen to what I'm saying, I *forgot* about the radio. A long time ago I stopped worrying about it. I came here to have a little visit with you."

Chaz shook his head. He wasn't going to let his brother just indulge a sick man. Since he was well now, not a savior or a prophet, just a Season's Greetings person like anybody else, he wanted to take responsibility for the way things really were. He said, "You shouldn't have given up on me, Ralphie. I understand completely, all the implications, it's getting through now, but you should have more confidence in your kid brother. Somebody else took the same very line with me. That shrink I sued, you know, the one messed me up like that, he kept saying not to worry about it, but I knew what he was really thinking—irresponsible. I had an airtight case, but he paid off the courts, the judge, he even got to my lawyer, the cops, the attendants, and had them give me that first series of electro. Treatments they call it, but it's electromadness, Ralph. I forgot about it for a while, just like he said I would, but then it came back to me. I'm still remembering facets, Ralph. All the facets come home to me. I admit seeing you again like this, with all your reproaches about the Zenith, how you slug it into me, doesn't help, Ralph."

Merian only had one brother, but there was also another life besides this one with Charles Merian in the Black Sun Tavern on Castro Street in San Francisco. He was beginning to chart exits. Plans and procedures occurred to him. Backward, before the walls closed down, into the doorway, and out; across the traffic and into a cab going whichever way it happened to be going under the sky. He would prefer to walk someplace alone. His heart didn't pound like this during a war or revolution. Why did a loved brother, a loved woman, do this to him? Just like a war or revolution, a person can't do anything about those things, either.

He could still see edges of daylight around Chaz. The walls hadn't closed down yet.

"I'll fix it now," Chaz said. "I'll deliver it personally."

"I have transistors," Ralph said. "That thing must be practically a museum piece, Chaz."

"Free of any charge and gratis. What you choose to do with it is your own business."

"Chaz, try to listen, we've got better things—"

"I'm not so irresponsible like that doc and you tried to claim."
He put his hand on Ralph's forearm. He was drawing him close
so that his attention would not wander. He believed in taking one
matter at a time; a person can't save the world without moving
very carefully. "Irresponsible means you not only don't do the
radio, you forget about it. Okay, so I didn't take care of it for a
while due to the situation, but I didn't forget about it, either. My
own personal situation wasn't too perfect, but nobody is. I understand that. And yet I didn't let it out of my mind, no matter
how I got irrigated by the course of treatments, Ralphie. They
told me shock is like kicking a radio to make it work. Sometimes
it does. That helped. New connections or the old ones get sharper.
I never forgot."

"Let go of it now," Ralph said. "It's okay with everyone."

He would not run away. He would sit here in the Black Sun
Tavern and live with it. He would give up whatever it took. He
would just let go and ride with it. That wasn't much to give for
a brother. He would listen, he would stay while Chaz presented
his case.

"And nobody's going to trap me into irresponsible, either. That
Zenith is a perfect example from the time when you didn't take
FM for granted, nobody did."

Ralph slowly moved his arm to see if the grip would loosen.

"It's a beautiful stained cabinet. It's got detailing. Come on,
stop jerking like that. People'll think we're fags? We look too
much like brothers. Course everybody here looks like related
brothers. That gold medallion with the Zenith lightning, the stars,
the earth, the whole universe with the Zenith crown on it. I had
a flash about that medallion right there on the speaker, Ralph.
That was just trim! It didn't mean what it said—the whole world
and more. It implied more than it delivered, if you get my drift.
It promised, but it was like Mom and Dad, you know what I
mean? Brought us into the world with a medallion on us and
then . . . Don't think I'm losing the train, Ralph. We both got the
same bellybutton. For the insides, I never got around yet to doing
the diddlypiss engineering. I'm sure it isn't serious. Not just

214

tubes, on the one hand, but on the other hand, it probably isn't really basic. A circuit. This isn't one of those cheap printed circuits the Japs bring in. The rice queens show up all the time around here, unlike some brothers I know. I think it's a frayed wire maybe, Ralph. Loose. It's not color-coded. Hard to pick it out if you're not trained in Zenith theory, and your handbook is long disappeared into the mists of history, Ralph—"

"Where that radio should be now," Merian said, "assuming it wasn't incinerated in the town dump—"

"Where we grew up," Chaz said.

"—would be an interesting story. The Story of the Radio." He thought he might try to tease his brother's grip off his arm. "In a dump, buried in man-made earth someplace, filling in part of a swamp or a development. Or who knows, like you say, maybe alive and chattering in the ghetto, if somehow it got to a used radio-teevee shop and some kid bought it."

"That kid'd prefer to rip off a new one, Ralph. You been out of the country and away from family too long. That kid'd put on his sneakers—did I say that? I didn't hear myself say that, Ralph. I have a policy not to make unfounded accusations against kids whose guilt has not been proven. I suffered too much from unfounded accusations myself."

Kidding might not be the best way to deal with a brother's little paranoia, little mania, little depression. The condition of being a brother was established for Merian, for both Merians, Ralph and Charles, and yet they had never mastered it. "Are you trying to hint on me," Chaz said, "a kid could fix what's wrong with that Zenith? Some talented ghetto kid with tricky moves? Or because I didn't get to it in time, due to being otherwise engaged, a course of shock, being picked up by the police like that when you weren't around to help me explain to them, it landed in a trash dump? Before they called it recycling, Ralph? Are you trying to blame me for what happened maybe twenty years ago, that very difficult period of my life, you were making a big career jump I suppose, getting that nomination for the Pulitzer?"

"It was a Nieman fellowship, Chaz. I went to Harvard for a year. No big deal."

"Easy for you to say, Ralph. Drinking coffee in a seminar with leather chairs and patches on the sleeves, tweedy stuff, and I was getting my forehead greased for the electrodes. The only leather patches were on my wrists and ankles. Straps. The Vaseline in the hair. It's all yucky, Ralph, the whole kick-the-wiring deal. You were wearing natural-shoulder equipment and fucking Nieman female fellows in pretty dresses, weren't you? I bet, your background in the Third World, you get lots of left-wing love. I was strapped down and buzzed."

"This isn't necessary, Chaz. Do you want me to go home?"

"Is that a threat? You got a home?"

Merian considered the question. "Not exactly. Not for sure." He thought of his high-ceilinged room for R and R on Riverside Drive, the grit and stale fabric smells that greeted him, grit in summer and steam heat in winter, and said, "I've got a rent-controlled place they'd like to condominiumize."

"Condo sweet condo," said Chaz. "With music and news in every corner, plus talk shows to your heart's content. How many speakers?"

"Chaz, you're my brother. The radio doesn't matter. I forgot it years ago."

"Easy for you." Chaz narrowed his eyes shrewdly. "Look how you remember the exact date. As I recall, you were using a car radio as your house radio. Now what I need to know is this: How did you happen to get a car radio to replace the one I was engaged to fix? Why a car-automobile radio? It doesn't make sense, Ralph, now be reasonable, no cabinet, rotten speakers—normally they count on the body of the car itself to provide resonance—why of all things a car radio with its guts hanging out? That's been bothering me, Ralph. Heck, as you are wont to say, it's time we got this straight. How could I work on a circuit—soldering takes a steady hand, you understand that—when I'm trying to figure why my big brother does a dumb thing in his decorating scheme like a car radio?"

Try, try, assume he would tire of it finally and get down to things. Brother and brother were the facts of the case. "I had this jalopy," Ralph said. "Paid a hundred for it, thought I'd drive out to the country sometimes, had a lady friend. But the garage costs. And the glass started to frost over. To fix the glass would cost more than the car was worth—"

"I do electrical. I don't do glazing or pane repair."

"I know, I know. Let me finish. So I sold it for junk, only it happened just when that radio went out—"

"Stop rubbing it in. I should have done it right away."

"No matter, Chaz. I used the radio from the jalopy until—that was how it happened."

Chaz curved his fist around an invisible glass. He knew enough not to take alcohol. Ralph signaled a waiter and mouthed the word "Coke." This lad in blue jeans and work shirt was the waiter, wearing the same general outfit as everyone else, only lumberjack shirts on the hunkier ones, or maybe boots rather than Adidas.... The lad was floating here and there with a tray, dollar bills between his fingers. It was easy to pick him out if you have a keen logical mind, as the V.J. did. The lad was on his mission and would return.

"You think it'd cost more to fix that frosted glass—that's what *you* say. But if you're telling me the truth, Ralph, whole truth and nothing but, and the car still drove good, you could go to a junkyard and pick up some old glass, make sure it's safety glass, laminated is how they do it, and install it yourself—well, not you, you're not handy, but get some handyman to do it, some talented kid, and you'll have a great little car again plus some talented ghetto kid picks up a nice few bucks. It's Found Money. I can't do it, Ralph, not my line. Everybody's a specialist. You do reporting and I do electrical. What kind is it?"

"Kind?"

The floating waiter fitted the mug of Coca-Cola neatly into the grasp of Chaz and lifted his fist and put it down on a square of paper napkin. Chaz did not seem to notice, as if the fist were catatonic, although the rest of him was not. "Brand," he said.

"Label, mark, kind. Dodge, Studebaker, Buick kind, Ralph."

"Chevy," Ralph said. "That was a long time ago. Chaz, can we ask other questions? Do you have friends you see in the neighborhood? Does the VA get your checks to you on time? If you don't want to write me, why don't we talk on the phone more often?"

"Chevy. Chevy. Hmm. I wouldn't necessarily of guessed that. It just doesn't make sense, Ralph, if it's as good a car as you indicate to me it is, get rid of it for junk. Just doesn't make very sense, Ralph, even a long time ago. That's planned obsolescence, Ralph, and you're falling right into their hands. You're a victim worse than me if you do that. And I know you're not. You're not the loser in this family, Ralph. I'm the loser in this family. Maybe you're not remembering so good. Maybe we ought to go back over it again and—"

"No, *no*," Merian said.

Chaz stared. The walls were closing down. There was a thick pulsating from the jukebox—"Blue Moon, I saw you standing alone"—the bass turned up. Chaz looked at his Coke, seemed surprised to find it, and made a series of neck-wagging gulps at it, like a cowboy taking his beer with championship efficiency. He licked his lips. "That's better. Who bought this round for me? Now you see why I don't call or write so often, Ralph, how hard it is to get a straight story from you. Plus you keep rubbing it in, don't you, how I let you down. You never did forgive—never. Some people say okay, let bygones be bygones, that's my understanding, big brother, but not you, not this guy I'm talking to straight for the first time in maybe many a year, laying it all out, because we're too close to fool around anymore, but not you, not this guy, he just keeps reminding me of the troubles of my past—"

Personal and private and enduring sorrow was everybody's right. Merian wished his brother might enjoy the general human privilege, even then, but the eyes of Chaz were distant and hooded beneath the agitation. There was a darkness that did not enclose his grief. He was talking and flashing unseen electricity from his

218

eyes. There was a storm rumbling from afar. He was sending messages of pain and Ralph Merian did not know how to ease him. Merian wished to drench his brother in memories of telling stories to each other, murmuring each other to sleep during humid summer evenings while the neighbor's radio throbbed at them from a screened back porch, "without a dream in my heart, without a love of my own," songs of crooning romance or excited night baseball games. They used to pretend to be sleeping when their parents came to shush them. It was useless to summon these memories when Chaz was not ready for them. He had another past in mind, he was chattering above the throb of the Wurlitzer, its base turned up and thumping, no one in this Black Sun space thinking of summer childhood and the love between brothers. He might have told him last year, another time, but this was today.

"Electro, plus all that life I wasted on the lawsuit, which was thrown out of court on my ass without even a Hello-I'm-sorry, and now here I am on the West Coast, trying to make a new start like any American got a right, and you, my only brother, probably the only one I'll ever have, you draw this picture of the perfectly good radio which it got wasted—*you* say—because of *my* neglect—"

Ralph Merian longed to see a woman in the Black Sun Tavern, a slovenly and beautiful one, or just any girl, neither beautiful nor slovenly, but someone real and fleshly and unwasted. He longed to see Susan.

"—and also junking a perfectly good little Chevy—"

"Chaz! What time is it?"

Charles Merian paused, sighed, lowered his voice to whisper the secret. Secrets always get a person's attention. *"You're* not wearing a watch, Ralph, and *I* don't even own a watch. So let neither of us, in this case *you,* feign surprise at how late it might suddenly have come to be. What it really very is: you wanting to avoid facing the consequences of this here conversation is what it is." And his voice rose again over the music of five synthesized all-boy disco cowhands: "Which was purely and simply how very sorry I am about not getting to your fucking goddamn

Zenith right away, like I said I would, because I just got hung up on psychological matters, legal matters, plus some personal stuff—"

"I'm trying my best to listen, Chaz. Don't get mad at me."

"I'm not mad, I'm just explaining. Excuse the language. I'll wash out my mouth with fucking soap. So they let me out on condition I didn't leave the state, didn't bother that rotten shrink anymore, the psychiatrist, didn't threaten him except once or twice when I couldn't sleep for thinking how he fucked me over, didn't do those things in the middle of the night anymore that I had to do because he got me beat in my case, and so after I tried everything I could try legally, writs and shit—excuse—naturally the physical thing was my court of last recourse, even as it was at the Court of Herod—"

"Chaz! Don't!"

"—but I left the state like they said, knowing you were bound to come through here on your way to some force and violence in the Philippines, say, or Vietnam or goddamn anyplace but your own head or mine, so then I could spend a few minutes with you and straighten out this difficult matter of the radio, between brothers in a decent way, make sure you weren't still causing me a lot of trouble, just ease right over it, sending out transistor signals like you practically admitted to me openly you were, Ralph, when we were kids and everybody thought vacuum tubes was all they had. Let's be honest at last, brother. I never do anybody any harm unless they ask for it. But it sure isn't what I consider a decent kind of behavior to spend twenty years after me, on my trail, and avoiding me with your high-beam signals, just because of a lousy inconvenient time it was to fix a radio, Ralph—stop! Don't think you can just step away from me! *Ralph, please!*"

Ralph Merian was standing by the table, his back to his brother, and it was like standing at a tomb, despite the young men nearby with their hands in each other's jeans, goofy smiles on their faces, not dancing anymore, merely standing there, waiting for the discovery which was the meaning of their lives. He turned and looked at Chaz. The orange skin. The puffiness. The drugs not working. He said, "You're flying, Chaz. I don't know what I can do. I never have known. If I could help you, I think I would, I think I'm ready to try. But I don't see how."

"Just sit with me, Ralphie."

"I've been doing that."

"What if I promise I'll talk slower?"

Merian wondered if he could do it.

"Does it seem like I been speeding in a fifteen-mile-limit area?"

Merian laughed and sat down. "Try, Chaz."

Chaz said, "I know you been making an effort. I been pouring it on and you been listening. I am aware, Ralph. I am disabled but not a hundred percent."

"You're upset."

Chaz nodded. Neither spoke. Ralph Merian wanted to put his arms around his brother. The Black Sun drinkers and dancers with hands in each other's jeans were on to a truth, but they had it mixed up with other matters. Merian said, "Are there people for you to talk to?"

"Dr. Michalski. The VA shrink. The Women's Movement made them an Equal Opportunity Employer, so this blonde shrink with the funny hair and the case load is dealing with a bunch of screaming Vietnam vets. I don't believe their nightmares or mine are anything like that lady's, Ralph."

Chaz was switching into a different mode. It gave Ralph hope for him, how he could usually pull back before it was too late. Now he was in the zone of irony. He understood that Ralph was ready to give up, get up, go; he knew it was on the verge, and so he was able to stop the rattling and shrilling. There had been all that swiftness with manic aim; now he was stopping to sight things. "Ralph, you got your head on one side at me. You're trying to listen, but I may be talking too much."

"We haven't had much of a chance lately. I came here for the pleasure of my only brother."

"I appreciate that, Ralphie. Thanks—trying to catch up too fast. A person can't play catch-up, anyway, that's not how it works." He too cocked his head, listening to the echoes in what

221

he had just said. "Can't play catch-up. . . . Look at that cowboy."

A man in an "Ask Me" tee shirt, with a metal belt buckle spelling the name WELLS FARGO hanging loosely from the jeans into which he had been sewn, was sitting alone at the bar, giving funky little slaps at the edge of it along with the music. He was inviting approval of his rhythm section. It was Human Offering Time here, and these were the humans to be first examined, then offered. Ralph believed it a good sign that Chaz seemed interested in the place where they were meeting. He seemed amused. They shared something recent. Good old Chaz. The Ask Me man caught their eyes on him, gave a final little tattoo in his finger drum solo against the bar, and turned to reveal the back of his tee shirt: "Then Tell Me."

Ta-*ta*, his uplifted hands and eyebrows stated.

"They start that go-away closer shit, they're worse'n women," Chaz said. "They start that I just rather have me a cold beer if I think my lithium'll take it. Thorazine, it definitely won't."

Ralph thought he might as well ask now as any other time, if he was going to ask at all. "Chaz, are you telling me something else? This place. I didn't know. Are you telling me you're, uh, is this your word—gay?"

Chaz measured his response carefully. "I'm going to answer that question," he said. "Mostly I'm occupied." And he stared at Ralph to dare him to ask what this meant. "Most women I got well acquainted with, though that wasn't true of Patricia Ann, they didn't have clean undies."

Ralph shrugged. "It's your business."

"I find the same thing is true of most men. They'll dress so precise, but then you take a good look at their jockey shorts—"

"Okay," Ralph said, "enough. That's why God invented the bathtub and the shower."

"I suppose I been running at the mouth, Ralphie."

"Less so now, Chaz."

They fell silent. In the throb and neon and smells and excess decor, connections were being made between others. These brothers also wished for a connection. Ralph Merian was thinking,

Well, why not meet here? Why not anyplace? "Let's forget the—" he said. He did not finish the sentence. "You've had a complaint about me so long it's practically legitimate. I know you mean it. The Statute of Limitations does not expire. Why don't you just finish? You always say I don't listen, but I'm listening now."

"Okay." Chaz also drummed with his fingers on the shiny black disc of table, but he wasn't slapping to the music. He was getting himself organized. He had a daughter in Miami he wrote to sometimes, maybe a letter a day for two weeks, then nothing for a year. Patricia Ann used to reply to his letters with finger paintings, then scrawls, then even words (DEAR DADDY I GO TO SCHOOL NOW), and there would be a note from his former wife, saying, Pay up, crud, I'm sending you her letters. And then Patricia Ann's letters stopped and Chaz believed it wasn't necessary to pay up. They all had it coming to them, including himself. That's what can befall a person whose brain works too fast for the rest of his mind.

"Okay," he repeated, "I used to be Jesus—what a crazy idea, how could I tell strangers a thing like that, a veritable recipe for trouble—till they put on the electro. They kicked my radio till I decided it wasn't worth it. I used to worry about your Zenith I promised you, but today I stopped worrying, maybe two, three, ten minutes ago."

"Right," said Merian. It might be safe just to assent to what Chaz offered and not add any new elements.

"The problem is, brother, here's the problem. It don't look fair. It looks like I get all the advantages of you, but aren't looks always deceiving—don't I know that! For instance, I get to sleep and you are working your very ass off. But why is that? Because you like it, snooping for a living, and all I get to do is sleep. I get *put* to sleep. See what I mean? So in the end it isn't fair to *me,* brother."

"Stay awake then."

"So you're working your very ass off and you like it and what good does staying awake do me? It only gives me the insomnia."

"The bad dreams," Merian said.

"You got it. I guess you know a little about that, too." Chaz considered the possibility. He gave it some thought. "You might worry a little. But you can also run off at the mouth, can't you, Ralphie, like I been doing? On some good occasion or other?"

Merian wondered if he should violate his recent resolution just to listen and give assent. Chaz seemed to get more nervous when he withdrew into caution; the brothers could still tune into each other's stations. Paying attention might include adding something of his own: how he too had love troubles. But would Chaz hear it as a trouble that a woman with a good nature was dumb enough to care about him? How he was growing old. But wasn't Chaz and everybody damn else just a couple of years behind him? How he was passing through San Francisco and worried about his only close family. But wasn't that something Chaz had to contend with, too, having a brother?

Instead of any of this, he clung to his professional modes, patience, caution, and watchfulness, as if he were in a Beirut basement or attending to an irate molybdenum speculator or President of an Indian nation. He said, "I'm like you in lots of ways."

"Sure, okay. A little heavier. In my own style I'm lighter, if a guy who doesn't tell anybody he could save the world and fix everybody's radio is light. Not anymore I don't. Trouble is, I think you lost the honky-tonk part of you, Ralphie. I got the cleanup detail."

"How do you know what I lost and need?" Merian was fraying despite his resolutions. Maybe Chaz wanted it that way. "How can you tell what I dream of when I can't sleep, which is often enough—"

"Which is never for me?" Chaz asked.

"What makes you think because you're sick you're more honest!"

Chaz grinned and showed the dark spaces between his remaining teeth. As a kid, he used to make Ralph laugh with his joke of putting a raisin on his teeth to hide them. Did he remember? Now no raisins were necessary. "I used to drive an old

224

Skylark till I ran out of, well, I ran out of Driver's License and Pattie Ann's mom was after me. What wheels you got, Ralphie? Probably a Mercedes?"

"I don't own a car. I travel a lot. I rent. I live in Manhattan."

"You rent for those weekends in the country, right? Take your ladies out in nice clean transportation, or maybe they own it themselves but you pay the gas?"

"Chaz, you want to fight with me? Is that what you're looking for? Aren't we too old for that?"

Chaz shrugged. "We used to wrestle. That's what we used to do. It was all in fun. We never fought, did we?"

"No, Chaz. I think we were close."

It was a Stony Apache story that told of brothers attached back to back, so that one saw the future and the other the past, and they saw nothing alike, and they struggled to go in opposite directions, pulling hopelessly. But they could never tear apart. They could never cut loose. They grew from each other's spines, they pulled and tugged and sometimes sprawled in ungainly awful intimacy that could never be ended.

"We're still close," Merian said.

A bulky man in an electric-blue leisure suit, carrying a black plastic zippered folder, out of place among the crowd of lean gray wolves in L. L. Bean casual, the chickens in less-safari jeans, was pushing through the dancers and loungers and conversationalists. He seemed to know Chaz. So Chaz had a friend in electric blue; better than none at all. "You're Ralph Merian! You don't remember me!" the man said.

"Of course I do," said Merian, trying to place the face, which must have been healthier once.

"Copy desk at the old *Trib* when you were there! You remember I told you to follow the Stations of the Cross in Jerusalem, that's the ticket?" the man asked. "Remember I told you to read the Book and then you'd know more about David Ben-Gurion than—"

"Yeah, yeah, yeah, I remember now. How are you?" Of course. That full-bore Christian on the copy desk—you didn't see many of them. In those days, the man had a delighted face, pink cheeks, the blissy smile; he had found it. "So what happened when the *Trib* closed?" Merian asked.

"Oh, man, I terminated that line of corruption when the Lord mentioned it. I didn't ask the Lord to lay down unnecessary signs. I left kind of abruptly, man, I was going to give part of my severance to God and keep part for me to continue His work, but they laid down a discharge for cause. The devil works in those personnel departments, that's a known fact. Jesus told it first when he told the eye of the needle. So I held out for medical, tried acting nuts up and down personnel . . . but you remember your radio?"

"Radio?"

"The radio, man! Your brother didn't tell you? You know—" And he twisted dials in his chest, saying, "Squawk-squawk, radio, that ain't a duck, what we use where we don't have video, man! When they want to talk or control a person, they radio into their brains through the teeth, man!"

"Sir?" Merian asked.

"You know what I'm saying. Chaz told me all about you. Chaz, you been settling with him about the radio between you two boys?"

Merian felt the labor going on in his brother. There was a metabolic surge in his eyes, almost a sea tide of clotted energy in his face, and this electric-blue leisure saint was shaking the gates and barriers. Merian stared hard at the man and said as coldly as he knew how, "Only awhile here in San Fran. Could you leave me alone with my brother, sir?"

"It's still SFO when you telex, isn't it?"

"Sir."

"Okay, okay, I'm going, bless you. I'm not one of those street-corner missionaries you can't forsake. May Jesus redeem your twisted soul. I'm going."

Merian watched him carrying his vinyl zippered case like a cross before him, separating the crowd at the bar. In a second or two he would have to turn back to Chaz, afraid of what he would find, just when Chaz had seemed to be lightening up, getting in control, in touch, which was even better. Chaz was his only brother and he knew the gates were now open. The rage would come breaking and foaming through.

"I found *him!* He found *you!* Do you see now what good moving around like that did you? You can't escape, Ralphie!"

"Chaz, what are you saying?"

"You mean you came out here, you ask credit for that, so brother, I give it. I *know*. But don't you think I arranged for you with those infinite powers we are granted?" He poked Merian on the forearm. He winked. "Infinitely limited, brother, just like you."

"Chaz, you're kidding, aren't you?"

"You thought Freddy there got to me? You think Freddy set me off? He used to be a chubby-chaser till he found Jesus again. Had a nice little couple of years taking runaway boys for milkshakes, french fries, eat up good, then whammo! The Lord came down and said, 'You wanna squeeze through the eye of the needle, you better not stuff yourself!'"

"Let's get on with it, Chaz."

"*I* was saying."

"Sure thing."

"So you can very slick it over, Ralph, but you got it from me and I lost it."

"I took something from you?"

"You said it, I didn't. I admitted it. I'm not an accuser anymore. I turn the other testicle."

"Chaz. What can I do for you?"

"I'll tell you a couple of things. Pay for your radio. That's a business deal, treat it as such, pure and simple. Plus, get unborn."

Merian stared. He was still waiting. He didn't know what else to do. He knew why it was easy to hide under bombardment, not too bad to discuss things with Hawkfeather. Those were the easy ways. They were the ways out of family. This universe of mind wreck was spinning away from any management by impersonal historical risk or by words. Here, in this arena of struggle, nothing came of words. Merian looked at the orangish face that resembled his own, but puffy with a history of Thorazine and lithium and Winchell doughnuts—the same pattern of gray and black in the hair, the same yellowish flecks in the eyes, but another history telling itself out in noise and static and words that did no work.

Chaz was still winking and grinning and wishing him dead. His eyes were shining. "Don't worry about what I say," Chaz said, "this is all selfish stuff. Don't even listen to me. Go home. Save yourself for something useful."

"Chaz, what can I do?"

"Mom and Dad are dead now, but not for long. We need them too much, Ralphie. For unfinished business."

"So we have to finish it by ourselves."

"If we can't though, Ralphie. I mean if we can't, we'll just have to ask them to come back. I think both of them would be nice, because they got unfinished business together, too, just like us."

"But while we're waiting?"

Chaz shrugged. He released Ralph's arm and leaned away in his chair, but Ralph could hear him over the music and laughter and the negotiations of the Black Sun Tavern. "Make it all better, brother, that's all. Save me. Save me! Can't we just go back to sleeping in our room and listening to our programs together?"

10

THE UNFORTUNATE PART about leaving the Stony
Apaches before tucking them into the paper's computers,
decently microfiching them with a final wave good-bye, but instead taking off on a wild tycoon chase to the Oxmans in Dallas,
and then adding an unscheduled cozy vacation trip in San Francisco to see a brother, was that the meat calculator kept on working. There was more about Danny Grand and the Hollywood
bankers. Jarls Coyote's sand-filled desktop coffee can kept in-
truding. There was more about the President of the Nation and
how it decided to spend tribal funds, how it decided not to spend
them on water, fences, and preventing hepatitis. Balance asked
to be tipped this way and that, new paras wanted to be added or
dropped, the steady wind down the main strip of the Nation kept
blowing on a tape loop in Merian's head. The story was ripening.

So do bananas on a refrigerator, he thought. Brown, spotted, soft, and hot. They don't necessarily evolve toward superior life past a certain peak in their time.

The Stony Apaches didn't let go of him. It wouldn't make any difference in the Syndicate, which would sent out a stripped-down economy-size version on the wires to Miami, Cleveland, Detroit, Rochester, and probably the up-scale Briefing insert in the *San Francisco Chronicle*, aimed at the brie and white-wine demographics, though maybe western papers would pick up on it more, even use the whole thing in Sunday magazines—Albuquerque if they weren't offended, Santa Fe, Phoenix, Tucson, the *Rocky Mountain Journal*, maybe an LA valley paper for the entertainment biz connection. But the neck-top meat computer was clicking away on behalf of Arnie Schultz, the New York outlet, and Ralph Merian's own childish dream of getting the story both free and right, telling the truth. Oh, boy. The dream of truth-telling was a reactionary fantasy he shared as a family trait with his younger brother, Charles Merian, the engineer and radio mechanic. Maybe they both got it from their mutual mother and father, now departed and unavailable for interrogation.

The unfortunate part about waiting, letting a story sit at home on the refrigerator, or even on a desk or imperfectly hidden from a Hawkfeather in a closet, was that it then was still sitting there, impatiently waiting, incomplete, unfulfilled, asking to be rewritten, and a person couldn't just bang it into the VA surplus metal file, politely murmuring, Too late, too late now, on to the next. A person couldn't just listen to the smoker's rasp of Arnie Schultz and turn the lock twice on Riverside Drive and say, Okay, another assignment, good-bye. A person was stuck.

All night, on the flight back to JFK from San Francisco, he was choked and hoarse about Chaz, his shoulders felt as if they had been pushing his jalopy together up the hill to the gas station, the battery was dead, it didn't turn over; and yet he was thinking about the Stony Apaches. A motherly flight attendant, maybe forty, once a swinging stewardess—aircraft were narrower bodied in those days—and now nice, treated him like a man heading too late toward an emergency. He must have looked worn out and griefy. On these night flights she had experience with accidents, sudden deaths, family disasters. Maybe it was only a home-office crisis. Did he want a drink, an extra pillow, a blanket, a rental car? The airline supplied aspirins and she personally happened to have Pepto-Bismol and hand cream. Was there something she could do to make him more comfortable?

She stopped coddling him and tended to other spongy-eyed midnight coffee drinkers when he took out his notebook and began scribbling. Goddamn Arnie, maybe the whole trip was a trick to get him to rework the Stony Apache story. Maybe he hired the Coke-machine shaped billionaire from a Rent-an-Oxman service. Goddamn Chaz drove Merian right out of himself, what he had to do, but now he was coming back. Work saves a person from thinking about what he can't do, should have done, didn't do, can't anymore. Goddamn Susan might be right about him.

She certainly was. Dats-a da trobble, as the wise psychiatrist said. Susan was right, smart, and dangerous. Get on to more fruitful lines of inquiry, Mister White Eyes.

Now if the Stony Apaches didn't take care of their ranges, didn't build the fences to keep the cattle in, they were going to continue losing cattle; but if they spent the money that they could otherwise use for wells, which merely gave fresh water, or for fences, which merely kept the cows from wandering off to eat the heebie-jeebie grass, they wouldn't be able to support Danny Grand's holy ambition to tell the unvarnished true story of Indians and cowboys, plus a couple of songs for the soundtrack album.... Something to keep a journalist busy. Great Satans are a fast kick, but pathetic ones come slow. Here was something nice, awful, and pathetic to keep Merian from personal business.

Here is how strange this world had become; Ralph Merian was ashamed of working.

> *Dear, you're in my mind even when I'm out of my mind;*
> *dear lady, everyone tries to make life worth living*
> *and I thought words do it but it's you.*

He woke on his couch at near eleven in the morning and his nose full of dust. He had worked through most of the night, then slept without knowing he was going to, and when he woke, one sock was off and the other dangling from his foot—dangling from the Stony Apache Nation. There were yellow sheets crumpled like snowballs around him. He was greasy and sweaty and clotted with words. He needed a shower. There was a pot of cold coffee on the table near his head; coffee dreams were full of words. He rinsed his mouth against the taste of his dream. He swallowed.

Dear, you're in my mind even when I'm out of my mind—

A person who dreamed words to Susan instead of mending his ways with her needed to do something about this error. His capacity to forgive himself was large—an older brother, wasn't he, Chaz?—but there were limits even for Ralph Merian. Another rinse and swallow of cold coffee.

Into the shower, nothing but icy water, his mouth open and gasping in the stream. Never fails to wake a person up. If I die, he thought, just put me in a cold shower and you'll see, I'll come out ready to write a smashing lead, full of the who what where when why and even—bless you, Arnie—the how of the great beyond. From One Who Was There. Our Reporter Across the Styx River.

Now into a terrycloth robe, hairy flanks still wet, and then straight to what, instructed by the barrenness of words in a dream, he needed to do. If he was reduced to words in a dream, he shouldn't blame it on coffee. It had grown dangerously late for Susan and him.

"May I come to see you?" he asked by telephone.

"It might not be a bad idea," she said.

This stopped him a moment. There were no tones in her voice. It was just a series of syllables coming out onto audio, like the receptor end of a voice scrambler. He tried again. "Susan, may I come on over?"

"If you like," she said in that toneless way.

He hung up and, with an edge of panic, laced his boots. He

shut the windows. He put a rock from a construction site—no souvenirs of war zones for him—on the pile of paper at which he had been poking. He expected no winds to sweep through his flat and scatter the work. The only wind in here was speculation and metaphor.

He didn't walk across Central Park to the East Side. Today he didn't take the bus, either. The generous unobstructed swerving of his taxi into the crosstown and the park gave him none of his usual pleasure. He didn't know what Susan had waiting for him, but he wasn't planning to like it. Apprehension seldom let him down. Arnie used to say he had a developed sense of apprehension, exactly what a correspondent needs. What really causes trouble is thinking you can cross that field, drink that water. The driver was driving, he was not the navigator, this was not a mission; they were speeding just because that's the way this cab liked to proceed when the road was clear. The tonelessness of Susan's voice filled Merian with unease.

The streets were cleaner on the East Side. For some reason, connected with street cleaning, there was less litter. Merian believed the West Side should demand representation at the United Nations as a Third World and proudly traditional mendicant state— one without oil. There was an unrealized fortune in combustible material on every West Side street corner. It was an undeclared war zone. But here on the East Side . . .

Why the devil had all the resonance gone out of Susan's voice?

He knew when someone was scared.

At the building on East Eighty-third Street he thrust bills into the driver's hand, sprinted through the lobby and past the doorman—"Hey! Hey, you!"—who decided it wasn't worthwhile to try to stop him; he might not be a burglar, anyway. The doorman stared and shrugged; assholes in this town, not like it used to be.

Merian stood with twitching legs in the elevator. Man the Hunter was not designed for perpendicular flight or pursuit. He was not intended to watch buttons lighting in serial order while he stood in mortal fear.

Lumbering, Merian ran down the carpeted hall beneath the flat

233

glare from the glass circle of fluorescent tube at every five long steps. The owner had replaced the bulbs, decided to save a few dollars a month on electricity. Had Merian been gone so long or had he just not noticed?

Susan's door was locked and he rapped sharply, then pounded on it. Silence. He decided he would count to five and then break it down. At four and a half he heard a hand on the lock. He stopped counting, he stopped breathing. The door opened.

There was a look of brutal calm on Susan's face. The nose seemed slightly coarsened and broadened, as if she had a cold; but her skin wasn't red, it was stretched tight, it was a bluish white. Her eyes were sleepy, not like someone who had just awakened but like someone who hasn't slept in too long. Her hair lay flat and, in the daylight flooding over her, looked almost white. Had he been away so many years? She opened the door, she let him in, she didn't speak.

Hawkfeather said, "You didn't want to settle with me—"

The words came out of Merian's mouth before he knew what he was seeing and hearing: "What are you doing here? What the hell you doing here, Hawkfeather?"

"It wasn't so hard to find her address, man. I mean it was all over your place if I looked under stuff. I figured there sure had to be a hometown girl you were sticking it to—"

His chest was blocked. He had the familiar nightmare sensation of pursuit through hallways, chased by punishing menace, while he ran light as a boy and then was suddenly caught like a child and cornered. He was innocent. He was impaled. He was a child pursued by stubborn enemies except that he was a man who should not be helpless, did not live in dreams, might choose not to be destroyed.

Also he had no hometown. Hawkfeather didn't get things right.

"—before you stuck it to Sandra and Claudia—"

An open fist shot out and cracked against Hawkfeather's face. Hawkfeather barely moved as the slap sounded. It was not Merian's hand—he did not have this habit; it was Susan's. Whose honor was she protecting and why did she dare?

234

Her face still wore that cold, withdrawn, almost sleepy pout, as if the hand didn't belong to her, either.

Hawkfeather touched his cheek, looked at his fingers. Then he looked at Susan. He was concerned for her. "You okay, honey?" he asked. "That was, I mean, a really dumb thing you did. I mean, assuming I might be a rational or normal, sweetie"—very politely, gently, and concerned—"and not likely to bust your bones, plus your previous—your previous—plus who knows what a crazy redskin like me has in mind—rape? double murder? chopping up into little tiny pieces? Who can tell, baby?"

It might be best to let him go on talking. It was a hijacking. Hawkfeather might tranquilize himself if he could be held to talking. It seemed to be his inclination just now, and it also seemed a better procedure to Merian. They were on the tarmac of some airstrip. Merian believed the only thing more difficult to handle than nonnegotiable demands was unstated nonnegotiable demands.

Hawkfeather stretched his arms in front of himself, cocked his wrists, cocked his head to listen to the sharp crack in his wrists, waited for Merian. There seemed to be no hurry in the whole wide world.

"What's your satisfaction in cruelty?" Merian asked.

"What's yours?" Hawkfeather said. "You don't do nothing but use, man. You use whatever comes your way. Some girl. Some dumb Indians. Whatever, you're a user, Mister White Eyes."

"Am I interfering with your conversation?" Susan asked. "Would you two brothers like to have a quiet place to talk?"

Merian turned to her and said, "You're about my only family, Susan. I have a brother in San Francisco. You're my family."

"Shit." Hawkfeather rubbed his cheek. "You go slapping at folks, lady, but I got lots of family, my own, my nation, my real bad people. I don't have to do like your old Mister White Eyes, make one up."

"So you're lucky," said Merian.

"You got that face," Hawkfeather said, "it's like those other Anglo faces, it just looks so tired and crinkly, like you want to

235

do something but you can't. And inside you're looking out for number two."

"I think you mean number one."

"To me you're just kaka," Hawkfeather said. "To me you're just looking out for that."

"You've made a study," Merian said.

"I've heard," Susan remarked, "American men enjoy having a good chat, but do you notice maybe you two are exaggerating?"

Hawkfeather didn't seem to hear her. "You like to have some fun, have a fiesta for a life, man, but you can't do that. You can't have everything you own way. At least I learned that one thing already."

"I get deadlines," Merian said. "May I make a suggestion? I have to work, some of us do that. I also have things between Susan and me—"

Hawkfeather shook his head. Merian was confusing matters. He had things all wrong. "That's another way not to have a fiesta, think everybody do like you do—right, baby?"

Frozen and distant, Susan remarked, "Thank you boys for expressing so much interest. But now this is my home. I don't feel like leaving while you finish your party, so maybe you two could—"

"Notice how he like to discuss?" Hawkfeather asked her. "Notice how he defend his woman by discussing? Notice how he let Sandra and that there *Claw*-dia—"

"Why are you doing this!" Merian shouted.

"I'd like you out, both of you, out of here," Susan said.

Hawkfeather shrugged and lounged. "Can't stop progress," he said.

"What good's it doing? It's only trouble!"

"Plus call to your attention," Hawkfeather said. "Like I previous mention, it don't blow you up for joy, do it? But it makes you think."

"You're crazy."

"This is my house," Susan was repeating, "will you go now?"

"Everybody knows redskins is crazy. We got the name, we

236

play the game. I learned all sorts of good stuff in Albuquerque, too, in the army, different ways to get crazy. Problem with us Injuns, we don't get *happy* crazy like the Africans. We get mean, okay, but we don't enjoy it so much. So I practiced drinking that Mexicali Ta Kill Ya and now here I am, smart as any other New Yorker. He fucked two little Chicago girls the same time, baby. I forget how to say that more polite—"

Merian threw himself forward. He had forgotten how to do this properly, he was old enough to be Hawkfeather's father, he very much regretted the clumsy butting of his shoulders, this wild fling of his fist, like a gloveless drunk exhibiting himself in a bar. Hawkfeather's arm where he hit it felt like thick uncured meat swinging from a pivot. Hawkfeather took the punch and then easily bloodied Merian's face with a flick of his fingers. Merian regretted this also. It was happening to someone in whom he had a benevolent interest and he regretted it. Despite the wet warmth trickling down his face—he often saw the blood of others, but seldom tasted his own—he plunged against Hawkfeather's belly. There was a kind of concussion. He bounced off a solid rubbery mass.

"Jeez, that's my dinner muscle, man," Hawkfeather said.

Without a weapon, he could do nothing. Without a weapon, the lad could kill him.

Merian pulled at a lamp—sparks, a snakelike cord whipping across the floor.

"Enough, goddamn you both!" Susan cried.

Unh, someone said, Merian said, grunting, so quickly breathless, not tired, just boiling with desire to kill.

Hawkfeather leaned back and studied him. "You broke her lamp, dummy," he said. "Shit, man, if you don't like me, I'm gonna depart."

Merian brought the lamp crashing down as Susan rushed toward him. The shade flew off like a tumbled hat. Susan hit him, deflecting electrical junk, and knocked him against the door. He stumbled against Hawkfeather, who was leaning against the door, covering his mouth with his hand.

"I don't need to rip you," Hawkfeather said. "You already done it to yourself." Susan tugged at the door, and Hawkfeather let it open and ambled out, kicking a pillow ahead of him. He waited there. Merian followed him, bent to pick up the pillow, and held it back to Susan. He felt the trickle of blood on his face. It would seem, when his mouth swelled up, as if he had finally taken care of his wisdom teeth.

"Now, you two," Susan said, "now you've had your little boys' game—both of you—let me close this door."

She stood there and took the pillow. He reached for her.

"Out," she said. "I want you *out,* mister."

"Let's get gone together," Hawkfeather said to Merian. "I don't think she wants either one. Hey, you got a—you got a—you got the words, man. You got a stinky face. Stinktimonious."

"Is that the longest word you ever used?"

"Could be."

"Well, you say it erroneously, chief."

Susan managed to push him away from the door. She slammed it. Merian waited a moment. It did not open again. Hawkfeather was grinning. "She don't want to see you, man."

Out through the hallway with its fluorescent tubes, down, back into the tunnel of street outside, sliding through the dense air. An afternoon crowd was sucking in what was required for life on the East Side of Manhattan; heavy weather lay on their necks. "Hey!" Hawkfeather was right behind, right with him. "Hey, man, you look rotten. You look like some drunken Indian got his welfare check, man. His Aid to Disabled."

Two tattered quarrelers were strolling together as if they had buffeted each other in their cages before feeding time. Hawkfeather gave him a piece of paper towel to hold against his lip. "Where we going now?" he asked. "What we doing?"

Merian stopped and turned to him. "You've made your point, leave me alone, will you? I got my own brother to think about. I don't need you. I got my own woman."

Hawkfeather's eyes were glinting and black. "You think so?" he asked.

11

OUTSIDE, ON RIVERSIDE Drive, a Latin phalanx was lined up for musical aggression at a park bench—two standing, three sitting, beating drums with the flat and balls of hands, with fists, sometimes with an elbow. The standing musicians were clacking things, piercing the air with inspired police whistles, and occasionally glancing up from their intense concentration to make sure the sound baffles, a row of apartment houses in front of them, a park, and the Hudson River behind them, were still in place. The acoustics were solid. A little further down the drive, two benches away, a darker boy with a silky adolescent mustache was playing his guitar as if the bongos didn't exist. Perhaps he was a Haitian. He was at peace with the world. He was picking out a baroque melody. Bach, Corelli, Vivaldi— Ralph Merian could never win music quizzes—as stiffly as a teenager in a Scarsdale music school. Strangely, though, the melody penetrated despite the swelling beat of bongos, clackers, and whistles from the other young men sweating and concentrating on their task.

All Merian needed was to look or listen from his window and he could see and hear the fumes of city grief, loneliness, boredom, ambition, flying up and down the streets; he could smell the fires. For many years he had escaped his own griefs by finding distant turmoils; there seemed to be war zones closer to home. "Uneasy truce" was a phrase that had satisfied him too many times. He smelled wet cartons burning at the street corner, an art form for kids who found music too slow and inexpressive. He sniffed, he shut the window. There had been oranges in some of those cartons.

Tasting various airs was a time-tested distraction for the V.J., but now he wished to engage the struggle between Susan and him. She was a powerful adversary. Hawkfeather was not the enemy. Hawkfeather had made his gesture and was roaming elsewhere in the city, finding other craziness to occupy himself with. Merian was not an observer in the present war. His condition took some getting used to. The next move was up to him, and as is proper, the normal procedure for a person in a weakened condition, he behaved foolishly. In war between nations, desperation does not usually risk ridicule, but Merian was not a sovereign nation. Dumb-dumb Ralph. He felt unqualified to predict how he might react to being laughed at.

He sent her roses that evening. Don't be rash, he advised himself. The next day he sent her flowers morning, noon, and night.

She wasn't answering her phone. Maybe she was listening to her Creole tapes.

Three deliveries of flowers had no effect on the telephone. He sent flowers again the next morning and a note saying, "It must be serious." This time she called and said, "Don't be funny," but didn't want to talk with him.

Progress. Rashness, foolishness, and abjectness. Was that a gain?

He called back in a few minutes, she answered, and he said,

"Your place'll turn into an overgrown garden unless you stop me. The only way you can stop me is by seeing me."

"I hate jungles," she said. "This is jungle warfare."

"Then you better see me. Susan, everyone needs to get over things."

"Some things people don't want to get over. Some things people shouldn't get over."

"Susan, let's not give up. Let's not stop before the end."

Silence.

"I'm coming to see you now, Susan."

Silence.

"You wouldn't let me make the trip all the way across town and then not see me, would you?"

He could hear the bundled wires bearing other voices while she considered what to do next. All she had to do was touch a piece of hard plastic and the connection would be broken. The dim electronic squawk of other voices continued until she said, "Why don't you take a chance."

He still wasn't sure. She had a right to be rude and vengeful. Or perhaps she didn't. The rules were unfamiliar to him. Living in the real world of wars and revolutions, observing history sensibly, he had cleverly avoided another real world. Chaz, Hawk-feather, and Susan were citizens of a mysterious and foreign place where obligation, devotion, and even deliberate cruelty between people who cared about each other was part of the normal procedures.

As he left the building, it occurred to him that the Puerto Ricans playing the bongos, the Haitian playing the guitar, were not making music about grief and mourning. They were celebrating their power to be alive.

The bongo players were gone now, anyway. He couldn't know for sure what their sounds meant, what they were emitting, and even if he had asked them, he would not know. All he did professionally was formulate convincing assumptions. He knew nothing. The Haitian boy was standing at the corner, holding his guitar case, staring at the smoldering wet ashes of the orange carton fire. Merian didn't know why the Haitian guitarist was standing there, why he wanted to play baroque music on his guitar, why he stopped.

In Port-au-Prince, Merian might have constructed a theory about it—escape, defiance of the Duvalier regime, something plausible or not plausible that the structure of sentences, subject, verb, direct object, could make convincing for readers who had half an attention to pay over their morning coffee. History had been the means for the V.J. to avoid his life; he worked at it, he developed the skills, like a flame-eater or high-wire entertainer. He had made his stunt into a gift for his readers, their morning half hour of distant terrorism and disaster, the breakfast of other people's war or revolution. Maybe the Haitian boy stopped playing his guitar because it was time for a hamburger.

The roadway from the West Side to the East, across Central Park, was leading Merian into a zone of trouble. He thought he would ask Susan what she meant and wanted and if she was celebrating anything.

When she admitted him, he stood there without asking anything, not even what had happened to the roses. There was a thick scent, very heavy and cloying, but she had put the flowers away, out of sight someplace. There was no welcome in her face. He thought he saw a kind of yielding, but no welcome, and wondered why she had let him come to see her. There was erosion, fatigue, a wearing down, nothing that pleased him. But he was there, wasn't he?

He listened to Hawkfeather, listened to Claudia and Sandra, listened to Chaz—listened to Jarls Coyote, Alamo Oxman, and Arnie Schultz—he had the habit of listening to people who were important to him and people who were not. It was his profession and habit. Now he had better listen to Susan.

She wasn't speaking. He sat in a chair without her asking him to sit, to drink, to eat, to do anything. He looked at her and waited. He had no pad of steno paper, no tape recorder, no telex machine chattering. This was unmediated between Susan and him.

"You don't mind the worm turning, do you?" Susan asked. "You thought I was too nice, but I'm not. Now what do you want?"

"Dunno," he said.

"Assume I will surprise you, how about that? I have a daughter to go back to. I have a limited time for stupidity. I might want to play. I might be a chained free spirit, Mr. Merian, so watch out."

"I see," he said.

"That may not do you any good, Mr. Merian."

He took her hand. In San Francisco he might have taken the hand of Chaz. Does it make any difference? Do hands say anything more than that hum of warmth? He should have held his brother's hand.

She suggested nothing. She offered no courtesy or kindness besides the loan of her hand. He was not sure what, if anything, she was offering. She let him hold on. Warmth, articulation of fingers, palm. Perhaps it was easier for her not to take her hand away.

He tried to follow her lead. He tried not to stretch out his legs as if he belonged here. He waited for her to decide.

She removed her hand and looked at it. She had allowed it to poke into a slot that had turned into a vise. This was not her intention. Susan controlled her own hand, fingers, opposable thumb, and the unwilled heat that ran through her body. She sighed. She frowned at her own thoughts and then at him. "How much do you know about my marriage?"

"Not much. I thought you didn't want to say."

"You respect my English Reserve, do you?"

He shrugged. Despite his avoidance of experience in recent years, he remembered that when a woman is angry and growing angrier, it was sometimes wise to listen and wait.

"How much do you know about me?"

He waited.

"About my marriage, about my daughter, about what I chose or choose, about my own self that were getting, that was getting—" She didn't want to give up her famous English Reserve and English grammar, and she was doing it. "All compromised!" she cried. "All changed! Not what I planned!"

"By me?" he asked.

"It's my fault, isn't it, that we're here? Because I'm here, I chose to be here, isn't that right?"

He said nothing. It was not what he had planned, either.

"But only for what happens to *me,* that's all I'm responsible for, not for you, Mister White Eyes."

He felt the heat flying to his face. "Don't you call me that."

"I'm taking responsibility," she said calmly. "You better take it, too."

Now they both chose to be silent. The hum of blood and anger gave way to the hum of the city through walls, the world through the city. Merian didn't know what came next. Susan would have to decide. He waited for her.

"How about a little lazy seduction, mister?" she asked. "Like kids at school, you know—that kindly urging?"

"I'm urging."

They were no longer touching. She was looking at her hand as if it had been imprinted or bruised.

"You're insisting, mister. You're not kindly." He drew back and showed his palms, empty of threat. "Well, maybe you are, but you're not *being* kind. I'm living in the moment, mister, just like people used to."

"Why are you being mean, Susan? If this is joking—"

"Don't trust," she said. "You know how I am."

But he didn't. He thought he knew what she wanted and what she would not permit herself to want, not with him. Anger was not supposed to be part of the deal. She might want a fix-up country house with tire ruts in the dirt, a tree, a pond, probably several trees, vegetables, and flowers to be tended in the garden, a place for her daughter. And he might want a passably clean hotel room with access to the National Palace or the War Room or the back-street dwelling of his underground contact. Since his early youth, those had been his pleasures, and he was no longer young. She might choose to want a late baby, another child, one of those late babies women were having these days, and to the V.J. it sounded something like retirement. He believed he wasn't suited to it.

Even if it wasn't retirement, it was normal life. Normal life had never been convenient for him. Like some freak on the evolutionary ladder, he found his calm browsing in whirlwinds. Wars and revolutions suited him nicely.

She wanted things that made a decent link with the past and the future. Destruction did not nourish her. She wanted useful objects and family celebrations. She might like to have both her daughter and Chaz in the house for Christmas. She had read about the new paper diapers that needed no pins, the nonsalt cereals for infants, the feasibility of a healthy mother nursing her child even in her late thirties, the new freedom to have a healthy baby, due to amniocentesis and the long lives and careful nutrition and nonharried personalities of intelligent new middle-aged parents.

He wanted to continue to have a harried personality.

It seemed that he needed to go to countries where people wore dashikis on state occasions. Or they might wear burnooses or khaki camouflage jump suits and green ribbons around the deadly weapons they got from the Soviet bloc via Czechoslovakia or Syria or former CIA American dealers. He had even been to Baghdad at a Third-World Peace-Lover's Conference, where the sandbags around the Iranian Embassy, behind which machine-gunners crouched, had been dressed in green slipcovers, signifying the unity of all Islam, including the delegation from the South Bronx. (The V.J. wasn't sure where Cuba fit in, although Fidel wore the unpressed green fatigue suit that he usually kept in the back of the closet during recent years.) The Peace-Loving Call to Guerilla Action and Oil Denial Against War-Mongering Hegenomonists Resolution, a progressive democratic unanimous decision, had been interrupted during Fidel's brief five-hour toast by a burst of gunfire from behind the green slipcovers. It was only a passing spat between the Iranians and the Iraqis, fourteen Shiites gone to paradise, no count on the injured. If any Iraqis had been hit, they weren't saying. Snarling hegenomonists with stars of David painted on their teeth had fomented misunderstanding within the Universal Reconciliation Bloc.

From Teheran it was announced that a division of Great Satan camel people was wiped out and the city of Baghdad lay in eternal darkness, its electrical system shorted by a suicide squad which then ascended straight to the celestial domain of the Ayatollah Khomeini, where the lights glow forever.

During the celebration of an hour of silence at the Workers Anti-Zionist Sports Stadium, while the bodies were being removed, Fidel finished his address, wiped his beard on an embroidered green napkin contributed by the Marching Girls Bazooka Cubs of Baghdad, and proceeded toward his next step in Bulgaria. Once again he had spoken six hours without notes, a feat without equal in capitalist history. During the peroration Ralph Merian went drinking with some other veteran journalists, including one Pole and his silent, hefty Russian assistant, a stringer for Novosti, in a hotel behind the Son et Lumière fountain contributed by the Confédération Generale des Travailleurs from several Third-World banlieux of Paris.

Merian, the Pole, a Frenchman, and an Australian tried to guess how many had died. The Russian from Novosti refused to participate in this sport, muttering, "Blood-drinking, blood-drinking," until he was gently corrected. "The word is bloodthirsty," Merian said.

The Frenchman, who had done time in Syria for *L'Express,* explained events at the conference by citing an Arab proverb: Kiss the hand you cannot bite, but call upon God to break it.... "God doesn't speak at these meetings," D'Artingues remarked. "He is off seeing if the Russians will sell him a nuclear reactor, maybe by passing it through the Indians."

The man from Novosti merely looked sleepy. But he had been paying attention. "Blood*thirsty,*" he said happily.

They could hear a crackle of firing at some distance from the hotel. It was only a wedding. They drank another round to the bride and groom.

This was a kid's life of killing, senseless perpetual killing, with occasional peace or war conferences, endless talk, quibbles over language, a routine of impatient politics, sometimes briefly resolved by an assassination or two, to which Ralph Merian was addicted. He had broken with tobacco and excessive drinking, but these other habits of fire, smoke, and flood kept a rougher grip on his metabolism.

There were supposed to be interesting PLO training camps in Bulgaria. He had not seen the Bulgarian countryside yet. How can a man settle down who has not seen the Bulgarian country-side?

Even Hawkfeather's anger seemed to distract him from Susan—why? Why should Hawkfeather, who made trouble, be more convincing than Susan, who gave pleasure and promised to continue to do so? Because Hawkfeather's trouble, like the pain of loss, could be worn out. And because Susan's pleasure was hard to dodge.

He was not able to dodge the troubles of Chaz, either. Merian gave himself credit for being better at dodging than he seemed to be. For a veteran journalist, this could lead to a loss of nerve.

The V.J. saw the world as a zoo in which all the animals were red in tooth and claw and he was not their keeper. Only writing it down, sir; not playing God, not even editor, just chronicling and trying to pay attention to the proper cage when the fur flew and the shrieks rose up. God claimed responsibility for the place, but had nothing to do with the shit in the corners. The V.J., with God absent, just stood there, pad and felt-tip pen in hand.

Susan didn't want to fit into the zoo. She wanted him in her world, and she had a right to insist upon it. Her world might even exist.

Sometimes in desert outpost or landlocked capitals, Merian met the fellows from *Time, Newsweek,* and other papers with wives and kids on stony mortgage ranches in Vermont; audio and visual media seemed to go more for Westport or the Hamptons. The reporters got drunk at sundown, thinking about their wives possibly running around, the kids not under control; no one was under control. But Ralph Merian was under control. He liked feeling superior to something—it was an unusual experience for him, it had lasted most of a career but it was still unusual. It was interesting even if sometimes boring. It was what he had chosen and made to work. Even if it was known he had not gotten the Pulitzer, it was also known he had been nominated several times. He had enjoyed his Nieman year at Harvard, and grown impatient waiting to hurry back to Africa, where the walls were caving in. Cambridge might be okay for boys who could move the family into a little sublet for a year. But when a fellow had it all organized so much better than the poor drunks worrying about their wives and kids in the Taranga Lounge of the M'Basa-M'Basa Ramada Inn, why should he, of his own free stupid will, disorganize it?

Prudence was not going to help him now. Even organizing it any other way was not going to make everything clean and unencumbered, like a new hard ticket item bought for cash. The woman expert on cultural linguistics might have an idea about her nest that was opposed to the erratic impulses emanating from Muammar al-Qaddafi or the various Assads via Arnie Shultz. Merian liked not practicing two availabilities at the same time; it gave him a leg up on things.

"Let's negotiate," Susan said.

They weren't thinking of the same thing. She wanted to get her hair uncaught from his shirt button.

Between Susan and Merian on this Manhattan afternoon and evening there occurred that gravitational lovemaking of people who stayed in the same town for months at a time and did not continually change continents, oceans, wars, friendships. They slipped into bed when they were already tired and thinking of sleep, and there was a dreamy roll and doze together, just floating and gently bumping—no all-star driving and shoving—like the planets turning in orbit, bound together by invisible force and yet a little alone in the universe. "Ummm, sleepy? . . . Yes, nice."

Merian could see why people liked continuity. It included, for example, kindly lovemaking, late night and dawn, of a sort people could imagine continuing forever. Though of course it usually doesn't, from what the V.J. had heard.

Later, lying awake on their backs and the sweat cooling and just their hands finger-fallen together on the pillows, palms up, not grasping, Ralph and Susan concentrated on nothing. Each could do this because the other was there. It was what love might be in real life if God hadn't decided to put people on trial continually and find them Guilty. Ralph wanted to love Susan so that his mother and father would say fine, you're a good boy, you're kind again. So that his brother might be his friend again. So that she would love him. So that he would love her. Maybe there were other and better reasons.

Swimming in the Manhattan evening, they stretched and curled sleepily at each other. The window darkened with diamond lights of reflected sky. Did she tire of this watching and thinking? She didn't say. Her hand was on him. Then later, and it was midnight now, their hands were again resting near each other, reckoning they were now two again.

Easy lazy cozy silent lovemaking proved nothing. It was not a demonstration of anything anymore. Distant griefs could not be transformed into present joys. Yet they can, they can be.

Maybe she too had complicated reasons for choosing to love him.

They each turned on their right sides and he curled against her back and his lips murmured nothing, just parted for breathing, against her shoulder. The articulations of her spine felt like the links of a chain.

Not Guilty.

It was morning and they had slept and he awoke not quite refreshed. He wanted to start a new day differently. He looked at a framed bedside snapshot of Susan's daughter, gap-toothed, younger then, as kids tend to be in the photographs kept by fond parents. A mirror, a closet door, a stirring curtain, a gray light.

The grinding of a sanitation truck. He tried to replace that whirring, worrying, wasting noise with the ardent sounds of birds. The birds were absent. Those calls in his head and memory did not make the present morning exactly what he wanted.

She too lay awake and waiting. He could stretch and get up or doze or, if he chose to be moderately foolish, ask if Susan's daughter wore braces to bring her front teeth together or, if he was very foolish, speak what was in his mind, had waked him, was making the morning dim, gray, distracted, cold.

"One thing I guess I'd like to know," Merian said.

"No, you wouldn't like to know that."

"I haven't asked you yet."

"You've been working on it."

"Did you sleep with Hawkfeather?"

"Did I *what* with him?"

"Did you?"

She didn't turn away. She put her arms behind her head in a peculiarly defenseless, therefore arrogant gesture. "Do you want to tell me about Sandra and Claudia?" she asked.

"That's nothing. That was nothing. You know."

She didn't move. Somehow she made her defenseless stillness into a slap, an insult. Her breathing seemed willed—too slow. She was in hiding and making plans. It didn't matter if she loved him. It was worse if she loved him; her anger was deeper.

"Whatever I know is enough," she said. "Whatever you know is enough, too."

The sanitation truck was grinding and moving on, and in the quiet, Merian thought he did finally hear a chirping. It was a doorman's whistle, trying to stop a cab.

"No birds," Merian said.

"Birds? What?"

"Did you sleep with him?" Merian asked.

She sat up and plumped the pillow behind her. "What a nice question! How elegant! Let's talk about city birds—mostly sparrows and seagulls, aren't they? We have sparrows in London, too, but in New York—"

"Why not simply answer?"

"I don't like the question."

"Isn't that an answer, Susan?"

She pulled the sheet tight over her knees. He was diminishing for her and he went on doing it, no matter how he made himself recede. "It's an answer, I suppose," she said carefully, "if you keep on asking the question. You're a persistent inquirer, dear— is that how you get answers from chiefs of state?"

"I don't specialize in chiefs of state. Is that what you consider yourself?"

She laughed and touched his hand. "Now we're talking. It's conversation now. Maybe you do better with guerrilla captains."

They had slipped from what he wanted to hear from her. They had dodged off and she preferred it that way. He was not content. "Why don't we just settle the matter?"

He was not only diminished for her; she was growing tight and blue-lipped with anger. This fever and freckling was not the color of her pleasure. Her eyes cast about. A naked woman, in her own bed, with only a sheet tucked about her, could not easily just get up and stalk away. Indignation and a wobbling pink rump seemed poorly matched. This was not a choice Susan enjoyed just now. She rolled her eyes, which was a futile way to find escape. All it did was communicate the desire to be off. But since she was put there somehow, by a choice she seemed to have made, tightly drawn up against the pillows, sheet pulled tight around her legs, she had to declare herself without walking away. She contracted any space left between the knees. The thighs were muscled together. She was concentrating on business.

There was a smell of apple. He had better concentrate on business, too, and not try for pleasant acidic smells. That was anger, and last night's love, and not apple.

"The matter is settled. Let us agree I don't know everything about you and mustn't care. And the same for me."

That nausea in his stomach, that childish lurch in his belly. *Well, what do you want? Do you want to lose her?*

He breathed deeply, as airborne officers had told him to do

before jumping. Maybe it was biofeedback or maybe it was just breathing deeply. Susan was silent. He said, "Okay. You're right."

She pursued her victory. She did not give up her anger. "Are you satisfied now? Will you accept that?"

"Yes. You're right."

"Good. You're a great big fellow. And as far as your question is concerned, dear—yes, of course I did. Now let's hug and be quiet about it."

It was what he wanted. For an Anglican, he thought, she has a good sense of rhythm. He wanted the truth and to be eased, which are contradictory desires, which was why he had given up love for so long. He did not believe it could contain contradictions, though that's what love needed. Containing contradiction was essential. They hugged like kids, chastely, careful not to touch too much, breasts, belly, stirrings that did not obey this consideration of chasteness. He was shamed and aroused. That was another contradiction. He was confused. He said nothing because she was right about being silent awhile. At this moment it was the correct procedure. He knew, and needed to know, nothing.

"I think you'll not get laid anymore," she said.

He tried for funny consternation; eyebrows, mouth, like a late-night network interview host. She was serious.

"From now on, mister, we'll make love."

Her gaze was wide-awake, wide-alert, watching him struggle in his confusions. "Well, a kiss then," he muttered.

Instead of laying her mouth against his, she only shut her eyes. He had no right to ask if she was offering or denying. Maybe he would find out in due course.

He received a postcard from San Francisco with a studio photograph version in sepia tint of Sitting Bull on a horse. He didn't remember telling Chaz what he was doing with the Stony Apaches.

Sitting Bull was a Sioux, not an Apache. Why couldn't he get things right?

The message said, "Pick up radio, free of any charge, no harm done."

Merian tried to call his brother, but got no answer. He called Dr. Michalski and her answering service said she would collect her messages at the noon hour. Perhaps she did, but she did not call back.

He tried Chaz again. Again no answer. He wondered if he was supposed to reply with a postcard.

The next day there was a busy signal all day long. Finally the operator told him the telephone was out of order.

Dr. Michalski's answering service again said she would pick up her messages at the noon hour.

They established the family routines of a modern couple with no children at hand and no impediments except the plenty of time that there is to kill. They found movies on both the East and West Sides, noticing that the lines were longer and more like singles meeting lines on the East Side of Manhattan. Merian wondered if some people didn't actually buy tickets, but just stood in the lines for the sociability and adventure of them. Susan smiled at his suggestion and said that English joking was different. Merian said this was no joke. "Jean Jacket, meet Wide-Wale Corduroy. Fine Egyptian Cotton Bush Jacket, I'm Guatemalan Shepherd Shirt." Susan smiled again in her version of a New Yorker turning palms up and said nothing. She was better at the linguistics of words than the linguistics of gesture, but it was not necessary to offer her the comment. It was only Merian's opinion.

People could go on like this forever, paddling in their jobs, visiting back and forth, trying out new restaurants; forever, or until they stopped going on like this. The people in the movie lines, nervous and funny, clowning with their New York cleverness or tucking themselves romantically together, cuddling until the feature started, had agreed to stipulate that it was forever. Merian found he had craved this sweet conviction, this sweetness of ordinary lazing through the weeks and months with a friendly person.

It was exactly the life that he had so often envied when he camped out in Manhattan between assignments. On wintry Sunday afternoons it would have been better to be alone with one other person, reading, having a glass or two, Dubonnet on ice, as Radio Station WQXR advised him, waiting for nightfall, instead of what he used to do on those wintry afternoons—he read, he had a glass or two, he waited for night, and he passed the time alone. Or maybe he met Arnie for chow, maybe someone he had met on a plane, or a friend of a friend. In New York his love life had been mostly with acquaintances of European reporters he met in Africa or the Middle East. They made love and they remained good acquaintances.

The situation was better now. It helped him to know it, remembering the chilled dusks when it was too dirty and too cold to go strolling on Riverside Drive (Wind Chill Factor) or Broadway (Detritus Factor). Usually he bundled up and went out anyway, asserting the well-known fact that he was still alive and could make the blood move.

He had been famished before he met her. Now he partook gingerly. "Help is on the way," Susan said as the ticket line lurched forward. Some of these people actually planned to enter the theater before the marquee changed, thanks to the magic of real estate, into advertised specials on Mazola and Ivory Snow.

"English joke is different. You see, I listen to you," Merian said.

When they bought the early edition of the *Times* after the movie, a Woody Allen movie, as it usually seemed to be in this East Side theater, Merian peered at a headline about new trouble in Iran. Killings of Bahai families; plots, threats, the International Masonic Bahai Zionist Conspiracy. "Can't get a visa," Susan said, snatching the paper away from him. "I just denied you a visa." Nicaragua was also percolating nicely, as were Chile and

El Salvador. "You don't like South American food," Susan said. "It's all rice and beans, especially when they're having civil strife. Let's get a hamburger—one of your exotic Yankee delights."

"Just curious," Merian said. "I need my warm bath."

"In Iraq?" she asked.

He let her keep him from the newspaper.

In fact, Arnie had suggested a follow-up visit to the Stony Apache Nation to do another story about their water and range rights, and to go before his series ran, but he didn't mention this to Susan. He didn't mention it until he mentioned it over their hamburgers in La Petit Cafe Sur Lex, and he said mildly, not meeting her eyes, that he hadn't spoken of it because he didn't want to bring up a distracting topic. Hawkfeather, Claudia, Sandra, and the general absence between Merian and Susan at a time when they especially should not have been absent from each other; well, it was a sore point. He did not quite expect her anger. Although he preferred looking elsewhere, at a Saint-Germain-des-Près mural, the great church, the Café Flore and the Deux Magots, the bookshop Le Divan smuggled in behind the little park, and since he was studying a decorator's pastel mural with such care, something in him knew it was a difficult topic. Okay, a tribulation here or there, but he didn't expect the loss of aplomb. From that delicate, rosy, English lip a shred of overpriced hamburger hung and she was asking, "What right have you to protect me? Who says I need that?"

Just like real marriage, Merian was thinking while his stomach clenched and ached and he watched her dear face with the curl of meat on it.

"Are you listening, Ralph? What if I decided, *I* decided, *I* seduced him while you were so busy with the work of the world as you call it?"

The waitress looked astonished. She was wearing black tights and a miniskirt with a white ruffled western shirt closed for modesty's sake, because of a broken snap, with a "Nuclear Freeze" button. Her acting class had not yet dealt with the emotion one feels when overhearing a woman confess infidelity to her man, so she merely refilled their coffee cups, murmuring, "A splash?"

Susan had grown thinner these weeks. It wasn't her best weight—a few drawn graynesses in the face and neck. That sensitive English skin seemed to change with the weather, no matter how determined, focused, and strong-willed the person was. She had frowned over her papers and journals as if they were strangers to her. She was discovering surprises in herself as a mother, as a modern parent, her daughter thousands of miles away in the care of a man who was now a stranger to her. Susan Pollet was in New York because of a man who might someday be the same kind of stranger to her. He was not so familiar even these days. It was not totally clear to her that her work on Creolization required Brooklyn and the West Side of Manhattan. She seemed to want the man she was in New York about, but she didn't want all the things that were coming with him. She wanted to be important to him and she wondered if, for him, that was part of the deal.

For reasons that were not entirely a puzzle to her, but had seemed quite friendly and determined and sensible and angry at the time—appropriately muddled, yet cleared by minimal calculation, by impulse, by desire—she had gone to bed with an American Indian called Hawkfeather. At the time, stocky, muscle-bound, angry and making her angry, he had seemed the right thing to do. It had seemed to be what she wanted. Even now, the idea was not one she wanted simply to forget. Or for another to forget.

"Another splash?" murmured the waitress, hovering, hoping to hear more, since the third act of plays often contained this kind of stuff. It could be useful. "How about if I decaf you, it's ninety-eight percent sleepy?"

Maybe this quarreling couple would look up at her, recognize her for a kindred spirit, and let her see if their eyes were dry or wet.

Merian was just looking at Susan without speaking, as sometimes happened; nothing to declare. He believed he knew what she was telling him. He didn't know why he didn't feel more sad. This is a hint of old age, he was thinking, not caring too much. Yet he cared for her more than he had cared about anyone. Ever, he decided. Maybe such caring was the shadow of his childhood, when he had seemed to need no one who did not bring pleasure or distraction from the sullen occupation of being a boy.

Yet this too was incorrect because he had loved his brother, Chaz, and had seemed to love a girl now and then, especially the wife he had married—love? love? something violent and painful—and not caring too much had been a talent developed through the years. It was a wilderness survival skill. It was a quality that removed pain, canceled loss, and freed a person for the marvelous risks that history brought his way. He loved his work. He was sure he still did. It never turned away, it never changed its mind about him, it was constant, he had never taken a permanent reproach from Arnie.

"Are you just going to stare?" she asked. "And you're not even staring at me—really, Ralph, right through me like that!—it's awful."

His voice was level and unwavering. "I don't care about Hawk-feather," he said.

"Your eyes are funny."

He shrugged, he tried to smile, he tried to think of something. "Who speaks of love has sad eyes. That's a song in French. You took my arm as if you loved me. That's another part of the song. A French friend of mine gave me the record. It's from a poem by Aragon, a Communist poet who—"

"I know who Louis Aragon is," she said with great irritation.

"Was. He's dead."

"You keep up, don't you?"

Merian felt he was watching her from a communications satellite. Since he was removed to this distance, her impatience was justified and normal. He was an inappropriate person and she was distraught. "Do I have sad eyes?" she asked. "No one ever told me that. Can you *see?* I didn't say your eyes are sad, just funny. New York is so dirty, dirt falling on everything, maybe it makes you squint that way."

"Or I'm just nearsighted." He had better eject from the satellite. What man hears his woman remind him she has had an affair with an Indian kid and then discusses French verse with her, the grit and grime of New York, the crinkles or squintings of eyes? What sort of man was this? "Susan," he said, "not when I look at you. When I look at you, I'm not sad. Susan, I'm trying."

She touched his hand.

"Otherwise," he asked, "who knows?"

"We can talk about other things, dear. You're not very clear, anyway."

"That's because I'm disorganized."

"And I was complaining."

"You were saying about the filth of New York. You know what'll happen when the bombs fall? All the mousetraps in town will snap. That's the snap we want to hear together. That click all over town."

"I appreciate your trying to tell me about your true feelings."

"Don't laugh at me. Don't ridicule me. I said together, didn't I? Go ahead, laugh at me and ridicule. It's just I'm not used to these things. I've worked on it so long. I've learned from experience. I've been very careful to become a pompous old fart. I've seen what the world is made of—not only puppy-dog's tails. I study trends. The trend is—I don't care anymore, Susan, I do love you."

Her face was turned with speculation toward him and then toward nothing. She was pale; this weather took the color from her face; steam heat was bad for her. She wondered if he happened to think she believed the world was puppy-dog's tails, plus a few incidentals. She wondered if he could be so ignorant about Susan Pollett—her marriage, her work, her daughter, her divorce, her risk far from home with an American stranger whom Hawkfeather called Mister White Eyes. She was hoping she would not pay too high a price for what she had forced him to say.

And he was trying not to think of Merian and Susan anymore. He was wondering if, as some eccentric physicists argued, time really did curve back on itself. Events in the future could cause things to happen in the present. For example, those mousetraps snapping tomorrow might have caused him to love Susan today.

Thus, despite his years of evasion in data, he was thinking about Susan and Merian after all.

The waitress waved an enthusiastic good-bye. She projected delight and a midnight dewiness through the long narrow room with its Left Bank motif, all the way past the other after-movie snackers. Romantic couples left good tips.

Arnie tilted back in his chair and said, "Now the piece is up to your minimum standard."

"Is that high praise from you, Arnie?"

"I don't mean it to be. It's a little downbeat. You get more happiness from open warfare than Indians getting screwed by Hollywood hookers. I mean it's open and shut, but not a banner. With your adds and fiddles, it's more complete than it should be. I mean, how much can we stand to know about Chief Charlie Cay-yoat?"

"I got interested."

"It's probably my fault for asking. It's heavy. From you we expect serious but not heavy. Well, you got to admit it's a leetle bit heavy, don't you, Ralph? Don't you seem to take it personally?"

"I guess I did."

"I shouldn't have let you work on it so long. Some of your best is when you phone it in, the shells are screaming overhead, you've got the clap—"

"Thanks, pal."

"We'll need some terrific art, lighten it up. If we can get the Chief with Danny Grand, powwow time on the new corral— 'Indian Moguls'—that might help. I'd say you covered it too complete was all."

Merian shrugged. "That's how it came out. He's a President, not a Chief. Jarls Coyote."

"It's not a bad job. Don't get sensitive on me, Ralph, but fair

259

warning. We're gonna make your five parts into three. You'll have to put up with some cuts. Even that might be too much, but we'll come out okay in syndication. The *LA Times*'ll probably use all three—the movie stuff, Danny Grand, the Wild West, they like fading grandeur and hepatitis, that's good, and then the *San Francisco Chronicle* might take a few hundred words in their Briefing section if we're lucky. Plus Albuquerque, Denver, maybe Salt Lake City, the *Sacramento Bee,* places they go for Indian stuff. Don't worry about us, Ralphie, we'll come out."

"I won't."

"But barely. Relax. You're not fired."

Arnie lumbered to his door and, before shutting it, yelled to Daphne to hold all calls but World War III or that the paper was taken over by Rupert Murdoch. This performance was for Merian; Daphne was accustomed to Arnie's games. So was Merian.

Arnie sighed and fell back into his chair, which tipped toward the window. For an instant Merian saw his friend crashing through the glass, somersaulting down past the World Trade Center like a very small but hairy King Kong and making a major obituary notice in the *New York Times* if they were feeling generous tomorrow and nobody really important, like a big insurance executive, had died; also news coverage in the *Post*:

EDITOR CATAPULTS ONTO NOONTIME CROWD, UNWED MOTHER CRUSHED

Leaves Grieving Buddy; Sen. Proxmire Defends Chair, Demands Stronger Safety Glass in High-Rise Construction, Hard Hats for World Trade District Picnickers

. . . The questions remain: What caused Arnold Schultz, 46, to lean so far back with shit-eating grin on his face? Was it murder most foul by his longtime friend, Ralph Merian, who resented criticism of his recent work and plotted a unique case of death by sarcasm and smugness?

Longtime friend Merian, 44, and longtime secretary,

Daphne DiAngelo, 38, are being questioned by longtime Coroner Wallace (Wally) Washington, 62, who issued only this terse statement:

"No coverup or sensation-mongering, such as was perpetrated in the cases of Marilyn Monroe, John Belushi, and John F. Kennedy in other jurisdictions, will be tolerated by this department. Mr. Merian, 44, will not be charged per se until we find the smoking gun, so to speak. In the meantime, he has been asked to keep in touch and we have assigned an ethnically balanced crew of plainclothes detectives to follow his every move."

He added, "Merian must be judged innocent until his rights are read to him and he is the proven slayer. Next news conference at two o'clock. Electronic media invited."

"Penny for your thoughts," Arnie said.

"Nothing. I was writing a story in my head in case you fire me and I have to go work cityside for the *Post*. Death notice for you."

"How'd I die, if I may inquire, or is that too nosy?"

"I give you a front-page death," Merian said.

"Spare the details, what good will it do me? I never read the *Post* anyway."

Merian and Arnie sat in silence awhile. Arnie found this negotiation difficult. He turned to clearing his smoker's throat. He had a whole para to insert. Why was Merian, a Benedict Arnold to the bachelor cause, deserting hs old friend? He betrayed the proud and ancient traditions of rootlessness. *Disponibilité*—over dinner one night at Harvey's Chelsea he had even given it the classiness of a French name, like a regular philosophy of life— demanded responsibilities. To be a disposable fella was a high calling. It allowed grown men to scatter their socks, just like an adolescent. This special person eats Dinty Moore stew from the can and anything else his black little heart desires. Sure, there were occasional discomforts, such as taking hotel dining-room meals on national holidays, depressions, loneliness, maybe a touch of prostate trouble due to various irregularities, either feast or famine in the sack department, but what are those compared with the steady good fellowship of an old friend like Arnie? Furthermore, didn't he understand that marriage, if that's what he had in mind, was doomed to failure when he continued to fly around the world, doing the only thing he knew how to do well?

"I might learn to do something else," Merian said. "Who said I have to keep mashing the soft parts of my brain against the bone in six-hundred-mile-an-hour machines? Maybe it's time I tried playing some other console."

"You thinking of retirement?" Arnie asked.

"Something else, that's all."

"Anything else is retirement for you, buddy." And Arnie stared with the enraged eyes of a man who read him adequately, understood him thoroughly, wanted only what was right for him, and consequently was ready to destroy. Hawkfeather, who seemed to want something else, looked at him with the same calculating red gaze.

"I'm thinking," Merian said. "That's not retiring."

"For you it is. You're not supposed to think. You're supposed to poke around and arrange words, buddy, that's what you're good for."

Merian grimaced and flicked at an imaginary hair on his nose. "I also have a good sense of smell I've kept from you. I'm going to develop my olfactories into cranial tissue. It's an evolutionary process. Gradually I'll get smart. I'm going to work on it."

"You found a lady, that's all," Arnie said. "You're scared. Who isn't? You're getting older. Who isn't? So you found a lady who smells sweet to your cranial tissue and you're acting like a big bold teenager."

Merian wondered why he should have to apologize to his oldest friend. He would not. "I got lucky," he said. "Can we let it go now, Arnie?"

To his surprise, Arnie suddenly eased up. He really wanted to figure out what Merian had in mind. Puzzlement was still a legal act between consenting adult pals, wasn't it?

Merian didn't know exactly what he had in mind; therefore it helped to explain it to a friend who might be persuaded to wish him well. Other people found a connection between work and love; he wanted some. Other people knew about balance. Aging and accomplishment might be part of an equilibrium. He wanted some of that, too. Nights that were not empty and sleepless or filled with racket and sleeplessness; mornings with more than his own bad breath for company.

Arnie's eyes were half shut, but he was paying attention. He waved a hand. Continue.

Yes, Merian felt responsible to the truth, he liked telling, writing it down, although most of the time he missed the truth in what he told. He liked getting things done, wrapping them up. But since it was impossible to tell the truth, he wasn't sure of what he had gotten done, what he would continue to wrap up. Didn't Arnie tell the publisher—the man who represented the paper on the parent company's board—he was the paper's official guy for putting cold water in their readers' warm baths? Equilibriums, except on the planetary sphere, tend to break down. Merian wasn't sure about the planetary sphere, either.

So he had found a Susan. He had found *this* Susan, Mrs. Pollet, acknowledged authority on Creolization. It was the biggest surprise in the world.

"Shouldn't be," Arnie said. "You were looking."

"I didn't know it."

"You wouldn't have found her otherwise."

"I prefer to think I was lucky."

"You tell me you're developing your nose into a brain? Pretty far to go yet, buddy."

They had a laugh. They had a beer from Arnie's little underdesk fridge. They had a moment of popping the cans and saying nothing.

Then Merian struggled to ask Arnie the questions Arnie was

asking him: How could he do his job and be what Susan needed? grow old and be pleased with his past? use words and expect to get something on paper without lying?

"Beats the shit out of me," Arnie said.

"I knew you'd be helpful," Merian said. "Since I don't take desserts, may I have another beer?"

Arnie wiped off the dew against his shirt and handed it to him. "Something else bothering?" he asked. "You didn't used to worry about the future. If that's intelligence, I'm not for it. Sounds like thinkpieces, columns, prognostication, viewing with alarm, and blah blah blah. No fret, no get. Your mother did not raise you to be a pundit, pal, any more'n mine raised me to be anything at all."

"There's more, Arnie. I'm trying to deal with some new things. Nobody can help me."

"What is it?"

"I don't hate Hawkfeather."

"That's no problem."

"I want to be good to Susan."

"Be nice to her then."

"My brother, Chaz."

Arnie stared at him and said nothing.

To run his hand round and round her ass so many times he could be the sculptor of it was impossible. It was her behind, her possession, the firm soft white pink rear parts created by inheritance, climate, God, and good luck especially for Susan Pollett, not her ass, and it was hers to dispose of, pinkly and sweetly. If she lent it to him, or shared it with him, for their pleasure together, she might also lend it and share it with Hawkfeather, and the would-be sculptor had no right to complain. It was hers to render as she chose.

But, oh, he treasured her love, if he could still have it. He would have to mention this to her and discover how she felt about the matter. And if the answer was a good one, he could easily spend a few years telling her about the sounds a radio used to make at night across a midwestern lake. Did they have such memories in England, did they have crazy loved brothers in England, would she listen to a foolish man with skin pitted and weathered by sun, wind, heredity, his own kind of good and bad luck?

Would she care to bring her own history up to date?

Love and the need to join with another was the thing he had overcome; he worked instead. He was like others and could not overcome it. Jealousy was the passion that did no work and he was jealous, possessive, scared, foolish, foolish, foolish. He didn't know Susan well enough. He felt deceived and had no right to deception. He might have to prepare for a troubled age with someone who gave him ease and comfort and delighted him and frightened him.

He wanted her.

"The death of innocence is only temporary," he assured her.

"Like a tooth," she said.

"You didn't used to be hard and cynical before you met me. Do I have an influence? I'll be fresh and alive before you can say Presto Change-o."

"You can get a shiny new false innocence." He was looking at her with his best professional don't-follow-you expression. "I don't believe you can grow a fresh tooth."

"Oh, gotcha. Let's not argue the future by means of metaphor."

"Then how?"

"I'm not dead yet. I'm grateful to you. I'm scared of being hopeful. Is that a good enough start?"

"Only a start," she said, "and I lost on a sure thing with my husband—he was perfect in every way. So I might as well gamble next time."

Merian looked at her and decided he would like to be with her when her hair turned white. He could imagine hoping he would still be there. We've talked a lot, he thought. Could be silent, too.

But I ought to tell her that.

"I'd like to be with you when your hair turns white."

He practiced saying it to himself. I want to be with you from now on. To live long enough to see your hair turn white. Forever and ever. Till—

It wasn't easy. He was getting there.

One evening Susan began answering after no question at all, after sharing an apple pared by a little device they had bought from a sidewalk peddler on an afternoon stroll, after a space of mere ticking Saturday history, ending a silence that had begun to be part of their routines: "I wouldn't even tell you if he forced himself on me. I wouldn't tell you if he raped me. Because it might be your thing to play Big Man Protector. For all that dramatic vision of yourself. For the Big Protector of it."

He shoved the *Times* and the Willy Brandt memoirs out of his chair and his eyes registered furniture, wall, shelves, the door. He did not plan to flee, however. "I'm only a man, Susan," he said.

"That's what I mean. Not on your life, mister."

"What would you rather I do? Why are you angry at what I might but didn't and won't do? Why bring this up again?"

"I've been thinking. You're right, I shouldn't be angry yet." She smiled and stretched and was embarrassssed. "Um, Ralph? He's a bright kid. He's really still just a boy. He needs... You can afford a few thousand, if that's what it takes, to send him back to school. To help, anyway. He ought to be a lawyer, not a thug. It's a more modern way to fight, isn't it?"

"What are you telling me?"

She just smiled. There was a faint gray saliva rind on her lips. She was moved. She licked it off.

He hadn't thought she was still seeing Hawkfeather. He didn't believe Hawkfeather was still a part of their life. He didn't know what she meant; maybe she only meant what she said. She wanted to help Hawkfeather, but the tribal funds for college scholarships had gone to Danny Grand. Merian did not choose to add Hawkfeather to his payroll. If he killed or raped or engaged the battle of the bottle, maybe Susan would know and care and maybe she shouldn't. Merian had always chosen to put the past where it belonged.

Susan no longer believed Merian had to know. She needed to tell him anyway. Merian had taught her this lesson and he might as well live with it, considering whether he wanted a partial truth—the most available to anyone—or try for something more important and filled with risk.

"Is he looking over our shoulders?" Susan asked.

"Not mine anymore."

"Good," she said. "Not mine, either."

"Let's put that burden down. Poor man."

"Poor mankind," Susan said. "Now it's our turn, isn't it? May we have a turn now?"

When he crossed to the West Side late Sunday afternoon, planning to spend the rest of the day tucking everything in the filing cabinets—Alamo Oxman, Stony Apaches, bills and receipts—get everything cleaned up for the next step, another assignment—Susan had work to do, too—he found the message on his answering machine, but it had also been delivered in a computer printout telegram to his downstairs neighbor, whose name he did not know; who was kind enough to slip it under his door, "Open by mistake, thot maybe important."

> YOUR BROTHER CHARLES FOUND THIS MORNING.
> CAUSE YET TO BE DETERMINED. REGRETS.
>
> DR. MICHALSKI

Thinking maybe it was a telephone, he picked up his Sony, looked at it, switched it on. There was music, not a dial tone. He stood looking at it.

He would tell Susan later, not tonight. He didn't want her to think he was making decisions about her for reasons that should not concern her.

267

He remembered lying with Chaz under blankets they had spread on chairs, playing the game they called Tent. They told stories in Tent. They went on desert adventures in Tent. Spaceflights in Space Tent. Other planets with Chaz in Tent.

Eventually he might mention to Susan one of the peculiarities of communication, how the message from Dr. Michalski omitted a word, probably by an error in transmission. Chaz had been *found*. Chaz had been found adjective missing.

When he began his story under the blankets in Tent, Chaz would say, "Look at me go, Ralphie. Lookit me go!"

Merian was still holding his Sony, the one he kept tuned for company to the baroque music station when he lived alone, and smashed it against the radiator. He heard scattered droplets of music. There was dust in the air. The radio couldn't be fixed.

He didn't have to wait to tell Susan. He had decided about her while Chaz was not yet found. The procedure now was for a person to tell himself. The procedure was not to think about it but to do what he was doing. He was standing over the sink. He thought he was sick and would void his stomach, but it was only his eyes that were exploding. He splashed handfuls of water into his burning eyes.

He had spent years telling the paper and the Syndicate about troubles elsewhere.

He stood at the sink and splashed water into his eyes. It did not put out the fires.